WICKEDLY UNRAVELED

A BABA YAGA NOVEL

DEBORAH BLAKE

Wickedly Unraveled (A Baba Yaga Book)

Deborah Blake

Copyright 2019 Deborah Blake. All rights reserved.

This book or any portion thereof may not be reproduced or used in any manner whatsoever without the express written permission of the author except for the use of brief quotations in a book review.

Support your favorite authors. Buy or borrow, don't pirate.

Cover art by earthlycharms.com

Interior design by Crystal Sarakas

PRAISE FOR THE BOOKS OF DEBORAH BLAKE

"Witchy and wild, this book has everything I'm looking for."
-Tanya Huff, author of the Peacekeeper series

"Paranormal romance at its best."
- Alex Bledsoe, author of the Eddie LaCrosse novels

"An addicting plot...I never had so much fun losing sleep!"
- Maria V. Snyder, *NYT* bestselling author of *Shadow Study*

"[Blake does] a fantastic job building layers in her world and developing interesting characters both old and new."
- RT Book Reviews

"An engaging world full of thoughtful, clever details, and a charmingly dangerous heroine...Tightly plotted, with great fidelity to the Baba Yaga stories from Russian folklore that inspired the book." - Dear Author

"An exciting new series."
- Tynga's Reviews

"[A] good tale with fantastical creatures described in vivid detail, and with a lovely romance woven in... Equally engaging and enjoyable."
- Harlequin Junkie

"[A] fun retelling of the Baba Yaga mythology in a modern urban fantasy setting."
- All Things Urban Fantasy

"The kind of paranormal adventure that will keep readers up at night."
- Fresh Fiction

ACKNOWLEDGMENTS

As always, this book took a village to create and polish. Huge thanks to my first readers—Judy, Lisa, and especially Karen, who said she thought it was my best book yet. (It's not, but I love you for thinking so.) Special thanks to Judy for final edits and catching my screw-ups and making me look good. Better, anyway. Sorry about the commas. But only slightly.

Huge kudos to my cover artist, Su from Earthly Charms, who accomplished the nearly impossible and came up with an amazing cover that was not only a great fit with the whole series, but matched as closely as possible the model for the first book. (Which came out from Berkley, so there was no way to duplicate her exactly.) Believe it or not, the dog was tougher to match than the woman! I can't thank her enough for gracing my work with the perfect cover and working with me until it was just right.

Big thanks as always to my agent, the wonderful Elaine Spencer, for her support and enthusiasm for all my writing, and for loving this series from the first. When I first sent her this idea, she accused me of being an evil genius eating bonbons in my tower while plotting dominion over other authors. No wonder I love her. (And no, I'm really not. Plotting, that is. The bonbons, well…)

But most of all, thank you to all my readers, who keep asking for more books about the Riders and the Baba Yagas. You guys are what keep me getting up in the morning and typing long into the night. Y'all rock.

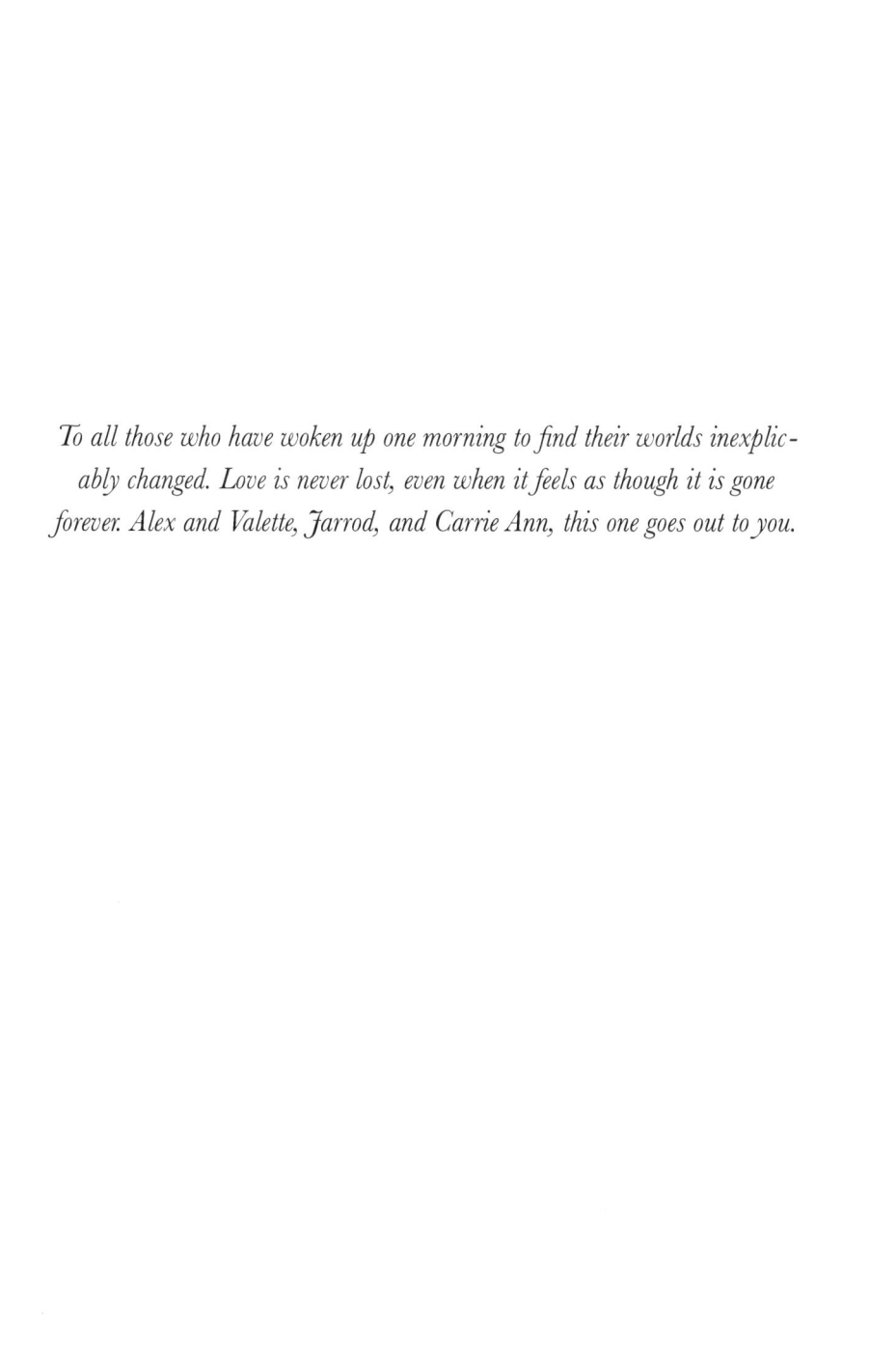

To all those who have woken up one morning to find their worlds inexplicably changed. Love is never lost, even when it feels as though it is gone forever. Alex and Valette, Jarrod, and Carrie Ann, this one goes out to you.

CHAPTER ONE

"I THINK WE SHOULD TAKE A FAMILY VACATION," LIAM SAID, gazing calmly across the knotty pine breakfast table. "We've never done that."

His wife Barbara blinked her clear amber eyes at him as though he'd just suggested they take a stroll through a field full of man-eating tigers.

"You really think that would be a good idea?" she asked in a deceptively mild tone. After all, there were reasons they'd never done such a thing. Like the fact that she was one of the Baba Yagas, a powerful witch out of Russian fairy tales whose job it was to maintain the balance of nature and occasionally —if she couldn't find a way around it—help a worthy seeker.

"What is a family vacation?" their adopted daughter Babs asked, looking up from her bowl where she had been taking precise methodical alternating bites of cereal and then strawberries, careful never to mix them both. Her asymmetrical pixie-cut dark hair and wide eyes over a snub nose made her look adorable, if slightly elfin.

Then there was that. That being Babs, who had spent the formative early days of her life trapped in the mystical Otherworld as a captive of a power-hungry rusalka and under the dubious care of Liam's insane former wife.

It had been almost four years since they'd rescued Babs and discovered she had enough innate magical power to convince the High Queen to allow Barbara to train the girl to become a Baba Yaga someday. Four years of living part of her life as normally as possible, while the rest was spent traveling with Barbara in her magical hut-turned-Airstream trailer.

Although, Barbara thought ruefully as she pondered the question, "as normal as possible" took on a whole different meaning when dealing with a child who thought nothing of having a best friend who was a talking dragon disguised as a giant while pit bull.

"A family vacation is when you travel with your family to someplace where you have fun together," Barbara said, feeling as though the explanation was probably somewhat inadequate. After all, she'd never experienced such a thing either. Her youth had been spent (a lot longer ago than one might think) living in a wooden hut on chicken legs in the great forests of Russia, her only family the bad-tempered old Baba Yaga who trained her, and the three mythical Riders who came and went periodically.

Plus Chudo-Yudo, of course, whose large white muzzle was

currently resting on her booted feet under the table. He had been her best friend too.

Babs pondered the statement thoughtfully, as she did most things. "But we travel in the Airstream all the time. We go places and fix problems. Is that not fun?"

Liam shook his head, dark-blonde hair flopping into his eyes until he shook it back out. Barbara felt a flutter of affection for the gesture, which had captivated her the first time she'd met him. He got regular haircuts now, so it wasn't as shaggy as it had been back then, but that one lock still seemed to have a mind of its own.

"Well for one thing, that's Baba's job. You both might enjoy it, but that's not the same as a vacation." He smiled at the girl, who, at more-or-less nine years old, was both more sophisticated and infinitely more innocent than any normal Human child that age. "Besides, I never get to go on those trips. I'm talking about all three of us traveling together."

Babs' large brown eyes lit up, although her face maintained its usual solemn mien. "All three of us together? Could we, Baba Yaga?" She gazed at Barbara, who sometimes got called Baba and sometimes Barbara, but never mother. That was okay by her, since she wasn't exactly the motherly type. Neither Babs nor Liam ever really asked her for anything…

"I don't see why not," Barbara said slowly. "It might be an interesting experience."

A huge smile spread across Liam's attractive face. "Seriously? That would be great! I have plenty of time coming to me, since I rarely take any off. And Belinda could easily cover for me." Liam was the sheriff of rural Clearwater County, where they lived, and Belinda was his most capable deputy.

Barbara felt a tremor slide down her spine, like tiny lizard feet scampering across her skin. With an effort, she dismissed the sensation. Probably just the occasional unsettled feeling that came from trying to adjust to the realities of everyday Human life and being married after eighty-plus years of magic and solitude.

"Sure," she said, pouring herself another cup of coffee from the enchanted coffee maker that usually lived on the Airstream, double-checking before she drank to make sure it was actually coffee, and not tea, or orange juice, or gods forbid, streamed yak milk. That one had been disgusting. "Did you have any particular destination in mind?"

"What about the Land of Disney?" Babs suggested. "Mary Elizabeth said her mom took her there and it was very fun. She said it was magical and there were fairies, just like the Otherworld."

Barbara snorted down her long nose. "Not exactly. Disney is make-believe magic, not real like ours."

A tiny line formed between Babs' brows and she glanced from Barbara to Liam. "That is just silly. Why would anyone want that?"

"Not everyone can have real magic, sweetheart," Liam explained. "So they pretend. I don't think you'd like it anyway. It is very crowded and noisy there."

Babs made a face. She still found large groups of Humans

overwhelming, although she would never admit it. They'd tried her at elementary school—way too much chaos and noise. After the third time Barbara had been called in to find the girl hiding in a back corner of the playground or inside a locker, they'd just given up and switched to home schooling. So large amusement parks were definitely off the table.

"Maybe something a little less…ambitious…to start with?" Barbara suggested. "How about a camping trip?"

Liam gave her a smug look, and put a colorful pamphlet down on the table, along with a couple of photos printed out from the computer. "What about this? It's within driving distance, it's beautiful, and shouldn't be too crowded since the summer tourist season hasn't quite started yet."

Barbara pulled the papers towards her and Babs jumped down from her seat, abandoning the soggy remains of her breakfast to take a look.

"Ah," Barbara said, pleased and surprised. "Niagara Falls. Good choice. Lots of great natural energy, not too many people. I haven't been there in years." She tapped one of the photos thoughtfully." I used to know a river nymph who lived in that area. I wonder if she is still around."

Liam winked at her. "It's also a traditional place for Humans to go on a honeymoon. As I recall, we never got one of those. It might be kind of romantic."

"I doubt most couples honeymoon with a miniature Baba Yaga trainee and a dragon," Barbara said, but her heart did a silent dance anyway. She was probably the least romantic woman on the planet, but somehow Liam could make her forget that fact.

"We are hardly most couples," Liam said with a grin, and came around the table to kiss her resoundingly before grabbing up his sheriff's hat from its hook. "But there is no one I'd rather take a belated honeymoon slash family vacation with. I'll arrange the time off while I'm at work today, and we'll make plans when I get home."

He tugged on Babs' hair before heading out the door. A reserved and self-contained child, she wasn't comfortable with kisses or hugs most of the time, so she and Liam had gotten into the habit of substituting affectionate hair tugs instead. It seemed like a small gesture, but she'd once made Liam drive all the way back from town to their yellow farmhouse just because he'd forgotten to do it on his way out.

Barbara admired his butt as he left, her lips still tingling from his kiss. That man. Oh, that man. She dragged her attention back to the table with difficulty.

Barbara gazed at her protégé. "So, what do you think about this idea? Do you want to take a family vacation? It would be a new thing, but not so different from what we do already, you and I."

Babs pondered for a moment. "I suppose it would be good. I like to travel in the Airstream, and I like it when we are all together. So traveling all together should be good, right?"

"Right," Barbara said, gathering up the breakfast dishes. "It should definitely be good."

So why did she have a feeling that disaster was lurking right around the corner?

"Are you sure we need all that?" Barbara asked as Liam brought another load of supplies into the Airstream. This seemed to be a box of board games, coloring books, and what looked suspiciously like the making for s'mores.

"It's traditional," Liam said with a straight face. "You can't argue with tradition."

That much was certainly true. When you were a legendary character out of old fairy tales, tradition was etched into your bones like the passage of water was carved into rocks. But surely there were limits.

"You packed sleeping bags," she protested. "We're traveling in a moveable house with beds. Comfortable beds. Why would we need those?"

"Tradition," he insisted again. "What if we want to sleep outside under the stars?"

Barbara rolled her eyes at him, but didn't bother to argue. Liam had thrown himself whole-heartedly into their first family vacation, and she didn't want to ruin his fun, as ridiculous as most of it seemed to her. Liam had been patient and understanding about the necessity of her going off on numerous Baba Yaga missions during the few years they'd been married. If he wanted to over-pack for a vacation with a woman who could manifest out of thin air just about anything they needed, she wasn't going to be the one to stop him.

He turned to her as if to ask a question, then stopped in his tracks as a loud humming sound filled the trailer. "What the—?"

Barbara got a sinking sensation somewhere between the bottom of her cropped red tee shirt and the top of her black leather pants. With a sigh, she put one hand out, palm up. A miniature man-shaped figure wearing leaves for clothing and an acorn as a cap landed lightly in the middle of her palm, his oversized wings vibrating slightly even when he was standing still.

"Hey, Baba!" Chudo-Yudo said as he bounded up the stairs and into the Airstream. "Did you see a—" He screeched to a halt as he saw their small visitor. "Oh. You did. Damn. I was hoping it was just a bug."

"Who are you calling a bug, you oversized mongrel?" the sprite said, waving a sword in the dragon-dog's general direction. The weapon in question wasn't much larger than a toothpick, but Barbara knew from experience it was much sharper. Her visitor didn't seem to be in much shape to do any damage, thought. He'd clearly had a tough journey—he was gasping like a marathon runner nearing the finish line. She could feel his whole body trembling.

She cleared her throat. "My apologies," she said to the wood creature. "Were you looking for me?"

Catching Liam's eye, she gestured toward the cupboard where she kept her herbal remedies. "Can you fill one of those tiny cups from the bottle marked *restorative honey*, please?"

To his credit, once the initial surprise wore off, Liam didn't hesitate. He grabbed a doll-sized goblet from the array available, and used the dropper on top of the bottle to fill it. He handed it to the sprite with a small bow and Barbara felt a swell of pride. Followed by a sinking feeling that their family vacation was about to be derailed.

"My thanks to you," the little man said, once he'd swallowed the potion and had caught his breath. "And to your consort. He is clearly not a bad sort, for a Human."

Liam rolled his eyes, but stayed where he was, eying the sprite warily. Since he normally made himself scarce any time there was Baba Yaga business, Barbara was pretty sure he, too, was worried that something would keep them from leaving that very morning as planned.

"What can I do for you?" she asked. "It's only, this isn't a very good time…"

The sprite raised one green-tinged eyebrow. "You are busy with a more serious matter?"

Barbara sighed. *Only my marriage*, she thought. "Not at all. Please tell me what brought you here, and how I can help?"

"I come from the wood to the north," he said. "Three days hard flight, as my people measure it. There is a wrongness afoot we thought you should be aware of. Magic ill-controlled, that threatens those in the surrounding area. We need the Baba Yaga to put a stop to it."

Uncontrolled magic. That was bad. "Where does this magic come from?" she asked. "Is it some creature from the Otherworld who is disregarding the queen's rules against blatant magic in the Human lands? Some fluke of the natural world?"

The little man scrunched up his face in disgust. "Worse," he said. "A Human."

"A Human with magic?" Liam said, forgetting that he was trying to fade into the background. "Is there such a thing?"

Chudo-Yudo laughed, his furry white sides shaking as though the trailer was being rocked by an earthquake. "Where do you think the Baba Yagas come from?" he asked. "Even our Barbara was once merely a Human child with an unusual potential for working magic. Not all such children are found, and some grow up to be adults with serious talent. Most never realize what they can do, but occasionally one figures it out and names herself witch. With enough practice, these Human witches can be quite powerful, although they rarely do anything that draws the attention of a Baba Yaga."

"And when they do?" Liam asked quietly.

"They usually get eaten," the dragon-dog said with an impressive display of sharp white teeth. It was hard to tell if he was joking or not.

Barbara ignored her furry companion. "Might we know your name, sprite?" she asked their visitor politely. "And the name of the place from which you come."

The small man bowed, handing her back the empty goblet with the same gesture. "I am Felixx," he said. "My home is simply called forest to those who live there. I know not the Human name for it. But I can tell you that something is very wrong there. The magic this witch does has confused the leaves on the trees, some of which are turning color out of season. Neither I nor any of my people have ever known such a thing to happen. Can you help us, Baba Yaga?"

She shrugged her shoulders in a "what can I do?" gesture to Liam. "Of course," she said to Felixx. "But first we have to figure out where exactly you came from."

"Maybe this will help," Liam said, unfolding a map and putting it out on the table in the Airstream's small kitchenette. Felixx flew over and hovered above it, his wings humming.

"I cannot see my home on this flat paper," the sprite said, drooping. "These scribbling mean nothing to me."

"Ah." Barbara thought for a moment and waved a hand through the air. The map wavered and spread, taking on a three-dimensional aspect, with lakes and rivers tinted blue, and the mountains gold and green. "Is this any better?"

The little man's face brightened as he fluttered lower. "Yes, I think…there. That big water is near my home." He pointed one tiny finger at a forested section of the map. "The place of trees by the big water."

"Hmmm. Cayuga Lake. It looks like maybe our new friend comes from near Aurora." Barbara wafted the image away.

"That's not all that far off our path," Liam said in a hopeful tone. "Maybe we can stop off there on the way, instead of putting the trip off?"

Barbara scowled at nothing in particular, feeling a gnawing sensation in her gut that had more to do with intuition than it did that third cup of coffee. But on the face of it, she could see no reason to argue. It really *was* practically on their way, only taking them a few miles off their route. And what kind of threat could a Human witch pose to a Baba Yaga? It seemed like a simple matter. Return Felixx to his home, find the witch, tell her to stop doing whatever the hell it was she was doing, fix the damage if necessary, and be back on the road in less time than it would take to stop for lunch.

She had always tried to keep Liam out of Baba Yaga business (except the mess that brought them together in the first place, where it was more or less unavoidable), but he could stay with the Airstream while she dealt with this minor issue, and then they could have their family vacation. Liam and Babs both stared at her with matching neutral expressions, neither of them putting words to the pleas she could see in their eyes.

"Very well," she said. "Why not?"

Dammit, nothing was going to get in the way of their family vacation.

CHAPTER TWO

FELIXX SPENT MOST OF THE TRIP NAPPING, LEANING UP AGAINST Chudo-Yudo's wide and furry side in the back seat of the large silver Chevy truck used to pull the Airstream. As with most everything else Barbara owned, it was more magical than not, and actually an extension of the former hut turned trailer, although it could be driven around separately if need be. She often thought that things had been simpler in the Olden Days, when witches and their enchanted houses and dragon companions had no need to hide what they were.

But in the modern era, it was easier to blend in and try not to attract attention. A pity. Barbara thought it was a lot more efficient when the general populous knew who you were and that it was a seriously bad idea to piss you off. Still, she always managed to get the job done anyway, even if she had to teach a few people that lesson from scratch.

As they neared their destination, Felixx woke up and guided them off the main roads to an area that seemed to be a mixture of rustic rural homes and small seasonal camps. Barbara pulled into the broad graveled lot of a campground that was mostly deserted mid-week in late May and turned to the sprite. "Here?" she asked. "This is where you live?"

Felixx chuckled, a sound like water flowing over rocks in a stream. "There," he said, pointing toward a thicker stand of trees that formed the edge of a forested section. "An hour's flight or so." He darted out through the open door as Barbara and the others piled out of the truck, and pointed in the opposite direction, down what looked like a narrow private driveway at the other side of the parking lot. "The Human witch lives down there, but I did not think your shiny metal home would fit easily down the path."

"Hmm. Good call," Barbara said. The Airstream would go wherever she wanted it to go, more or less, but it would be easier to walk from here. Besides, she wanted to make sure that Liam was out of range of any stray magic, just to be on the safe side.

"Did you wish to come with me?" she asked Felixx.

The sprite bowed in mid-air. "I would rather return to my family, if you have no further need of me, Baba Yaga. I have been away too long as it is." Tree sprites were uncomfortable being far from their personal trees for any length of time. This was the reason they couldn't relocate to the Otherworld along when most of the rest of the Paranormal peoples made their exodus from the lands of Humans. Most sprites lived and died without ever traveling more than a few miles from home, which was why Barbara had taken his request for help so seriously, despite its bad timing.

"I will do my best to resolve this issue," she said, returning his bow. "Give my regards to your family."

Felixx nodded again and then flew off in the direction of home. Barbara turned to Liam. "Why don't you make us some lunch while I deal with this? I doubt it will take long."

"I'll help him," Chudo-Yudo said, pink tongue lolling.

Barbara rolled her eyes. "Try and leave some for the rest of us, you giant bottomless pit. The last time you 'helped' Liam with the food prep, there wasn't actually any food to be seen when you were done."

"May I come with you?" Babs asked. "I have never met a Human witch before. I would like to see what one is like." The spark in her bright dark eyes and the way she cocked her head to one side made her look like a curious crow, intrigued by some new shiny object.

Barbara shrugged. She took Babs along on plenty of assignments more dangerous than confronting a witch who probably had no idea what she was doing. "Okay," she said. "Let's get this over with, so we can get back on the road. I can't wait to show you the falls."

Liam tugged on Babs' hair, and she tugged his back. Barbara got a big hug and a passionate kiss on the lips, which she returned—with interest. Even after more than three years of marriage, she never got tired of Liam's kisses.

"Hurry back," he said, just as he did whenever she left for an official Baba Yaga job. He raised her hand and placed his lips gently on the ring he'd given her, a round circle in the shape of a golden dragon with a sparkling diamond held in its mouth. "I'll miss you."

"I'll miss you too," she said, with a tiny smile. Traditions must be upheld after all. "But you know I'm going to be right down the road, and we'll be back in no time."

"It will seem like forever," Liam said, clutching at his heart in an exaggerated gesture.

"Oh for the love of Chernobog," Chudo-Yudo growled. "If you're trying to make me lose my appetite, it's working." He nudged Barbara's leg with his massive white head, almost knocking her off her booted feet. "The sooner you go, the sooner you get back. Yeesh, you two."

Barbara sighed, the twinkle in her amber eyes hidden by the wild cloud of dark hair that fell in front of them. "Very well," she said to Babs. "Let's go see what all the fuss is about, shall we?"

They marched down the road together, although Babs tended to dart ahead to look at something that caught her eye, then straggle as she took a moment to analyze anything new. The path they followed seemed to be a shared driveway or possibly a very narrow back road used by only a few houses, and they walked about a mile before they came to the one they'd been looking for.

They were clearly in the right place, because just as Felixx had said, some of the oak trees had new spring leaves, while others were adorned with bright autumnal colors. A bed of tulips showed off frilled pink flowers under raspberry bushes that shouldn't have held fruit until the end of summer. The purple berry Barbara popped into her mouth tasted perfectly normal, even if it was growing out of season. *Huh.*

The house at the end of the road was a small wooden cabin, neat and well kept, with freshly painted white shutters and a plume of smoke rising from its chimney. An extensive herb garden was planted next to it, and Barbara recognized some more exotic magical herbs mixed in with the usual culinary and medicinal ones. Definitely the right place.

It hardly looked threatening, though. There wasn't the slightest hint of a "wicked witch" vibe about it, and there was nothing in the aura of the house that made Barbara think that the owner would be much of a problem. The woman was probably just in over her head and needed some stern correction. Luckily, Barbara was just the person to give it to her.

They marched up to the front door and Barbara banged on it decisively. There was no answer, so she banged on it again.

"Hello?" The door swung open to reveal an attractive middle-aged woman, perhaps in her fifties or early sixties, with dyed blonde hair flatteringly cut to frame her heart-shaped face. She wore a tidy blue dress covered with an embroidered apron and had on full make-up, despite the fact that as far as Barbara could tell, she was in a house in the middle of the woods all by herself.

Barbara blinked, marginally taken aback. The woman didn't look like any witch that Barbara had ever met, but she can smell the magic on her, and in the air of the cabin, so this was almost certainly the person they're looking for.

"I'm sorry," the witch said politely. "But whatever you're buying, I'm not interested." She glanced at Babs, who gazed impassively back at her. "It isn't Girl Scout cookie season, is it?"

"I wouldn't know," Barbara said. "But I can tell you that it isn't raspberry season either, and yet you have some beautiful berries growing on the bushes in your yard. I think you had better explain to me why that is."

The woman's blue eyes widened and she quickly tried to shut the door. Barbara's foot in its heavy motorcycle boot somehow seemed to be in the way.

"Look, I don't know who you are, but I'm busy and don't want to talk to you."

"That's too bad," Barbara said, not moving her foot. "Although if it is any consolation, I don't particularly want to talk to you either. You're actually interrupting my vacation. And I've never had one of those, so I have kind of been looking forward to it. Let's just get this over with as quickly as possible, and then we can both get on with our lives."

"Who *are* you?" the woman asked, still trying to shove the door closed.

"I'm the Baba Yaga," Barbara said. "And you are starting to get on my nerves."

"Oh, oh," Babs said quietly, and took a step back.

Barbara snapped her fingers and the door vanished, leaving the woman clutching at air and wobbling off balance. Barbara righted her with a fierce stare and said, "Now, I suggest you invite us inside. We need to talk."

The woman sputtered, but didn't act at all astonished by her disappearing door, which told Barbara that it wasn't likely she'd have to go into a lengthy explanation about what a Baba Yaga was.

"Very well," the woman said. "But I hope this won't take long. I'm in the middle of something important." She pressed red lips together. "And I'm going to want that door back before you leave."

"Not a problem," Barbara said, snapping her fingers and returning the door with a whoosh of displaced air. "I'm Barbara Yager, the Baba Yaga in charge of this section of the country. This is my ward, Babs. And you are?"

"My name is Katherine Chanter," the woman said, leading the way into the rear of the house, where sharp green odors, touched by an acrid hint of something metallic, scented the air,. "And I'm not doing anything wrong."

Barbara gazed around with interest at what might have been a perfectly normal kitchen if it weren't for the cauldron bubbling over a low flame in the fieldstone fireplace. Or the various herbs lined up neatly in jar after jar on open shelves or hanging down in bunches from hooks on the walls. She reached up to touch a couple of the more unusual varieties.

"Datura," she said, of one with faded pink flowers and a spiny unopened fruit. "Lovely. And look, here's some deadly nightshade to go with it, some hensbane, and a nice mandrake root." She tutted at Katherine. "You're at risk of becoming a bit of a cliché, with all these 'witches' weeds.' What about a few roses or daisies for variety?"

Katherine looked unimpressed. "I actually use rose petals in my elixir, for your information." She pointed at a jar labeled "Rose, petals" on a bottom shelf between "Rose, hips" on one side and "Rosemary" on the other. Barbara was reluctantly impressed. None of *her* herbs were in alphabetical order. Or any kind of order at all, really.

"And datura was historically used in Ayurvedic medicine as an aphrodisiac. It is only poisonous if used incorrectly."

"You're making an aphrodisiac?" Barbara asked, raising an eyebrow. Somehow the woman didn't seem like the type. But you never knew.

"What's an aphrodisiac?" Babs asked, gazing up at the datura plant.

"I'll explain later," Barbara said. "And don't touch that. It's very dangerous."

Katherine sniffed, moving over to stir whatever was in the cauldron. "No, I am *not* making an aphrodisiac, although I fail to see how it would be any business of yours if I was."

"It is my business," Barbara said, "because whatever it is you're up to is disrupting that natural flow of nature. I've had complaints. I do not enjoy complaints." She scowled at Katherine, irritated as much by her attitude as by the annoying orderliness of the woman's work space. "So whatever it is you're doing, you're going to have to cut it the hell out."

"Don't be ridiculous," Katherine said, stirring counterclockwise three times before setting the large wooden spoon aside on a blue and white porcelain spoon rest. "I'm not hurting anyone. I've been working on a potion to turn back time, creating a remarkable serum that will make women look younger."

Barbara snorted. "You're making face cream?" She couldn't believe she'd put her vacation on hold for this.

"Not face cream," Katherine said in a huffy tone. "A serum that gives women back their youth. Well, to some extent, anyway. It can actually turn back the clock. You don't believe me? I'm in my seventies, and just look at my skin. The wrinkles around my eyes are getting tinier every day. I look fabulous, I feel fabulous, and it is going to make me *rich*." Her blue eyes glinted with a combination of pride and avarice.

A sinking feeling made Barbara's stomach feel as though she'd swallowed a dozen writhing snakes. "You created a youth potion that actually works?" Her words dropped like stones into a pond, but Katherine somehow missed the ripples.

"I did! Isn't it amazing? Scientists have been trying to come up with something like this for decades. Who knew they should have been consulting a witch, instead of a bunch of chemists?" She let out a silvery peal of laughter.

"It's not amazing," Barbara said grimly. "It's against all the laws of nature."

"Oh, piffle," Katherine said, waving one slim hand through the air. "Don't women deserve to look better and feel good about themselves? What is the harm?"

"The *harm?*" Barbara gritted her teeth. "The harm is that you are messing with powers way beyond your control. Hell, they're beyond any witch's control, even mine. Time is not an element to be trifled with. Change the air or the water, sure. They're meant to have a certain mutability. Make a hill into a mountain or the other way around? It takes a certain effort. But time is only designed to run in one direction. Forcing it to do otherwise will only lead to catastrophe."

Katherine stirred some more, then added exactly six drops of something from a tiny brown glass bottle. "Catastrophe," she sneered. "What do you know about catastrophe? Catastrophe is gazing into the mirror every day and watching your beauty fade, your skin wrinkle, your jowls sag, and not being able to do anything to stop it. You wouldn't understand. You're still young and beautiful. But someday you'll find out. And then you'll be glad I came up with this elixir."

"Not all that young," Barbara muttered. She'd turned eighty-six on her last birthday. Luckily she had the Queen of the Otherworld's Water of Life and Death, which boosted a Baba Yaga's power and kept her aging at a slower rate than most Humans. "But someday I will grow old and wrinkled, and I hope I will do it with dignity. It is part of the natural cycle of life. Things are born, grow older, die, and are reborn. You cannot change that."

"I can," Katherine said. "I am. With nary a catastrophe in sight, I might add."

"What does that word mean?" Babs asked, sniffing at a pile of chopped greenery sitting on a cutting board. She made a face and shook her head. "That does not smell good. You should use something else."

"Little girls should be seen and not heard," Katherine said.

Barbara hid a laugh behind one hand. "Not this one. She's probably smarter than you are. At least about magic." She turned to Babs. "A catastrophe is a disaster. Something really bad happening."

Babs thought for a moment. "Like what Jazz did?"

"Exactly like that," Barbara agreed. Her stomach clenched just thinking about how close her sister Baba, Bella, had come to losing her apprentice.

"Jazz tried to change time," Babs said to Katherine in her usual solemn manner. "To give the Riders back their immortality. It was a nice thing to try, but it was a *catastrophe*." The girl said the word slowly and carefully, making sure she got it right. "She accidentally made herself ten years older. She almost died. If Baba Yaga says you should not do this spell, you should listen to her."

Katherine's hand shook. "Someone made herself ten years older? That's awful."

"She was sixteen," Babs explained. "Then she was twenty-six."

"More or less. As far as we could tell," Barbara added grimly. "Plus don't forget the nearly died part."

"Well, twenty-six," Katherine said dismissively. "That's still young. It's a pity about your friend, but I'm no teenager playing with witchcraft for the first time. I know what I'm doing, and it isn't hurting anyone."

"Not now. Not yet." Barbara shook her head. "I'm sorry, but I simply can't allow you to continue. Enough chat." She really wasn't the chatting type. "This is forbidden magic and I intend to put a stop to it."

She took a step forward and gathered a ball of energy in one hand. "Move away from the cauldron. Do it now."

"No!" Katherine shrieked. "You can't destroy my work! It has taken me years to perfect it. I'm going to be rich. And I won't go back to being *old*!" She raised her wooden spoon as if it were a wand and began to yell the words of an incantation so vile, they colored the air around her head a sulfurous yellow. A few droplets flew off the end of the spoon and into the cauldron, where they sizzled and stank and spat.

"STOP," Barbara commanded, feeling the potential power in the room shift and build. She grabbed Babs by one thin shoulder and shoved the girl behind her. "There's too much magic loose in here already. You're going to—"

But it was too late. Before she could even get the words out, the other witch had finished her incantation and flung her curse at Barbara's head. Barbara threw up a hasty shield, which shuddered as the hex hit it and then bounced back toward the one who had cast it.

Katherine flew backward as if she had been punched in the gut, her screams reaching up to shred the herbs hanging from the painted white rafters. Bits of dried greenery drifted down as she slammed into the edge of the cauldron, tilting it sideways so that some of the contents slopped over the side. For a moment, the flames underneath flickered, as if undecided about which path to take, then they shot upward and outward, like the breath of a dragon. Instantly, the kitchen was on fire, the bright red tongue of destruction licking at the checked gingham curtains and devouring the wooden cabinets with crackling glee.

"Out!" Barbara said to Babs, shoving her in the direction of the door. The air was already so thick with smoke it was hard to breath, and Barbara snapped her fingers to create a small bubble of clarity and oxygen. She cast one quick backward look toward Katherine, but the Human witch lay unmoving on the floor as the room dissolved in chaos around her. Barbara suspected she'd been dead the minute her own spell hit her. There was a certain irony there that Barbara would take the time to appreciate later. For now, she just wanted to get herself and Babs to safety.

Once outside and a cautious distance away, they turned around to look at the inferno that moments ago had been a charming little house. The fire burned with a fury that far exceeded anything natural, and would soon threaten the trees nearby. Barbara shook her head, thinking of the tree sprite who had brought them there, and made a few arcane gestures toward the ponderous clouds above, which responded by letting loose a torrent of rain neatly centered over the blaze. Before long, there were nothing left but steaming ashes, and a few charred beams reaching up to the sky as if marking the spot for a future cautionary tale.

"Are you okay?" she asked Babs, leaning down to give the girl a rare hug. It was an indication of how shaken the child was that she not only allowed it but gave Barbara a brief squeeze in return.

"I am not harmed," Babs said. Her solemn pixy face was as composed as ever, but her dark brown eyes were wide and troubled. "Is that woman dead, Baba Yaga?"

"Nothing and no one could have survived that," Barbara said, straightening up and waving her hand in the direction of the smoking ruins. "But she was gone before the fire started, a victim of her own curse and an unfortunate clash of two powerful and incompatible magics."

Barbara muttered a curse of her own under her breath, although this was a much more mundane one. She didn't know how things had gotten out of hand so fast. It was a little late now, but she kicked herself for underestimating the other woman's power. Just because Katherine had been Human, and seemed so…ordinary, Barbara had made the mistake of assuming she was harmless. This is what came of spending most of your time fighting Paranormal threats and people who were outright evil. Barbara hadn't expected so much trouble from someone who was simply misguided. Not an error she would make again. It was a pity the price for learning the lesson had been so high.

"I'm sorry you had to experience that," she said to Babs. Barbara's own magical mentor had had no qualms about exposing a small child to the more brutal realities of a Baba Yaga's job, but Barbara had hoped to make Babs' childhood a little less traumatic than her own. Although truth be told, the girl's harrowing and unconventional start to life had probably prepared her for almost anything.

Babs patted Barbara's hand. "It is all right. I know bad things happen. She should not have attacked you. That was not wise."

Barbara gave her ward a crooked smile. "People are often unwise when fighting for things that are very important to them. If I had realized just how significant that elixir was to her, I would have approached Katherine differently." She tugged on a strand of dark hair. "I would still have destroyed it, but there would have been less talking first."

Ah, well. What was done was done. "Come on, little one. We have places to go that aren't here, thank the goddess. Let's go see what the boys have rustled up for lunch, shall we?" She looked at the witch's house one more time, shook her head, and they headed back down the road.

It was a relief to see the Airstream sitting in the parking lot, its silver exterior gleaming in the sunshine. Barbara practically leapt up the three metal steps to get inside, skidding to a stop when she saw Chudo-Yudo dozing on the hand-woven carpet and no sign of food preparation.

"Hey," she said indignantly, nudging the dragon-dog with her boot, "What happened to lunch? You didn't eat it all, did you?"

He lifted his huge white head and woofed at her indignantly.

No doubt he'd just said something rude in Dog. "Welcome back from your walk and what the heck are you talking about? Since when do you expect me to cook?" He looked past her as Babs came in. "And who is that? Are you picking up strays now?"

"Very funny," Barbara said. "Where's Liam?" She glanced around, but there was no sign of him.

"Liam who?" Chudo-Yudo said, lumbering to his feet. He walked over to sniff at Babs, looking a bit baffled. "Wait. I know you, don't I?"

"Of course you do, you silly dragon," Babs said, patting him on the head. He was so large and she was so petite that their shoulders were practically at the same height. "You are my best friend."

He sniffed her again, then licked her hand. "Right. Babs. For a minute there…huh." He subsided onto his back haunches, a confused expression on his furry face.

"Seriously, Chudo-Yudo, where is Liam? Things went horribly wrong out there and I just want to eat our lunches and get back on the road." She walked toward the back of the trailer to check the bedroom and the bathroom. Empty. "Liam? If this is some kind of game, it's not a good time."

"Baba Yaga? Who are you looking for? There is no one here but me."

Barbara stared at Chudo-Yudo. He didn't look like he was kidding. A sharp-edged sword of dread gripped her heart and for a moment, the room swayed around her.

"Barbara?" Babs whispered her name, clearly picking up on Barbara's unease. "Where is Liam?"

Biting her lip, Barbara headed back to the bedroom without answering. She held her breath as she opened the sliding doors to the closet that ran along the side wall. Black leather and crimson silk still hung where they always had, alongside the few formal outfits she kept for the times she had to dress up to visit the Queen. But there were no blue jeans or men's tee shirts, or overly large boots shoving her own shoes out of the way.

Leaving the closet, she ran to the small bathroom and yanked open the miniscule medicine chest over the sink. No men's toiletries or extra toothbrush. Nothing to show that Liam had ever been there. In the back of her head she could hear a muffled screaming as her heart broke into a million pieces.

"He's gone," she said calmly, as if her world hadn't just burned down as surely as the witch's house had done. "I don't know why, but he's gone."

CHAPTER THREE

"Who is gone?" Chudo-Yudo asked, and Barbara stared at him briefly before walking on numb feet into the living area and subsiding onto the couch. "What's wrong with you? You're acting weird. I mean, even more weird than usual."

"You really don't remember him at all, do you?" she said, some puzzle pieces beginning to slide reluctantly into places they shouldn't fit. "Liam McClellan. Sheriff of Clearwater County. My husband."

"Your *what?*" Chudo-Yudo's mouth dropped open. "Are you hallucinating? You don't have a husband."

Could she be hallucinating? There had been a lot of fumes filled with powerful magic floating around in that kitchen. Was it possible that all her memories of a tall, rugged lawman were just a figment of her own imagination, created in an instant out of years of loneliness and longing? It didn't seem possible, but then, much of what she did and experienced came down on the far side of impossibility anyway.

She dropped her face into her hands, but then sat up straight as cool metal met her skin. "Look," she said, holding out her left hand so the ring on it was clearly visible, the diamond in the dragon's mouth winking up at her. "This is the ring he gave me. It's real. He's real." Her insides shuddered with mixed relief and fear. He was real. Gone, somewhere, somehow. But real. She hadn't imagined him.

Chudo-Yudo swung his ponderous head between her and Babs, still standing near the doorway, her face pale and set. "You remember this person, little one?"

Babs nodded. "Liam. He is Barbara's husband. My foster father. He is kind. We all live together in a yellow farmhouse." She turned to Barbara. "Do you think he went back to the farmhouse? Maybe we should go home and look." Hesitant hope glimmered in her eyes.

Barbara pulled herself together with an effort. Something was very wrong here. Liam wouldn't have left her—left Babs—without a good reason. And why couldn't Chudo-Yudo remember him at all? She had a *really* bad feeling.

She reached into her back pocket for the phone she had reluctantly started carrying at Liam's insistence. Technology instead of magic. Bah. But sometimes it was handy. She tried their number at home, and then his cell. Both of them mocked her with a recorded voice that told her the numbers weren't in service, and it was all she could do not to melt the useless gadget into a lump of black plastic and electronic bits.

"When did you start carrying a cell phone?" Chudo-Yudo asked. "What the hell is going on here?"

"I don't know," Barbara said. "But something is very, very wrong. An hour ago, I had a man who loved me and we were all headed to Niagara Falls for our first family vacation. Now he has vanished and you don't even remember that he existed. For a minute, you didn't remember Babs either, and you've barely left her side since she came to live with us almost four years ago."

"Did the magic do this?" Babs asked quietly. "The not-compatible magical powers and the bad witch's curse?"

"I don't know," Barbara said. "But I have to believe there is something uncanny at work here. None of this makes sense, otherwise." Hell, it didn't make sense anyway. But she had to start somewhere.

"I can't think of any reason why Liam would have gone on to Niagara Falls without us, so let's head back home and see if we can find him there, okay?"

Babs nodded. "Yes, please. I would like to go home."

Chudo-Yudo glanced around at the interior of the Airstream. "We *are* home," he growled. "No, wait, don't tell me. We live in a yellow farmhouse." He stalked off to lie down in the kitchen, gnawing loudly on a large bone he pulled out of a cabinet that normally held plates.

Barbara could still hear him muttering under his breath as she and Babs headed out to the truck. She couldn't blame him.

Hopefully, things would get clearer when they were back in Dunville.

"We lived in *that*?" Chudo-Yudo said as they stood in the driveway looking at the farmhouse on South River Road. "In what century?"

He had a point. The yellow farmhouse clearly hadn't been inhabited in some time. In fact, it looked exactly like it had when she had bought it—derelict and abandoned, with a yard full of overgrown bushes and weeds, and a couple of windows boarded up where they'd been broken by time or vandals. There was no sign of the garden she had sweated over for the last three summers, or the tree house Liam had built for Babs in an old oak tree on the other side of the drive.

They walked up and peered in through the dusty glass of the windows that were still intact, but the house was as empty as it looked. No furniture, no cozy kitchen, no clothes or books or pictures. Apparently everything they owned now was in the Airstream. Oddly enough, after a lifetime spent in just that situation, she felt absurdly bereft to have lost the few things she and Liam had collected in their life together. As Babs snuck her cold hand into Barbara's larger one, Barbara suspected the little girl felt the same, for all her calm demeanor.

"Maybe we should ask Anna if she has seen him," Babs said in a small voice.

"Anna?" Chudo-Yudo asked. "Is this another imaginary friend?"

Barbara rolled her eyes at him. "Liam is not imaginary. Just temporarily misplaced. And Anna is the ghost who was here when we got the place. She's pretty harmless, so I never bothered to make her leave."

She took out her key, which slid into the rusty lock under protest but then turned easily enough when she gave it a nasty look. Not that she couldn't have unlocked it with magic, but she was trying to prove a point. To Chudo-Yudo or to herself, she wasn't sure. Either way, the house might look as though they had never lived there, but she still had the key that opened the door. That must mean something.

"Hello? Liam, are you here?" It was clear from the layers of undisturbed dust that no one Human had walked on the wide wood boards in years. "Anna? Anna, it's me, Baba Yaga. Will you come talk to us?"

A vaguely female shape wavered in the dim light that curved around the edges of the open door. If you squinted, you could barely make out shadows that hinted at long fair hair and an apron over a nondescript ankle-length dress.

"Who are you?" a thin voice asked. "Go away. Boo."

"Boo yourself," Barbara said acerbically. Anna's attempts to frighten people off were pathetic at best, and most visitors never even sensed her. She'd been murdered by an abusive husband many years before and the gory and notorious crime was the reason the house had sat empty for so many years before Barbara finally came along and bought it for a song. Once they'd had a nice chat, Anna had actually been happy for the company.

But it appeared that the ghost's memory had been affected too. A brief interchange—before she disappeared again—made it clear that she had no idea who Barbara and Babs were, had never heard of Liam, and thought the big white dog was going to bite her. Although how he would do that, Barbara wasn't sure.

Sighing, she locked the door behind them and they walked back up to the Airstream. Babs' sneakers with their cheerful red laces scuffed dispiritedly through the bits of leaves and debris that cluttered their once neat lawn.

"What do we do now, Baba Yaga?' she asked. "Where do we look if he is not here?"

Barbara could only think of one other place he would be. The other place he considered home. "We're going to the sheriff's department," she said.

"Going to turn yourself in for crimes against sanity?" Chudo-Yudo said.

"Ha," Barbara responded. "No, but keep up the wisecracks, and they might have to arrest me for animal cruelty."

"Oh, great. Woman bites dog. Again," he said. "Film at eleven."

※

The Clearwater Sheriff's Department served both the town of Dunville and the rest of the county, neither of which had the money to support a police force on their own. The building that housed it was unprepossessing at best—a long narrow single story built out of red brick, with straggling shrubbery and dirty windows. Barbara was simply relieved that it looked the same as the last time she'd seen it. If Liam was inside and okay, she swore she would kiss the cracked linoleum floor.

She left Chudo-Yudo and Babs in the Airstream, although it was hard to say who was keeping an eye on whom, and rode her classic royal blue BMW motorcycle over instead. Tucking her helmet under one arm, she pushed open the stubborn old glass door and headed to the front desk. An older woman with a narrow homely face and short gray hair sat behind it perched on a stool while she talked into a headset, simultaneously typing what looked like an incident report. She held up one finger for Barbara to wait, hit a button on the computer and another on a complicated-looked switchboard.

"Idiots," she said, without much vehemence. "Who calls the sheriff's department because the neighbor's cows are in their yard again? Call the damned farmer to come get his cows. I'm sure as hell not going to send a deputy to go round 'em up."

"Sorry," she said, looking directly at Barbara. "I've been doing this job for a long time. You'd think I'd get used to the stupid."

"Ha," Barbara responded, having spent many years complaining about the same thing. "You never get used to the stupid. It's the gift that keeps on giving." She nodded. "Hello, Nina. Is Liam in?"

Nina raised a sparse eyebrow. "I'm sorry? Have we met?"

"Barbara Yager," Barbara said with an internal sigh. "I'm—" She didn't know how the hell to finish that sentence. Luckily, Nina finished it for her.

"Oh, wait, aren't you that professor that came through town about a year ago? Studying local herbs or something." Nina nodded at her. "Sure, I remember. You were only in town for a week or so. Sorry it took a minute to come back to me."

A year ago? That didn't make any sense. Neither did her only being here for a week. "Right, uh, I was looking for Sheriff McClellan. Is he in, by any chance?"

Nina's face fell, the lines around her thin lips deepening. "I'm sorry, Ms. Yager. Liam isn't the sheriff anymore." She jerked her head over her shoulder, in the direction of what had been Liam's office. A pudgy stranger sat behind his desk, reading a magazine with his feet up on an open drawer. "Is there anyone else that might be able to help you?"

"Um," Barbara thought for a minute while her mind raced. Liam wasn't the sheriff? That job was his life—she couldn't imagine him without it. Then again, he had been on the verge of losing it when they'd met. Another puzzle piece she didn't like clicked into place.

"Does Belinda Shields still work here?" Belinda had been Liam's deputy, and her mother, a Russian immigrant, had set everything into motion by *Calling* for the Baba Yaga when Belinda's daughter Mary Elizabeth had gone missing, along with three other local children. The family had ended up becoming friends after Barbara and Liam rescued the little girl, and Babs occasionally spent time with Mary Elizabeth, although Babs still wasn't all that good at "playing."

"Sure," Nina said. "I can get her for you." She spoke into an intercom, then gave Barbara a serious look. "But if you met her when you were here before, don't be surprised if she seems different. She hasn't been the same since her daughter disappeared. Changes a person, that kind of loss does. So don't take it personally."

Mary Elizabeth was never found? They didn't rescue the children? What the hell was going on?

Before she could ask, Belinda came up to the desk. The petite woman was noticeably thinner, the already unattractive tan polyester uniform hanging on her as if it had been made for someone else. There were lines of strain permanently etched around her warm brown eyes and pale pink mouth, and the smile she gave Barbara was superficial at best. Even her light brown hair in its neat braid seemed to have faded. Barbara, who would have sworn she didn't have a heart, could feel it cracking around the edges.

"Hello," Belinda said. "Nina said you wanted to talk to me?" The deputy gestured toward her desk, tucked toward the back of the main room. "Why don't we go sit down. Can I get you some coffee?"

"Ugh. No thank you," Barbara said, possibly with more vehemence than she'd intended.

Belinda gave a short laugh. "I can see you've had our coffee before." She slid into her chair and waited until Barbara had taken the seat in front of the desk. "It's Doctor Yager, isn't it? I remember there was some sort of fuss about a permit the last time you were here. Then I saw you talking to Sheriff McClellan a few times at Bertie's. Things were a little…hectic around that time." She shook her head, as though to dismiss unwanted memories. "Anyway, I'm sorry I didn't have a chance to talk to you while you were in town back then. What can I do for you now?"

"I was looking for Liam, actually," Barbara said. "But Nina told me that he doesn't work here anymore?"

Belinda sighed, her breath gusting across the desk to ruffle one of the many piles of paperwork that seemed to have taken over every bare surface. The only spot free of clutter held a framed photo of a little girl of six or seven, with long blonde hair and laughing blue eyes. The edges of the frame were worn in spots, as if it were picked up often.

"I'm afraid not," Belinda said. "I'm not sure if you were aware of it during your visit, but three children went missing before you got here. When Liam, Sheriff McClellan I mean, couldn't find any trace of them, the county board fired him. It was pretty damned unfair, if you ask me, because the state troopers didn't find anything either, and the entire department searched night and day without coming up with a clue. But they fired him anyway, and replaced him with Frank Smith, the son in-law of Clive Matthews, the president of the board."

"I see," Barbara said. How Liam must have hated that. "And did Sheriff Smith solve the cases?" A glance at the man in the office showed he'd put down the magazine and seemed to be hard at work on his computer. Barbara was betting on a difficult game of Solitaire.

A bitter laugh escaped tight-pressed lips. "Frank Smith couldn't find his own ass if you drew him a map," Belinda said, although at least she kept her voice down. "Honestly, he's a lousy sheriff. Luckily Dunville and the rest of Clearwater County are pretty quiet most of the time, and the other deputies and I can take care of the occasional bar fight or domestic dispute."

"Were any of the children ever returned?" Barbara asked. She held her breath, although she was pretty sure she knew the answer already.

Belinda bit her lip. "No. They weren't. They vanished without a trace, and we never found so much as a stray fingerprint or the sighting of a suspicious car."

"Your daughter was one of the missing children, wasn't she?" Barbara said, as gently as she could manage. Gentle wasn't her customary mode, but she'd gotten a fair amount of practice in the last few years of having Babs around.

"She was," Belinda said, reaching out to stroke the picture. "It really killed Liam that he couldn't bring her back to me. I never blamed him, though. He would have walked through fire for that child."

Barbara's mind raced. None of this was right. They had found the children, who had been stolen by a rusalka who'd used a doorway that had been accidentally opened between the Otherworld and this one. The nasty creature had disguised herself with a glamour to look like a beautiful Human woman and had taken a job with Peter Callahan, whose company's use of fracking had opened up the portal in the first place. Together, Barbara and Liam had gone into the Otherworld and brought the children back, along with Babs, who was an unexpected bonus.

But it sounded as though none of that had come to pass. Something was terribly wrong with the time line. Barbara suspected that Babs was right when the little girl asked if it had something to do with all the magical chaos that had erupted back at the witch's house. But how?

"Did any more children go missing after your daughter?" Barbara wondered out loud.

"No, she was the last," Belinda said, sounding tired. "Whoever took them must have moved on somewhere else, although I check constantly to see if there is any news of similar incidents happening elsewhere, and so far I haven't come across anything."

"How odd," Barbara said. And it was. She was a little worried that the other woman would wonder why Barbara was asking so many questions, but from the look of it, Belinda was probably too exhausted and worn down to care. Although possibly she was also too polite. Not a problem Barbara had ever had.

"I met your mother the last time I was here," Barbara said, more or less randomly. She needed answers, but she didn't even know what questions to ask. "We had a nice chat about our mutual Russian roots. Is she well? I'd love to see her again now that I'm back in town."

"I thought you had a touch of an accent," Belinda said, a corner of her mouth turning up. I hadn't realized you'd met my mother. It must have been right before her heart attack."

"Her *what?*" Barbara gripped the edge of the desk. She rather liked the elderly woman, who she'd seen last week baking cookies with Babs and Mary Elizabeth, seemingly in perfect health.

"My mother was so upset about my daughter's disappearance, she ended up having a minor heart attack," Belinda explained. "She's better now, but she was in the hospital for weeks and hasn't really been the same since. She and my father gave up their farm and moved in with me."

Barbara drummed her fingers lightly on her leather-clad thigh. She kept coming across things that were different from what she remembered, but she wondered if this particular event wasn't somehow pivotal to the rest of the changes. If Mariska Ivanov had a heart attack and never *Called* on a Baba Yaga to help find her granddaughter, then it was possible that Barbara had come to the area a year ago for another reason and had never gotten involved in the search for the missing children at all.

Which was a pretty important piece of information, if it was true, but Barbara had no idea how it was at all helpful. Dammit.

"Thank you." Barbara stood up. "I appreciate your time."

She hesitated, not sure what else to say. "I'm going to fix this and get your daughter back" seemed rash and overly ambitious. "I'm sorry I seem to have somehow screwed everything up" wasn't at all useful and would probably just confuse the woman. And Barbara was already confused enough for both of them.

In the end, she just shook Belinda's hand and walked away, glaring into the sheriff's office on her way out of the building.

It was probably just a coincidence that the poor man's computer blew up just as she walked by. Probably.

When she got back to the Airstream, she loaded the BMW into the back of the truck and then sat in the front seat, trying to figure out what to do next. Babs slid into the rear seat, along with Chudo-Yudo, and tugged gently on a strand of Barbara's long dark hair.

"Where do we go now, Baba Yaga?" the little girl asked.

Barbara ran through several answers and discarded them all as too profane to utter in front of the child. "I'm not sure," she said. She could park the Airstream behind the yellow farmhouse and probably no one would notice, but the thought just made her sad. In the end, she could only think of one spot to go—the spot it had all started.

"I remember this place," Babs said, almost cheerfully as they pulled into the patch of meadow overlooking the Clearwater River. "This is where you brought me when I first came back to this side of the doorway. It is pretty here."

It was, too. An untidy half acre of crabgrass and wildflowers set at a wide curve in the road, Miller's Meadow was a perfect example of what a nice job nature did when left to itself. Its isolated location and the soothing babble of the river gave it a feeling of calm and serenity that had attracted Barbara to it in the first place.

She parked the Airstream carefully as close as she could

remember to the spot she'd put it originally, as if that action alone could magically make things go back to the way they were supposed to be. Then they all went inside and sat despondently in the living area.

"I take it you didn't find your sheriff?" Chudo-Yudo said after a few minutes of silence. He chewed on a large bone. Barbara and Babs each had cookies, although Barbara felt like she might choke on hers, and finally gave up and set it down on the plate mostly uneaten.

"No," she said shortly. Then sighed. "Apparently he's not sheriff anymore. They fired him when he couldn't find the missing children."

"But, Baba, you did find them," Babs said, her brown eyes even wider than usual. "You did. You found them and you found me. Liam helped. He was a hero."

"That was before," Barbara said. "Somehow everything has changed."

Babs put her cookie down too, and Chudo-Yudo helpfully snapped up the rejects.

"But how could this have happened?" Babs asked, a little plaintively. She found the Human world confusing enough on a daily basis, no matter how hard Barbara and Liam tried to make it make sense. Their current situation was obviously much, much worse. Barbara felt a little plaintive herself. Or like throwing something, which was closer to how she usually dealt with frustration.

"I'm not really sure," Barbara said. "I have never heard of

such a thing, even in the old tales my own Baba Yaga told me. But I have a theory of sorts. Let me see if I can explain it."

She snapped her fingers and a ball of yarn appeared, plucked from its usual resting spot in one of the storage cabinets that lined the walls. Barbara knitted occasionally, a skill her mentor had taught her to pass the time during the long, cold Russian winters, although Barbara had never really developed a knack for it. It was too fiddly for her, and when she missed a stitch or the yarn knotted up, she had an unfortunate tendency to turn it into something less annoying. Like a book. Or a potato.

Still, it would do for an illustration, as well as anything could.

She held up the coil of rough gray wool.

"Imagine that this yarn is our timeline. The one you and I remember, Babs, where everything turned out okay, and you and Liam and I ended up together." She rolled the ball along the floor, where it unrolled as it went. "Somehow time has moved backwards, so that we have moved backward a few years, and are now about a year from the events that culminated in the children being rescued." She retrieved the yarn and rewound it.

"Obviously, that shouldn't be possible, but since we're here, it clearly is." She growled quietly to herself. She only liked the impossible when *she* made it happen.

"But I don't remember this timeline you're talking about at all," Chudo-Yudo said, dropping cookie crumbs on the floor. "I don't remember Liam, or any of the other events you have talked about. If we went back along the timeline together, wouldn't I remember those lost years too?"

Barbara resisted the urge to throw the yarn across the room. Barely. "One would think so. But in this case, I think something else happened. A part of the witch's spell moved time in the wrong direction," she gazed at Babs, "which is one of the reasons why we never, ever, ever mess around with time when doing magic. It is just too unpredictable and hard to control."

Babs nodded. This was one lesson she was unlikely to forget.

"More than that, though," Barbara said, holding up the yarn again. "I think that when the witch's time-reversing potion mixed with my magic, and spilled over onto other herbs and tools in her kitchen, it caused an even more drastic reaction. Time didn't just move backwards, it unraveled."

She pulled apart the strands of yarn until the end was frayed and messy. "It would have been relatively easy to rewind time the way I rewound this ball of yarn. Unraveling, however, is a lot more complicated." She plucked at one strand. "Some pieces have stayed the same, like Babs being with us, and me having at least visited Dunville." She held out another one. "But other pieces have changed beyond recognition. The trick will be twisting them all back together so that they put us back where we should be. Where we started out."

Chudo-Yudo shook his massive head. "Can you do that? Is it even possible? Isn't there a chance that you might make things worse? I don't want to end up being an actual dog instead of a dragon. Or being stuck with some other Baba Yaga. I've barely gotten you trained the way I like you."

Barbara squeezed the ball of yarn until it squeaked and turned into a little gray mouse. "Oops," she said. "Sorry." She put the mouse down on the floor, where it scampered off to hide among the ever-changing flowers of the embroidered rug.

"I don't know, Chudo-Yudo." She rubbed her hand over her face, suddenly feeling exhausted beyond measure. "But I can tell you this. I am going to keep trying until I manage it. I waited eighty years to find Liam. I'm not going to lose him now."

CHAPTER FOUR

CHUDO-YUDO PONDERED THAT FOR A MOMENT. "IF YOU INSIST on doing this, I think you're going to need some help," he said. "More help than one very handsome dragon disguised as a pit bull and an adorable, very talented, but untrained miniature Baba Yaga can give you."

"Maybe we can ask the Riders to come," Babs said, perking up. She loved all three of her honorary uncles, who were always happy to play with her or teach her interesting things, like how to build a fort or navigate through a forest or kill a man using only one finger.

Barbara snorted. "Tempting, but this is a magical issue, not a brute force one. I'm not sure how much good Alexei, Gregori, or Mikhail would do us. My sisters, on the other hand, could definitely be useful."

Bella and Beka weren't her sisters by blood, exactly, but the three of them were all Baba Yagas, and together they dealt with any problems that fell under their job descriptions within the United States. They usually each worked on their own, but they were always willing to help each other out if necessary. They felt like sisters, and that was what mattered.

She pondered her choices briefly and then pulled out her cell phone and hit the number for Beka, the youngest of the Baba Yagas, who usually took care of issues on the Western third of the country. She lived by her beloved ocean in her hut on chicken legs-turned converted school bus.

Of course, Beka's phone, being magical as well as practical, recognized the call as coming from Barbara.

"When did you get a cell phone, Barbara?" the younger woman asked, sounding amazed.

Barbara rolled her eyes. "Never mind that," she said. "I've got an emergency. It's too complicated to get into on the phone. If you're not in the middle of a Baba Yaga task, is there any chance Marcus can spare you to come help me for a few days?"

There was a moment of silence on the other end of the call. "Marcus who?" Beka asked.

The writhing snake already taking up residence in Barbara's stomach suddenly had friends. She had a terrible feeling she was about to discover another unraveled piece.

"Former marine," she said carefully. "Currently a fisherman. Your husband. Marcus Dermott."

Beka laughed. "It can't be too bad a crisis if you're making jokes. You know perfectly well I'm not married." Then she added in a more sober tone, "Besides, Brenna isn't likely to want me to go. She's currently got me working on some menial project she has me doing as one of my tests. You know how much of a stickler she is for me finishing those once I've started them."

Barbara was aghast. She almost dropped the phone in her alarm, and then spoke without thinking. "What? Brenna is there? But Bella's Chudo-Yudo Koshka killed her after she tortured the Riders and stole their immortality!"

"What the *hell* are you talking about?" Beka sputtered. "Are you okay? Is all this nonsense supposed to be some kind of code to say you need help? Are you under an evil spell? Or have you just lost your mind?"

That one was distinctly possible. "Brenna is still a Baba Yaga, after everything she did to the Riders?" Barbara couldn't believe her ears. Surely the Queen would have punished Brenna, even if for some reason Koshka hadn't killed her in this timeline.

"Brenna has never done anything worse to the Riders than scold them when they showed up late," Beka said, worry coloring her voice. "And how could you have forgotten that the Queen let Brenna come out of retirement to continue my training?"

"The Queen did what? Why?"

Beka sighed. "Brenna talked her into it after I failed to help the Selkies and the Merpeople when that mysterious illness forced them to leave their homes, and then I allowed the Water of Life and Death to be stolen out of my bus. You knew all that. I'm really starting to worry about you, Barbara."

"Brenna stole the Water herself, and plotted with the Selkie prince Kesh to poison the Selkie and Merpeople's home with radioactive waste," Barbara said. But she was pretty sure she was wasting her breath. Clearly that whole situation had worked out much differently this time. "I don't suppose I showed up when this was all going on, and gave you advice?"

She'd been on a kind of honeymoon trip with Liam and the newly adopted Babs when this happened in the real timeline, and since there was no Liam in this one, she suspected that trip had never happened. How much difference had her talk with Beka made, and how much did it matter that Barbara hadn't been around to boost Beka's wobbly self-confidence?

"No, of course you didn't," Beka said in a resigned tone. She sounded defeated, and Barbara's chest tightened in sympathetic pain.

Brenna had spent years subtly undermining Beka's confidence because the older woman was jealous of Beka's youth and beauty, and hadn't wanted to give up the power that came with being a Baba Yaga. She'd only retired once the Queen of the Otherworld had insisted on it, and now, somehow, she'd weaseled her way back into the position. And back into chipping away at Beka, bit by bit, from the sound of it.

"I'm sorry, Beka," Barbara said. "Look, I know you won't believe me, but you did a great job as a Baba Yaga. You're smart and capable and kickass. Don't let Brenna tell you otherwise."

"You're being almost nice. Now I know there is something wrong with you," Beka said. But she did sound a little more cheerful. "Seriously, are you okay? You're sounding kind of nuts."

"It's complicated," Barbara said. "I promise, I'm not crazy. And I really do need to see you, if you can get away."

It wasn't as though Beka would have to drive across country, after all. Each of the Baba Yaga's former huts had magical doorways that opened into the Otherworld, and they could simply make their way through from one moveable house to another (although admittedly, that journey could be long and tricky or short and easy, depending on what mood the ever-changing Otherworld was in at the time).

"I'll see what I can do," Beka said. She hesitated. "You take care of yourself, okay?"

"You too," Barbara said, and ended the call. Beka had always been the most kind-hearted of the three of them. Barbara wasn't sure it was a trait that worked well for a Baba Yaga. She was glad that she was mostly cranky and difficult to get along with—it made it a lot more challenging for anyone else to play with her head.

Not that she needed anything to do that more than this damned situation already had.

"Is everything all right?" Babs asked, her normally smooth brow creased with worry.

"Not even a little bit, sweetheart," Barbara said. "But I think we've had as much bad news as we can handle in one day, so

I'm going to wait and call Bella tomorrow. For now, I think we should make something nice for dinner. Good food always cheers me up."

"Me too," Chudo-Yudo agreed happily. "Can we have steak? I know a steak would make me feel much better."

Barbara wasn't sure that even a three-course, five star meal made out of chocolate would make her feel better, but she knew she needed to keep her strength up. Something told her she was going to need it.

After dinner Barbara read Babs her favorite story, *The Little Prince*, a tale the girl seemed to identify with for some reason, and tucked her into bed. This was normally Liam's job when they were at home, and Barbara could tell that it was a difficult moment for Babs. For them both, if the truth be told.

Ironically, when they were on the road in the Airstream, Babs simply put herself to bed in the tidy sleeper cot that swung down from its hiding spot in the ceiling, and had from the very beginning. She had always been incredibly independent, no doubt because she'd mostly had to take care of herself during her years in the Otherworld living with an only sporadically sane woman to act as her parent. Babs had seemed perfectly content to continue her pattern of self-sufficiency, which suited Barbara—not the most maternal of women—to a tee.

Liam, on the other hand, had thrown himself into fatherhood with obvious enthusiasm, and Babs had indulged him, at first tolerating his ministrations with barely-disguised discomfort, but eventually coming to enjoy them as much as he did. Reading to her in bed had been his idea, as had tucking her in, even when she grew old enough that the action was more figurative than literal.

Barbara wasn't sure what moved her to take over his role that night, despite their being in the trailer, where they didn't normally bother with such things. She supposed she'd hoped it would bring them both some comfort. She wasn't sure she'd succeeded, although she had gotten a tiny smile when she'd given Babs her customary hair tug.

Once the girl was asleep, Barbara turned down the lights and went to stand by the window that looked out on the meadow. A nearly full moon shone brightly on the field and road, empty of life other than whatever small creatures roamed in the night. No shaggy-haired former sheriffs appeared out of the darkness, although she watched for over an hour.

Chudo-Yudo eventually came and stood next to her, leaning his warm bulk comfortingly against her leg. His weight almost knocked her over, but it was still a sweet gesture.

"I don't understand what's going on," he complained—quietly, so as not to wake up Babs. "But I'm sorry you're sad."

"Thank you, old friend," Barbara said, in an equally quiet voice. "I'm afraid sad doesn't even begin to cover it, but thank you."

They stood there in silence for a while. No one came. Barbara wasn't sure why she'd though someone might. Too many fairy tales in her formative years, perhaps, complete with charming princes and miraculous love stories. She'd gotten that once, against all expectations. It was probably too much to hope for that she would get it again.

"You were really married?" Chudo-Yudo said finally. "To a Human?" He clearly found the concept nearly impossible to wrap his head around. Barbara didn't blame him. If you'd suggested such a thing before she met Liam, she would probably have laughed. Or cold-cocked you.

"I was. I am." She twisted her dragon ring around on her finger. No matter what happened, she was definitely still married. "I know this all seems crazy to you, since it doesn't match up with any of your memories. As far as I can tell, Babs and I are the only ones not affected by the magic that rewrote the timeline, probably because we were at ground zero when it all blew up." The thought that Liam might not even recognize her when he saw her made her heart clench in her chest. She'd once been gnawed on by a pack of hyenas. It had been less painful than this.

"Would you mind keeping an eye on Babs? I want to go out for a while."

Chudo-Yudo raised one furry eyebrow but didn't comment. Instead he simply walked across the Airstream and plopped himself down heavily underneath Babs' bed. After a moment, he produced a large meaty bone out of a nearby cupboard, and settled down to gnaw on it in a desultory fashion.

Barbara let herself out of the trailer and set off on the motorcycle in perfect silence, not even disturbing the fox and her cubs that were out on an evening stroll. Magic had its advantages.

Drawn like a moth to the flame, Barbara followed the tugging of her heart as if it were an invisible string that connected one broken half to the other. A series of back country roads eventually brought her to a small house with black shutters and an uncut lawn. In the driveway, there was a familiar truck that bore an unfamiliar sign. It read: Liam McClellan, Handyman. No job too small or too large.

She parked the bike by the side of the road and walked on soundless boots to stand about three feet outside the house. From her vantage point, she could see into the living room, where the only man she had ever loved sat in a battered old recliner, watching a ball game and drinking a beer. His hair had gotten too long again, and to her eyes he seemed worn and sad.

Barbara wanted more than anything to open the door and walk inside, into this house he had once shared with a wife who betrayed him, where he now sat without solace in his sorrow and his loss. She had saved him from that once, but she didn't know how to save him from it now. So instead, she simply stood outside and watched him, and loved him with every atom of her being, until the light went out and she was left alone in the dark.

CHAPTER FIVE

Babs and Barbara were sitting at the kitchen table picking at a breakfast that neither of them really felt like eating when there was a knock at the door. Barbara's heart skipped a beat, but then she realized that Liam had no reason to know she was here, much less care enough to come by.

When she opened the door, she saw Belinda instead, clad in her unbecoming uniform and trying to look stern and official.

"Good morning," Barbara said. "This is a pleasant surprise. What can I do for you?"

Belinda coughed. "I'm afraid I've been sent to tell you that you can't park here without a permit, Doctor Yager. Any more than you could the last time you came to town."

Barbara would have resented the implication that she hadn't learned from experience, except of course that it was true. She'd been so preoccupied yesterday, she hadn't even thought about that stupid permit. Mind you, now that she had, it was easy enough to deal with. She put one hand behind her back and made an arcane gesture or three.

"I'm sure you're mistaken," she said lightly. "I think if you check into it, you'll find that all the correct paperwork is in place."

"I'll have to wait until I get back to town," Belinda said. "There's no cell service out here and even the radio in the police car doesn't usually work." As if to call her a liar, the radio squawked and Nina's voice came through, announcing that the permit had been found, never mind.

Déjà vu.

"Since you came all the way out here, would you like a cup of tea?" Barbara had a sneaking suspicion there was more behind this visit than a missing piece of paperwork. Her tea wasn't exactly a truth serum, but it did tend to encourage the people who drank it to speak whatever was on their minds, eventually. Another twitch of her fingers set the kettle to boiling on a previously cold stove.

"I suppose I could take my break now," Belinda said. She walked back to her car and spoke briefly into the handset, then took off her hat and entered the trailer cautiously.

"Wow," she said, looking around. "This isn't at all what I expected. It's…cozy. And surprisingly luxurious, at least by my standards, although I'm the first to admit that my idea of decorating is to toss an old quilt on top of the sofa to make it look less ratty. I've seen some RVs in my time, but none of them looked anything like this."

Barbara's lips twitched up in a tiny smile. Most people had a similar reaction when they entered expecting the usual staid colors and man-made fabrics and were greeted by rich brocades, velvet, and silk instead, in vivid jewel tones that set off the cherry and walnut cabinets. But this was her home—at least it had been before she created one with Liam, and was again for however long it took to fix this mess—and she liked a place with comfort and class.

"Thank you," she said. "I'm quite fond of it." She patted the nearest wall, and the slightest vibration, almost like a purr, rippled through the space.

Belinda looked startled. "Did you feel that?"

"Oh, that's just the wheels settling as the day heats up," Barbara said, and gestured to the table, which had miraculously been cleared of the debris from breakfast. Babs looked quite proud of herself, although there was a suspicious hint of toast crumbs around Chudo-Yudo's mouth to suggest he'd helped on a non-magical level. "Come sit down and I'll get the tea."

"Hello," Belinda said to Babs, sliding into the banquette seat. "I'm Deputy Shields. Is that your dog? He is very handsome."

Babs glanced at Barbara, clearly struggling with how to treat someone who was usually a friend as if she was a complete stranger. Barbara winked at her, and nodded.

"He is very handsome," Babs agreed solemnly. "But Barbara says if you tell him that, he will get a swelled head, and that his head is already large enough. He is not my dog, though. It is more like I am his girl."

"I have a cat," Belinda said. "That makes perfect sense to me. Is it okay if I pet him? I like dogs."

"How do you feel about dragons?" Babs asked in her usual serious tone.

Belinda blinked. "Uh, they're cool, I guess."

Chudo-Yudo rose gracefully to his feet like a mountain deciding it was tired of staying in one place, and considerately moved himself into the perfect position for an ear scratch.

"Holy crap, he really *is* large," Belinda blurted. Chudo-Yudo often had that effect on people. But she reached out and petted him anyway.

Barbara put three mugs of tea on the table, with lots of extra milk in Babs' cup. An equally milky brew was placed in a bowl on the floor in front of the dragon-dog.

"Your dog drinks tea?" Belinda said. "That's unusual."

"He's an unusual dog," Barbara said.

Belinda glanced around. "I suspect there isn't much about you that isn't unusual." She looked at Babs thoughtfully. "Shouldn't you be in school?"

"She's home schooled," Barbara said. "Well, technically trailer schooled at the moment, I suppose. This is Babs. And Chudo-Yudo."

The dragon-dog woofed.

"He says hello," Babs translated.

Belinda looked a bit bemused. "Hello, Chudo-Yudo. You know, my mother used to tell me stories from Russia that had a dragon in them with that same name."

"Isn't that a coincidence," Barbara said blandly.

"So, Babs," Belinda said, obviously trying to find some more normal topic of conversation. "What is your favorite subject?"

As always, Babs gave the question some serious thought before answering. "Magic. Well, perhaps mathematics. I am very good at math. So magic and math are both my favorites."

"Magic and math," Belinda repeated, blinking rapidly as she digested that. "You would get along well with my mother. She was a scientist when she was younger, back in Russia. She's very good at math too. And she loves stories about magic, especially the ones from the Old Country."

"Like the stories with Chudo-Yudo," Babs said in an approving tone. "Those *are* good stories."

Barbara took pity on Belinda, who bore the slightly confused look of someone who has wandered into a fairy tale when she was expecting a nice safe detective novel.

"How is your mother?" Barbara asked. "I was sorry when you told me she'd had some health problems." Babs looked concerned at this, but Barbara just shook her head and the girl subsided.

"She's well," Belinda said. "Frailer than she used to be, before…before everything happened." Mary Elizabeth's name hung in the air, unsaid, like the smoke from a burned out fire. "In fact, my mother is part of the reason I came out here."

"Is that so?" Barbara said, picking up the teapot. "Here, have a little more tea."

"It's very good," Belinda said. "What kind is it?"

"Russian caravan," Barbara said with the hint of a smile. "Appropriate, isn't it? Now, what were you saying about your mother?"

"I happened to mention you to her at dinner last night," the deputy said. "I told you my parents lived with me now, right?"

Barbara nodded.

"Anyway, my mother seemed quite intrigued by what I told her about you and the Airstream and everything, and she was kind of upset that she hadn't gotten a chance to meet you when you were in town last year. Maybe it's the Russian connection, I'm not sure." Belinda shrugged. "I told her you only had a slight accent, so you probably hadn't been there in years, but she was still quite adamant about getting to see you. I'm not sure why, but she hasn't shown this much interest in anything since her heart attack…" her voice trailed off.

"Ah," Barbara said, the other shoe dropping. "So you came to check me out and see if I could be trusted with your mother."

Belinda twitched. "Not exactly."

Chudo-Yudo gave a coughing laugh that sounded almost like a normal bark, and nudged her leg with his large head.

"Okay, pretty much that." Belinda covered her mouth with her hand, as if surprised to find the truth sneaking out. "Although I hadn't intended to say so."

"It's very strong tea," Barbara said. "And the answer is that I am extremely untrustworthy under many circumstances, but not when it comes to old Russian ladies. I assure you, Mariska is quite safe in my company."

"Mine too," Babs piped up.

"Ah, good to know," Belinda said. "Perhaps you would like to come to dinner, both of you? It would make my mother very happy. Which would make me quite happy."

"It is always good to have the law on your side," Babs said, quoting something Liam said often. It was kind of an inside joke between him and Barbara, who tended to find trouble and vice versa.

Belinda opened her mouth and then shut it again. Babs often had that effect on people.

"We'd love to come," Barbara said. "We might be staying in the area for a while, so it would be nice to meet some of the people who live here."

She fingered the end of her long nose. "You know, there was someone who was here last year that I was wondering about. Perhaps you know if she is still in the area. Her name is Maya, and she was the assistant to a man named Peter Callahan, whose company was buying up property to do fracking on. Is she still around, by any chance?"

Belinda shook her head. "I remember her, but no, she and Mr. Callahan are long gone. Maybe you didn't hear about it, but not long after you left, the governor actually banned fracking in New York State." She gave the first genuine smile Barbara had seen since they'd met up the day before. "Some people were disappointed, obviously, but a lot of us were really happy about the ban."

"Oh, right," Barbara said. "I vaguely remember hearing something about that." At the time, she hadn't given it much thought because she had already driven Callahan off and taken care of Maya. "So they left after the ban was passed?"

"Sure," Belinda said. "Nothing for them to stay for, thank god. At least, the company packed up its operations, and I assume that Peter Callahan was sent to some other state that wasn't so lucky, and Maya went with him. Was she a friend of yours?"

"Hardly," Barbara said dryly. Her friends rarely tried to kill her. Almost never. "We merely crossed paths. That's all."

She realized that she needed to do two things before she pursued the issue of Liam any further. One, check on the unauthorized door to the Otherworld that Maya had been using, and make sure it had really been closed.

And two, visit the Otherworld to see if she could find Maya and the children she stole. If Maya wasn't here, perhaps she'd gone back there. If a year had really passed since the children were taken through the doorway in this timeline, it might be too late to get them back. But Barbara had to try. Not just for the woman sitting in front of her, but for all the parents whose children had never come home because Barbara hadn't gotten involved. There was no way in hell she wasn't going to try and make that right.

The next morning, Barbara left Babs doing her homework with Chudo-Yudo (the dragon was a lot better at fractions than Barbara was) and rode her motorcycle to the dusty back road that led to the cave where the doorway had been.

On the way, she drove past the small farmstead owned by a young couple she'd taken a liking to after Maya had contaminated the herbal remedies Barbara had been selling to the local folks. When Barbara met them, Lily, her husband Jesse and their two small children had been struggling to make ends meet. Barbara had helped them out in the short term by magically getting Jesse a minor lottery win, and long term by teaching the couple to grow herbs they could sell to restaurants and farmers markets, as well as making soaps and lotions out of them. Barbara wasn't exactly known for her soft heart or her generous nature, but she believed in helping people who were willing to help themselves.

She'd hoped to stop in and say hello, but when she got to their farm, the house was deserted and there was a "for sale" sign at the end of the driveway. Barbara decided she was liking this new unraveled reality less and less.

A couple of miles away, a narrow road led to a barely visible path, impassible even by her BMW. So she left the bike humming a show tune quietly to itself and made her way carefully to the entrance of a cave. It was so well hidden by shrubs and overgrown trees that she would never have spotted it if she hadn't been there before. But now she shoved her way through the prickling thorns and springy green saplings until she found herself in the Stygian darkness underground.

Summoning up a glowing light from her outstretched palm, she peered around her at the damp walls, jagged rock floor, and uneven ceiling that threatened to put a dent into even her hard head. It was nice to see that something hadn't changed. Even the squeaking of the bats seemed melodically familiar.

She followed the path she remembered until she came to the place where the doorway had once stood, a shimmering arch into a forbidden world. Now there was only a relatively new rock fall, a solid wall of stone that blocked any movement forward. Barbara sniffed the air, and ran her fingers over the outer edge of the wall. Familiar magic tingled as it coursed its way up her arm.

Excellent.

Well, that answered one question, at least. The magic she sensed was her own, so she had clearly closed the doorway, either because she'd found it herself or at the Queen's command, if its existence had been discovered from the other side. Of course, that left plenty of questions unanswered, like why had Barbara hung around for a week, if the doorway had been dealt with? Had it taken her that long to find it, or had something else happened? It was maddening to have the memories of one timeline while wandering around in another.

She complained about it to Chudo-Yudo later over lunch. "It's as though everyone around me remembers a fake life, and I'm the only one who remembers the real one."

"I remember too, Baba Yaga," Babs said around a mouthful of tuna sandwich with its crusts cut off.

Barbara nodded. "I know, sweetie."

"Well, it doesn't seem fake to me," Chudo-Yudo growled. He had an entire tuna—fins, scales, and a glittering silver tail that hung out of one side of his mouth as he chewed. "And if you want to know what you did, why don't you just ask me? I mean, I was there for some of it, and you told me about some of the rest. Mind you, you were being oddly secretive there at the end, but still, I ought to be able to fill in some of the blanks."

"I'm an idiot," she said, smacking herself on the head with the hand not holding her own (scale-free) sandwich. "Why didn't it occur to me that if you didn't remember the timeline Babs and I do, that meant you'd remember the other one?"

"Well, you have been preoccupied pining over your lost sheriff," Chudo-Yudo said indulgently. "Although at first I thought you'd just lost your mind. It was a lot easier to believe that than it was some story about altered timelines, or that you'd actually fallen in love. With a *Human*, no less." He looked thoughtful. "I'm not sure insanity is completely off the table."

"Very funny," Barbara said, giving him the rest of her lunch. She still didn't have much appetite.

He shrugged, his furry white shoulder almost knocking the

table over. The table, being used to such things, righted itself with an indignant huff. There were advantages and disadvantages to living in a semi-sentient former hut and sometimes it was hard to tell one from the other.

"It isn't, really," he said. "You have to admit that your tale is hard to believe. Even without the mind-boggling love story. Even I might have been excused if I doubted your sanity—although probably not. We've been together for a long time and you have always been the sanest person I know. The crankiest, maybe, but also the sanest. But if you *and* Babs both insist on the same version of the truth, I have to believe it. Even if it is hard to wrap my brain around the concept of you being married." He gave her a sharp-toothed grin. "To a Human."

"Yes, you mentioned that part." Barbara rolled her eyes at him. "Feel free to stop mentioning it; there's a good dog."

Babs ignored their bickering from long practice. "It is good that Chudo-Yudo believes us, Baba Yaga, but what do we do now?"

The humor fled from Barbara's eyes like a frightened rabbit running from a wolf. "Now we go to the Otherworld and visit the Queen," she said.

"Oh," Babs said. "The Queen."

"Crap," Chudo-Yudo agreed. Nobody argued.

CHAPTER SIX

BARBARA DECIDED, AFTER MUCH DISCUSSION AND NO SMALL amount of argument, that it was important for all three of them to go see the Queen together.

She changed into her formal "going to court" attire—in this case, a red silk tunic embroidered along the hem with sinuous black Oriental dragons, and black velvet leggings tucked into high-heeled black leather boots that made her look even more imposing than she already was. Her normally wild dark hair was corralled into a bejeweled mesh woven out of silver to match the silver sword that hung at her waist from a matching gemstone studded belt.

"You look very pretty," Babs said as Barbara bent down to tuck a ruby-tipped barrette into the girl's asymmetrical pixie-cut hair. Babs was dressed in a miniature version of Barbara's own outfit, except that her tunic was a muted sky blue and its matching dark blue boots had flat heels.

"Thank you," Barbara said, straightening up after giving the girl's outfit one last tug. It didn't do to appear before the Queen in anything less than perfect order, if you could help it. Her Majesty was nothing if not a stickler for protocol. "You look nice too."

A barking cough drew her eyes to the massive white pit bull waiting patiently for them to finish. His preparations were much simpler, since they were limited to having Barbara buckle on the jeweled collar that attached to the flask of precious Water of Life and Death he guarded. If the dragon-dog was going to the Otherworld, so was the Water.

"You too, Chudo-Yudo, but you are always so handsome, it hardly seems worth commenting on."

He gave her a lolling pit bull smile. "Well, you're not wrong," he said. "Can we go now? The sooner we get this over with, the happier I'll be."

It wasn't that he didn't like visiting the Otherworld, which was the only place he could change back into his natural form and literally spread his wings, but the High Queen of the Otherworld was as temperamental and unpredictable as she was gorgeous, and any visit to her court came with its own risks.

Once they were all ready, Barbara opened the closet that doubled as a hidden entrance to the passageway to the Otherworld. She stared at the rows of mostly black shirts, pants, dresses, and jackets that hung there, sighed, and closed the door. Then she rattled the wonky handle and gave the bottom of the door a forceful nudge with the tip of one boot.

The closet let out a tiny squeak of protest, but when she

opened it again, the interior was filled with a swirling mist through which barely visible sparks could be seen flitting to and fro. The three of them trooped through until they came out the other side into a landscape of rolling chartreuse hills dotted with oddly shaped trees under a faintly lavender sky. Three giant blue rabbits played a complicated game of tag made more interesting by the large wings that unfurled from their backs at the sight of the newcomers.

Barbara exhaled in relief at the (relative) normality of the scene before her. When Maya had been traveling back and forth through the illicit doorway with the stolen children, she had thrown off the balance between the Human world and the Otherworld, causing major unsettled shifts on this side of the door. Now, as then, Barbara's closing that passage seemed to have corrected the imbalance and returned the magical land to its usual uncanny splendor.

It was good to see the Otherworld looking as it should, but it wasn't completely unchanged. Glancing up, Barbara saw that all three moons, two crescents facing in opposite directions with a full moon in between, hung straight in the sunless yet still bright sky. In the original timeline, one of the crescents had ended up slightly crooked as the result of the Queen's fit of temper. Clearly that hadn't happened here. At least not yet. Barbara wasn't sure *what* that meant.

They followed a path lined on both sides with tall orange and yellow sunflowers whose chatter rose and fell with a sound like chimes. A winding river accompanied them most of the way there, adding its melodic murmuring to the background. A water elemental waved at them gaily as they passed.

The castle appeared when it was good and ready to, as usual, its stone walls glittering under graceful towers that seemed to reach upward with impossible fragility. Gaily colored pennants flew from the tops of tall spires. The castle grounds rolled out before them like a perfect carpet of moss and grass, dotted here and there by oversized mushrooms that acted as seating for the elegant lords and ladies of the court.

The group wandered past a life-sized game of chess being played using goat-legged fauns for pawns and various other magical creatures for the other pieces. A particularly shaggy set of disgruntled looking centaurs towered over the rest.

A helpful brownie carrying a tray of crystal goblets pointed them toward the back of the castle. There they found the Queen, her consort, and some of her majesty's more favored courtiers dining al fresco by the edge of an azure blue pond the size of a small lake. Barbara recognized the six white swans floating near a fountain that shot rainbow-hued streams of water into the air. Something else that had changed in her world but not here.

"Baba Yaga, how lovely!" the Queen cried when she spotted them. "Were We expecting you?" She used the royal "We," of course.

As always, the Queen looked ethereally beautiful. Her silvery-white hair was piled atop her head in a complicated arrangement of curls and braids, adorned by a gold tiara studded with amethysts, diamonds, and tiny pearls. A matching necklace hung around her long neck, and her gossamer white silk gown was covered with a fine netting hung with yet more pearls, each more delicate than the last.

She was a vision of perfection, set off even more by her handsome consort's striking dark hair, neat pointed beard, and dove gray tunic and leggings. They sat side by side on carved wooden chairs that weren't *quite* thrones.

Barbara bowed so deeply, her forehead nearly brushed the ground. "I am afraid not, Your Majesty. I hope we haven't come at a bad time."

The Queen waved one languid hand. "Not at all, dear Baba. Our lunch is mostly a forgotten memory, and We merely nibble on its remains. Do come and talk to Us. Things here have been remarkably boring of late, and you always manage to entertain."

Barbara hoped the Queen still thought so after she heard the latest strange tale.

"Thank you, Your Majesty. You remember my apprentice Babs, I hope." She had no idea if they would or not, after Chudo-Yudo's initial reaction.

"Of course," the Queen said. The King gave Babs a friendly smile. Children were highly valued in the Otherworld, because most of those who resided there were both long-lived and rarely fertile. "You brought her to meet Us when you first decided to take her in and train her to follow in your footsteps." A tiny wrinkle disturbed the otherwise perfect royal brow. "How odd. One does not remember the exact circumstances of that meeting, although We are quite certain it occurred."

She turned to her consort. "My darling, you must remember. Where did Baba Yaga say she found the child?"

The King looked, if anything, more baffled than she did. "I must confess, I do not remember ever seeing this charming urchin before, although it is clear from her aura that she is, in fact, Our Baba's trainee. How is this possible?"

Barbara bowed again, hoping she wasn't going to be turned into something unpleasant sometime in the next minute or two. "I am afraid there has been an accident, Your Majesties. A magical accident, resulting in the unraveling of time and circumstance. The history you remember is not the one that I and Babs have experienced. This current reality is a lie."

There was a stunned silence around the table as her words sank in.

"Impossible," the Queen said, sitting up even straighter in her chair. The wooden arms sprouted bright pink flowers that blossomed and died almost immediately. "How would such a thing even happen?"

Barbara could feel the muscles in her jaw tighten, and it felt as though her words had to fight their way past clenched teeth. But not speaking wouldn't help her now.

"It is difficult to explain, Your Majesties. To be honest, I do not completely understand it myself. I can only tell you that a few days ago, I was living in a reality that was very different from the one in which I find myself now. I was on my way to take a family vacation when I was *Called* to deal with a Human witch who was in far over her head. This witch had created a potion that could actually turn back time."

The court gasped in unison.

"I confess, with some chagrin, that I underestimated this woman." Barbara grimaced. "It was an error completely of my own making, Your Majesties, although I have paid a steep price for my hubris. I assumed that because she was a Human, and because her intentions were more prosaic than evil, that she could not be any real threat. I was, alas, proven completely wrong in that assumption."

"Do continue, Baba Yaga," the Queen said. "We are on the edge of Our seats with suspense."

The King nodded in agreement. "What happened? Did this woman summon demons to her aid? Invoke ancient and arcane powers handed down to her by her ancestors? It must have been something quite dramatic."

The courtiers present held their collective breath and waited for her to continue her story. Barbara almost hated to go on, since there was little doubt that the facts would be much more disappointing than whatever their imaginations had dreamt up.

"Nothing so exciting, I'm afraid, Your Majesties," Barbara said. "This Human had become obsessed with halting the natural course of aging—both her own, and others, for a price, of course. You would be amazed how much these mortals will pay to slow the inevitable forward march of the clock." She shook her head.

"When I arrived, I discovered that this woman, Katherine, had done what should have been impossible. She had somehow created an elixir that affected time itself. It was clear from her own face, which appeared many years younger than her actual age, that she had immense natural powers. I learned too late just how strong she was, when she attacked me in an effort to prevent me from destroying the potion she had crafted."

Another gasp. The penalty for attacking a Baba Yaga was death. Of course, most Humans had no way of knowing that. And whether or not she had, Katherine Chanter had certainly paid the penalty in the end.

"She attacked you?" The King's tone was a mixture of dismay and reluctant admiration. "Did she not know who you were?"

"She knew," Barbara said with a grimace. "But I was threatening all she valued most, and I suspect she would rather have died than to have lost that which she had sought for so long." One corner of her mouth twitched up. "Besides, you must remember, I am mostly a legend in the lands beyond the doorways. It is unlikely she took that legend seriously enough."

The Queen tapped a lacy ivory fan on the edge of her chair before flicking it open and waving it gracefully through the air. "One assumes you corrected that misapprehension, Baba Yaga." It was a statement, not a question.

Barbara sighed. She had the sneaking suspicion that her reputation wasn't going to be at all improved by the rest of the tale.

"Yes and no, Your Majesty." Next to her, Chudo-Yudo gave an obvious wince. She couldn't blame him, since he knew what came next.

"The witch had a large batch of her potion boiling over an open fireplace in her kitchen when I got there, and there were many herbs and other tools of her trade in the nearby vicinity," Barbara explained. "When I told Katherine that I could not allow her to continue interfering with the natural course of time, she hurled a magical curse at me. A curse of the most violent and malignant kind, intended to kill me."

Another gasp rose from her audience.

"Whatever did you do, Baba Yaga?" one of the courtiers asked.

The Queen rolled her violet-colored eyes. Daintily. "We assume you killed her first, of course," Her Majesty said, as if any other outcome would have been too ridiculous to mention.

"I did," Barbara admitted reluctantly. "But *mostly* accidentally." This was not to say she wouldn't have killed the woman on purpose if given the chance—that curse had been cast with complete disregard for the presence of Babs, and while Barbara could excuse someone trying to do away with her, attacking her adopted daughter was a guaranteed way to end up mangled, dismantled, and altogether deceased.

"Katherine caught me off guard and I only had time to put up a defensive shield. The shield reflected her own curse back upon her, and that was what actually killed her."

The King stroked his beard thoughtfully. "Hmmm," he said. "Not as impressive an ending as One might have hoped for, but still, the witch was dead and you were not, so that is satisfying enough. We do not quite understand what this has to do with this disruption of time you claim has occurred, however."

"I'm afraid I hadn't finished, Sire," Barbara said. "The blowback from the Human's curse mixed with my magic, and she was thrown up against the cauldron containing her illicit time-reversing brew. The potion spilled into the fire, various herbs were blown into the conflagration, and before you could say 'abracadabra,' the entire place was on fire. A fire fueled as much by magic as by flame, so that the entire house went up in an instant and Babs and I were lucky to be able to make our way out in time. By the time we had gotten to a safe distance, there was nothing left but ashes and regret."

The Queen shrugged one silk-clad shoulder. "Unfortunate, but these things happen to those whose reach exceeds their grasp. You are not responsible for the end result, Baba Yaga."

"Perhaps not, Your Majesty," Barbara said, not willing to let herself off the hook that easily, but not foolish enough to argue with the Queen. "But it wasn't until Babs and I returned to the Airstream—our traveling hut—that we discovered that things had gone much more seriously awry than I had initially supposed. Upon our arrival, we found Liam, my husband, had vanished, and Chudo-Yudo had no memory of his existence in our lives. It took Chudo-Yudo a moment to remember Babs, and further developments showed us that time had not only unwound itself to a point almost three years previous to the last moments that Babs and I knew we had lived though, but also unraveled so that the reality that remained no longer resembled that which we knew to be true."

There was silence for a moment after she finished her recitation, and then the Queen said in a shocked tone, "My darling Baba Yaga…did you say *husband?*"

Barbara sighed. This was going to be even tougher than she'd thought.

CHAPTER SEVEN

CHUDO-YUDO SHOOK HIS MASSIVE HEAD. "I KNOW. THAT WAS the part I found the most difficult to believe as well, Your Majesty."

Barbara nudged irritably him with the toe of her boot. It was like kicking a rock. Why was the idea of her finding love so damned shocking to everyone? Just because she never had before, and because she had a *tiny* tendency to be antisocial and a little short-tempered…

"Yes, Your Majesty. In my timeline, I have been married for three years to a Human named Liam. He is a sheriff, one who enforces the law, and he was of great help to me on a mission you assigned me. I assure you, in the history I recall, you gave your blessing for the union, and even allowed me to share very small amounts of The Water of Life and Death with him, so he would age more slowly than normal."

The Queen shook her head. "How remarkable. It is not that

We doubt your word, Baba Yaga, but you must admit that this story sounds quite fantastical." She gazed thoughtfully at Babs, who gazed thoughtfully back, her dark brown eyes old beyond their years.

The King leaned forward. "Is it possible that you are under some sort of spell, or suffering from exhaustion?"

Barbara's hands curled into fists at her sides, more out of frustration than anger. She couldn't blame them for not believing her. The story *was* fantastical. No less true for being so, but she wasn't sure she would have believed it if anyone else had told it to her.

"I assure you, Sire, I am quite well," she said. *Broken heart aside.* "And my tale, although bizarre, is quite real."

The Queen pursed her perfect rosebud pink lips. "Do you have anything that can prove the veracity of your saga? Some token of this time We cannot recall as you do?"

She tapped the fan again, a sure sign of agitation. Barbara sympathized with the Queen's frustration. How could she make them accept the impossible, the incomprehensible, even in this land where the impossible happened in one form or another every day?

Babs pulled on Barbara's tunic to get her attention, and Barbara bent down so the small girl could whisper a suggestion.

Barbara rewarded her with a smile and a quick tug of the hair before stepping closer to the Queen's chair.

"I have this," she said, sliding her dragon ring off her finger. "Liam gave this to me when he proposed." (Admittedly, after she had asked him first.) She held it out so that the diamond in the dragon's mouth glinted in the three moons' light. "He clearly searched for just the right ring for me."

"Why Baba Yaga, are you blushing?" the King said, humor coloring his voice. He turned to his wife. "That alone makes me think there must be something to this. Our Barbara, blushing over the thought of a man. Never did I think I would see the day."

Barbara's cheeks heated even more, and Babs gave a rare giggle.

"They kiss all the time," she told the Queen. "It is very silly."

"Indeed," the Queen said. "We can see that it would seem so. Wait until you are a little older." She bestowed a radiant smile upon her consort, who returned it filled with the accumulated devotion of millennia. "It will, perhaps, make more sense to you then."

Her beautiful face grew stern again as she put out her palm to receive the ring. Barbara hesitated for a second, unwilling to let her one last connection to Liam out of her grasp. Despite the wide open vistas around her, it felt as though she couldn't get enough air into her lungs.

"We shall return it, Baba Yaga," the Queen said softly. "But We must be able to touch it to sense its whole essence." She reached up and plucked the ring out of Barbara's fingers, then closed her hand around it and brought it up to her chest, eyes drooping shut as she tuned in on the energy contained within the piece of jewelry.

"What is she doing?" Babs asked in a low voice. "Is it magic?"

"Of a sort," Barbara explained. "Any item that belongs to someone takes on some of the aura of the person who owns it. Things that have great emotional meaning, especially those which are worn or carried for a long time, absorb that emotion. Those who have a gift for it can sometimes sense feelings or even memories that have attached themselves to the item."

"It is called psychometry," Chudo-Yudo added, leaning around Barbara's legs to put his face next to the child's. "Even some Humans can read the history of an object, if they happen to have that talent." He gave a snuffling woof, as if dubious about such skill residing in a mere Human. "The Queen, of course, has much stronger abilities than most, since her magic is drawn from all those who inhabit the Otherworld."

"Shhh," a lizard-like courtier hissed, his green tail lashing. "I want to hear what she says."

The Queen was silent for a moment. When her violet eyes opened, they had darkened to a vivid amethyst hue, her irises rimmed with gold.

"So much love," she said in an almost reverent tone. "We would never have thought you capable of it, Baba Yaga. But it shines out like the glow of a thousand suns. Love, and respect, and loss, and fear, and determination. But most of all love. We can see an image of a tall man with dark blond hair and broad shoulders. He is not unattractive, for a Human, and his love too is held in this ring."

She grimaced. "We have caught glimpses of memories and images that make no sense to Us. Some of them are quite horrible—something to do with the Riders? Human children. And...a rusalka?" The Queen sighed and handed the ring over to her consort, who had been eying it eagerly. "Feel free to try it yourself, my treasure, but it is unlikely that it will mean any more to you than it did to me."

The King held the golden dragon for a moment, then dropped it back into Barbara's eager hand. "As you say, my dearest. Many images and strong emotions. No doubt I perceived it even less clearly than did you, but still…it seems that our Baba is telling the truth. However incredible that truth might be."

"This is very bad," the Queen said, leaning back in her chair and pondering all the permutations. "Such a thing should not have happened, but since it has, something must be done about it. We cannot know what changes have been wrought that We are as yet unaware of, but time is not meant to be trifled with or changed. It is a very serious matter."

Barbara took a deep breath. She'd survived the first part of the explanation; it remained to be seen how well she would fair after the second.

"I am afraid it is worse than you think, Your Majesty. Those children you saw in my memories were stolen away from their Human parents by a scheming rusalka who used an illicit doorway to bring them from my world into yours. Once here, she traded them to a few of the more influential members of your court for power to boost her own. In my own timeline, I was able, with Liam's help, to retrieve the children and return them to their homes. In this current universe, the children are still missing, and I regret to say, are likely still hidden away here."

"What?" The Queen rose from her seat, pale cheeks suffused with anger. "You must be mistaken, Baba Yaga. No member of my court would be so foolish. It breaks Our strictest rules."

The Paranormal people had once lived on the other side of the doorway, coming and going as they pleased. But as the Human population grew, it became harder and harder for the magical folks to hide, and it became more dangerous to continue to try to coexist. The Humans tolerated the tiny pranks and mysterious ways of their uncanny neighbors, but the occasional theft of their children aroused such fury, the Queen eventually forbade it altogether.

Such actions had been part of the reason she eventually moved as many as could go to the Otherworld for good. She would have no tolerance for those who broke this particular edict.

Barbara prayed that she was right, and the same folks who had been involved the first time had the children now.

"I can tell you which of your lords and ladies were involved in the original timeline, Majesty, and you can send your guards to search their homes." She swung around and pointed at three different couples, all among the highest level of the King and Queen's inner circle. One strikingly beautiful pink-haired woman immediately prostrated herself on the ground, sobbing and begging for mercy.

The royal couple looked grim. "Do as the Baba Yaga says," the King commanded three sets of fierce-looking guards in gleaming silver armor. "Search their houses and bring us anything untoward you find."

Barbara held her breath the entire time they were gone, which thankfully wasn't long. The guards returned with three dazed and blank-eyed children, a tall girl whose light brown hair was already taking on a vaguely silvery hue, a small boy of about two who was seemingly unchanged from the day he had been taken, and a small girl Barbara had once known well. Mary Elizabeth had the same blonde tresses, blue eyes, and stubborn chin Barbara was so familiar with, but she looked closer to the age she had been when Barbara set out on her vacation in her own timeline, eleven, than the eight years old she should have been in the current timeline. She had aged faster in the Otherworld than she should have.

"Damn it," she muttered. "I was afraid of that."

Chudo-Yudo growled under his breath. "They've been here too long, haven't they?"

"Yes," Barbara said. "Two of them are older than they should be, and one hasn't aged at all." Time flowed differently on this side of the doorway, which is why there were legends of people stumbling through a crack into the lands of faerie and coming back years later completely unchanged, or a day later and seemingly twenty years older.

But one crisis at a time.

The Queen stood up as the guards brought the children into the room. She twitched a finger and the three couples were marched over to stand in front of her and her consort. "*You,*" she said, pointing her fan at each one in turn. "You dare to break Our laws and risk the safety of every denizen of the Otherworld? You sat in Our court every day, ate at Our table and *lied to Our face?*"

There was an explosion high in the sky, and one of the crescent moons was suddenly hanging canted at an angle, burning a little dimmer than the rest. Tiny sparkling fragments rained down upon the ground, causing the emerald green grass to sizzle and hiss. A splashing sound heralded the high-pitched shrieks of six lovely maidens as they materialized in the middle of the pond, shedding pure white feathers as they made their way to shore.

Barbara watched the erstwhile swans wobble as they attempted to use legs for the first time in years. The Queen ignored them. No doubt whatever minor offenses had gotten them turned into swans in the first place paled in comparison to the crimes she was dealing with now.

Ironically, Barbara felt almost cheerful. In her own timeline, the Queen had blown up the moon and changed the ladies in waiting back from swans. So at least something was back on track, although an angry Queen is never a good thing.

"Explain yourselves," the King said in a deep voice.

The three couples babbled and pleaded and protested, sounding for all the world like a flock of some kind of exotic twittering birds. Unfortunately, there wasn't a helpful word in the bunch. None of them had seen the rusalka who called herself Maya since they had traded her a portion of their magical powers for the children she had stolen. None of them had any idea where she was now.

"Enough of this," the Queen finally said, shouting to be heard over the noise. "You are all an embarrassment and unworthy to a part of Our court. You betrayed Our trust and broke Our most immutable law. There will be no forgiveness. Instead, let you stand as an example to the rest, lest others forget the price for such a crime."

She waved her fan as if it were a magic wand, and where the six courtiers had stood, there were only elegant stone statues which bore their likeness.

"Take them to the south gardens," she said to the guards, her expression icy. "I do not wish to look at them any time soon."

She turned back to Barbara, her amethyst gaze softening only slightly.

"So, Baba Yaga, it would seem that yet another part of your unlikely tale has been proven to be true. We wish it had been otherwise." She returned to her seat, taking her consort's hand as if seeking comfort. "That such a thing could happen right under Our nose is quite distressing.

They all turned and looked at the small Humans still standing with the guards who had brought them in, seemingly unaffected by the fuss or the transformation of those who had been caring for them. The little boy was playing with a purple toad wearing a jeweled collar, and the girls watched a trio of colorful butterflies the size of dinner plates flit around over their heads.

"We assume you will return the children to their parents now," the King said, a hint of regret in his tone. Children were rare in the Otherworld, and therefore treasured. "One supposes they are missed."

"You have no idea, Your Majesty," Barbara said, gazing at them with regret. "Their loss has nearly destroyed those who love them. But alas, I can't take them back, not like this."

The Queen narrowed her eyes. "What do you mean, you cannot take them back, Baba Yaga? This wrong must be righted. It is your duty."

"Indeed, Your Highness, there is nothing I would like more," Barbara said, staring at Mary Elizabeth—so close that a few strides would bring the girl to her side, and yet so far from being truly found. How was Barbara supposed to face the girl's mother now? Another band tightened to add to the already crushing pressure around her chest. She would have liked to have blown up a moon too, if she thought she could get away with it.

"They have been here too long," Barbara explained. "When I rescued them the last time—" *Argh. Time shifts. There was no good way to talk about them.* "That is to say, in the timeline I experienced, the children had only been here a short time. In this timeline it has been a year or more, and they have either aged too much or not at all."

She looked at their blank eyes with sorrow, and added in a quieter voice, "And your enchanted land has worked its magic.

I suspect they no longer remember where they came from or who they truly are. Unless I can somehow change things, these children can never be returned to their parents. It is too late."

The King and Queen exchanged frustrated glances, and the Queen turned her basilisk glare in Barbara's direction.

"Well then, Baba Yaga, it is clear that you will have to find some way to fix this unraveled time line of yours. There is nothing We can do, since Our magic rules only the Otherworld, not that which lies on the other side of the doorway. So it is up to you."

The fan tapped one more time on the arm of her chair before coming to rest, quivering. Much like Barbara's knees.

"You *will* fix this, Baba Yaga." The "or else" went unsaid, but clearly implied. "And you will fix it soon."

"Crap," Chudo-Yudo muttered.

Barbara couldn't have said it better herself.

CHAPTER EIGHT

"I will do my very best, Your Majesty," Barbara said, straightening her spine. "But before I go, there is one more matter I need to speak of."

She looked around at the members of the court who still watched them avidly, their faces alternately either amused, appalled, or coolly unaffected by the drama unrolling before them.

"But it is of an extremely sensitive nature, and perhaps best kept between ourselves," she suggested, as tactfully as possible.

The Queen raised one elegant silvery-white eyebrow, but following Barbara's gaze around the clearing, nodded to acknowledge her point.

"Go away," the Queen said to the courtiers, waving her fan gracefully through the air.

The courtiers went. The Queen was clearly in no mood to be argued with.

"Very well, Baba Yaga," the Queen said when it was just her, the King, Barbara, Chudo-Yudo, and Babs. "What can possibly be so important and so delicate a topic that We cannot discuss it in front of Our court?"

She took a dainty sip of effervescent wine from a goblet on the golden table next to her. Barbara couldn't be sure, but she suspected that the Queen had only acquiesced to Barbara's request to buy herself a few moments to recover from her shock and anger.

"It is about Brenna," Barbara said. "I spoke to Beka, and she told me that you'd allowed Brenna to resume her duties as Baba Yaga. You know that normally I would never question your actions, Majesty, but I have to tell you, you have made a terrible mistake in doing so." She held her breath and waited to be turned into something.

The King cleared his throat. His ebony stare pierced her to her core. "I beg your pardon?"

"Brenna," Barbara repeated. "She is evil. A menace to all we hold dear. And she is undermining Beka's confidence so much you are likely to lose her as a Baba Yaga entirely. Which is exactly what Brenna wants."

"My dear Barbara," the Queen said in a cool tone. "We admire your loyalty to your sister Baba, but it was necessary to return Brenna to her role as Baba Yaga—on a strictly temporary basis—in order to allow Beka more time to grow into her position. She failed spectacularly on her first major solo assignment, and even allowed her portion of The Water of Life and Death to be stolen out of her traveling hut when her Chudo-Yudo abandoned his post to assist her. We had no choice."

Barbara was afraid that the sound of her teeth grinding together would be audible to their majesties. "You don't understand. Brenna tricked you." She backed up a little. "That is, she fooled us all. But I promise you, what I say is true. In the timeline I lived through, she did horrific things."

"What horrific things?" the King asked. He sounded more amused than alarmed. "Admittedly, she was becoming somewhat erratic toward the end of her career, a tad eccentric, even for a Baba Yaga, which was why We insisted it was time for her to retire. But peculiar is far from evil. Surely you exaggerate."

"I only wish I did, Your Highness," Barbara said grimly. She shuddered as she remembered everything Brenna had put them all through. "Brenna spent years chipping away at Beka's confidence and persuading both Beka and Your Majesties that she wasn't ready to assume the mantle of Baba Yaga. Brenna didn't want to give up the power, or the longevity that comes from drinking The Water of Life and Death. Of course, none of us realized that until it was too late."

"Most Baba Yagas are happy to finally set down the burden of their obligations and live out their retirement in a comfortable corner of Our lands," the Queen said. "Yes, Brenna resisted more than most, no doubt from an overblown sense of duty, but eventually We persuaded her it was time to hand over her role to Beka, who she had trained so ably. Or so We thought, until the girl made such a mess of things."

"Brenna hurt the Riders," Babs said, her face set and stern. She had been so quiet, they had all nearly forgotten she was there. "And she tried to kill Bella. So Bella's Chudo-Yudo Koshka turned back into a dragon and incinerated her." She looked up at Barbara. "Incinerated. Is that the right word?"

Barbara nodded, tamping down a smile. "Yes. Yes it is." She turned back to the Queen. "What Babs said is true. In our reality, Brenna captured the Riders through trickery and deception and then held them captive with magic, torturing them for weeks in an attempt to steal their immortality for herself. By the time we found them, it was almost too late, and only a massive dose of The Water of Life and Death allowed us to save their lives. It was too late to save their immortality, which was gone forever."

The Queen's already pale complexion turned ashen, and she reached out for the King's hand without taking her amethyst eyes off Barbara's amber ones. "The Riders lost their immortality? Such a thing is impossible. And one Baba Yaga trying to kill another? We cannot believe this."

"I realize it is difficult to comprehend," Barbara said in a marginally softer tone. "I would not have believed it myself if I had not seen it with my own eyes. But I assure you, Brenna is quite insane. She may be able to mask it with her patchouli-scented aging hippie persona, as she did in our time, but behind that mask lies cunning madness and an unquenchable thirst for power and immortality. *She* was the one who stole the Water of Life and Death from Beka's hut-turned-bus. Remember, Brenna knew exactly where it was kept, because she had once lived there."

The King tapped one slender finger against his lips. "That *would* explain how someone got past the hut's defenses. Even without Beka's dragon there to defend it, the Water should have been safe. We did wonder about that at the time it happened."

"No," the Queen said sharply. "We have, reluctantly, accepted that there is something very wrong with the timeline. But this, this is simply Too Much. We saw the Riders not long ago and they were just fine, and as immortal as always. We simply cannot believe what you say."

"But Your Majesty," Barbara protested. Or started to.

The Queen held up her fan, a signal that the conversation was over. "We shall summon Brenna here and speak to her about your accusations. That is as far as We are willing to go."

Barbara held back the bitter and argumentative words that rushed up her throat and threatened to spill out of her mouth. Talking to Brenna was the absolute worst thing the Queen could do. Better to say nothing than to provoke a woman so insane that the last time around they had barely survived her machinations.

But a subtle shake of the head from the King told her that she had pushed the Queen as far as she could go. One more word and Barbara might well become the first Baba Yaga statue to adorn the royal gardens.

So instead she just bowed, and said nothing. The King let out a barely perceptible sigh of relief. No man, not even a King, likes to be caught between two stubborn and strong-willed women.

"We have given you an assignment, Baba Yaga," the Queen said. The fan tilted so that it pointed in the direction of the path back up toward the castle. The audience was clearly at an end, along with the Queen's patience. "Fix this mess. Repair the unraveled time line so the children may be returned to the other side of the doorway where they belong. That is all."

Oh, wonderful. That is all. Just accomplish the impossible, Barbara thought.

She and her two companions all bowed and made their way out. There was nothing else to do.

"That could have gone better," Chudo-Yudo said thoughtfully as he, Barbara, and Babs climbed back through the cupboard door into the Airstream. "But it could have gone worse."

"I don't see how," Barbara said, overwhelmed both by the immensity of her task and the lack of support she'd gotten to achieve it. Not that she had really expected otherwise.

Chudo-Yudo let out one of his barking laughs. "Well, you're not quacking or saying ribbit. Under the circumstances, I'd count that a win."

※

The three of them spent a while down by the creek, mostly decompressing from the stress of their visit to the Otherworld, or in Barbara's case, thinking madly. (Although not necessarily productively.)

She watched idly as Babs cast a line into the slow-moving

water, and then stood resolutely with her fishing pole waiting for a bite, guarded by her faithful dragon-dog. Liam had taught the girl to fish last summer, and it was one of the activities they'd shared with each other. Barbara wondered if Babs was missing Liam too. The girl was so self-contained, it was hard to tell.

Of course, Barbara was hardly one to talk. She was missing Liam so much it hurt to breath, but no one would have seen the aching of her heart if they were looking. She wasn't the crying type. More like the kick ass and take names type. She just needed to figure out whose ass to kick, that's all.

She spent part of the time debating whether or not to tell Belinda her daughter was safe. Would it comfort the woman to know her daughter was well, but forever beyond her reach unless Barbara pulled off a miracle? Perhaps not. For the moment, Barbara decided reluctantly, it would probably do more harm than good.

Kind of like knowing that Liam was alive but had no idea who Barbara was. Or that in another life, they had been deeply in love. Of course, Barbara thought, it wasn't as thought Liam was as out of reach as little Mary Elizabeth. He was only a few miles away, although for all he knew of her, he might as well have been on the moon.

Or maybe not?

She hopped up, brushing dirt and grass off the bottom of her black leather pants, and strode over to where Babs and Chudo-Yudo were standing. Babs was crouched over, hands on her knees, having an intense conversation with a large carp. Her fishing pole lay on the bank beside her, forgotten for now.

"Excuse me," Barbara said to the carp. "I'm sorry to interrupt. It won't take a minute."

When you grew up in a fairy tale, more or less, you learned to be polite to everyone, just in case. You never knew when a fish was an enchanted prince or a powerful elemental in disguise. Even if it was just a carp, good manners cost nothing.

"What's up?" Chudo-Yudo asked, showing large, very sharp teeth in a big yawn.

"I've had an idea," Barbara said.

"Great Chernobog, no," Chudo-Yudo said, flopping down on the ground dramatically. "May the Black God deliver us from your brainstorms."

"Oh, shut up, you overgrown lizard." Of course, sometimes good manners were simply a waste of time.

Babs emitted a giggle, a rare and precious sound. In the early days, she would get upset over these kinds of exchanges, thinking that Barbara and Chudo-Yudo were genuinely fighting. Now she knew better and mostly found them entertaining.

"What is your idea, Baba?" the girl asked.

"It's a surprise," Barbara said. "But I need to go into town for a little while. Will the two of you be okay here by yourselves?"

Most Humans would probably be appalled by the idea of leaving a (more or less) nine year old alone with only her gigantic dog as a babysitter. Of course, most Humans wouldn't realize that the dog was really an ancient and intelligent dragon who could keep her safe in almost any situation, or that the petite and pixie-like child was surprisingly capable of taking care of herself. She'd had to do so in the Otherworld from the time she could walk and talk.

Barbara only hoped that no well-meaning social workers stopped by while she was gone. Chudo-Yudo would probably eat them.

"We will be fine," Babs reassured Barbara. "I am having a fascinating discussion with Clive about the local wildlife."

Barbara looked around. "Clive?"

Babs gestured at the carp.

"Ah, I see. Well, you and Clive have a nice time, and I'll be back as soon as I can. Remember, we are having dinner with Belinda and her parents, Mr. and Mrs. Ivanov, tonight, so after your chat, be sure and get washed up. I'll be back in plenty of time for us to go."

Babs nodded and went back to talking to the fish.

"What are you up to, Baba Yaga?" Chudo-Yudo asked, resuming a more dignified position.

She winked at him. "You'll see, old friend. You'll see. You might say I'm hedging our bets."

"I have no idea what you're talking about," the dragon-dog said. "But there better be treats in it for me."

"Hopefully there will be treats in it for all of us," she said, and strode off to ride the BMW into town.

Barbara and Babs rode over to Belinda's house around five, leaving Chudo-Yudo lying on the sofa contentedly chewing on a giant rawhide bone Barbara had brought back with her from town. (Hint: if your dragon demands a treat, it is probably best to give it to him. Or her, as the case may be. Your furniture lasted a lot longer that way.)

The deputy's small white house sat a little way off the road, a row of pine trees along the front edge and a patch of colorful tulips lining the path to the front door. Belinda's cruiser was parked in the driveway next to an older model Honda Civic. An unused swing set sat forlornly toward the side of the yard, its bright plastic seat hanging crooked, one chain banging rhythmically in the breeze, as though to say, "Come play with me."

But when they knocked on the door, delicious aromas drifted out over Belinda's shoulder. The deputy looked much the same as she always did: mousy brown hair pulled back into a tidy French braid, tiny gold studs in her ears, wearing neat but well-worn jeans under a blue tee shirt that hung a little loosely on her thin frame. Her smile seemed a tad forced, although it widened when she spotted Babs.

"Hello, Dr. Yager," she said. "Come on in." She motioned them into the house and down a small hallway into a cozy living room. "I'm sorry, I wasn't expecting an extra guest. I should have realized."

"I brought Babs. I hope it is okay," Barbara said. "And please, call me Barbara. I don't go in much for formal titles." *Ha. Except the one that only a few people knew.*

"Of course. The more the merrier. Would you like a cookie, Babs?" Belinda asked. "My mother just baked some this afternoon."

Babs shook her head, making her asymmetrical bobbed hair swing back and forth. "No thank you, I do not eat cookies before dinner," she said with her usual formal manner.

"Ah, yes," Belinda said, sadness visible in her already shadowed eyes. "We used to have that rule here too. Now I wish I'd broken it a little more often." She shrugged at Barbara. "But parents do have to set parameters, I guess."

Barbara snorted. "Babs mostly comes up with these rules on her own. I'm not sure where she gets them from. Books, I suppose, since we don't watch television. I'm not much on rules, myself. I think the only ones I ever gave her were 'don't set anything on fire' and 'no practicing magic unsupervised.'" She almost added something about her husband being the one who took care of the mundane do's and don'ts, but stopped with the words on her tongue, remembering she didn't have a husband. Dammit.

"Uh, sure," Belinda said, looking a trifle confused. "Setting things on fire is usually a bad idea, unless you are having a barbeque." She looked up as an elderly couple entered the room. "Oh, there you are." She turned to Barbara. "I don't think you had a chance to meet my parents the last time you were in town. This is my mother, Mariska, and my father, Ivan."

Turning back to her parents, she said, "Mama, Papa, this is Barbara Yager and her daughter Babs."

Mariska Ivanov smoothed back her snowy white hair, which was braided and wound into a bun, and tugged at the embroidered tunic she wore. "Dobriy vyecher, Baba Yaga," she said. "Dobro pozhalovat' v nash dom." *Good evening, Baba Yaga. Welcome to our home.*

"Spasibo, chto prinyali menya," Barbara replied in the same language. *Thank you for having me.* "You wished to see me?" She knew that Mariska spoke perfectly fluent English, so Barbara wasn't sure if the woman was simply being polite in greeting her guest in their shared tongue, or if there was something Mariska wished to say without being understood by her daughter.

"You *are* the Baba Yaga, aren't you?" Mariska asked, her voice weaker than Barbara remembered, but her posture as upright as ever.

Barbara made the tiniest of bows in her direction. "I am," she said, still in Russian. "Shall we speak later?"

Mariska nodded. "Come, dinner will be getting cold," the older woman said in English. "I will get another plate for the little one. I hope she likes beef stroganoff."

"I like almost all foods," Babs said. "Except snails. I do not like snails. The French are very silly to eat them." She had insisted on trying escargot at a restaurant once. That might have been when Barbara had decided to institute the "don't set things on fire" rule.

Mariska gave a creaky laugh. "I don't like them either. The French eat many strange things. Come, come and sit down. My stroganoff is much better than snails."

They followed her into the kitchen, where a long farmhouse table was set with cheerful red pottery plates and blue glass goblets. Sturdy wooden chairs with bright flowered cushion were pulled up around the table. Mariska hurried to set one more place, although there already seemed to be enough plates for the five of them.

They'd no sooner sat down than the back door flew open and a familiar man with dark blonde hair and broad shoulders came hurrying in. He put a six pack of beer down on the table and leaned over to kiss Mariska on one wrinkled cheek.

"I'm sorry I'm late," he said. "I was fixing a fence for someone and time got away from me."

Mariska clucked her tongue at him. "You work too hard, dear boy. Sit down and eat. But don't give Ivan one of those beers. You know they make him silly."

Ivan waggled bushy gray eyebrows at Babs and said, "Don't listen to her, *malyshka*. I am never silly."

"Oh, you have guests," Liam said, sliding into his space at the table.

"You remember Barbara Yager, don't you, Liam? She was in

town for about a week last year. I think I saw you two chatting a few times at Bertie's," Belinda said, putting a beer mug down in front of him and then sitting down across from her mother. "Barbara, Liam comes to dinner a couple of times a week. My mother worries he doesn't eat enough, otherwise."

Barbara ended up sitting between Babs and Liam. Her right side, the one closer to him, felt hotter than the left, and she struggled to keep a neutral expression on her face.

Liam gave her the crooked smile that had charmed her from the very beginning. "Yes, of course I remember her," he said. "Hello, Barbara, I hadn't realized you were back in town."

She had to clear her throat before she could speak. "Yes, well, we just got here. This is my adopted daughter Babs." Barbara gave the little girl a sideways glance from under lowered lashes, worried about how she would react to Liam's sudden appearance. What if Babs forgot that she wasn't supposed to know him?

But she should have known better than to underestimate the girl.

"Hello," Babs said. "We are having beef stroganoff for dinner. Mariska is a very good cook."

"Yes, she is," he said. "I didn't realize you had a daughter," he said to Barbara. "I don't remember you mentioning her the few times we talked." His cheeks flushed, and Barbara realized to her delight that their mutual attraction had clearly been as real and immediate in this timeline as it had been in the other.

"Ah," she said. "I hadn't adopted her then. How have you been?"

He flushed again, this time more out of embarrassment, she thought. "Life has been challenging for all of us," he said with a shrug. "I'm doing okay." He opened a beer, and handed one across the table to Belinda. "Would you like a beer?"

"I'd love one," Barbara said. "So, I hear you're not the sheriff anymore. I'm sorry. I know you really liked the job."

He shrugged again, pushing a shaggy length of hair out of his eyes. "I'm doing handyman work these days. I like that too. There is something very satisfying about taking something that is broken and fixing it. The law was rarely quite that simple."

"I expect it wasn't," she said. Then added casually, "You know, I will probably be needing a handyman. I just bought the yellow farmhouse out on the South River Road, and it could use a lot of work."

Babs sputtered milk onto the table, her face lit up by a smile. "You bought our house? That is wonderful!"

Barbara bit her lip, trying not to smile at this rare show of enthusiasm. "Yes, I bought us a house. That was the surprise."

"You're staying in the area?" Belinda asked, looking amazed. "I hadn't realized anyone was even looking at that house. It has been empty for long time." She widened her brown eyes. "You know they say it is haunted."

Mariska chuckled. "Oh, I doubt this one is afraid of ghosts."

Her own brown eyes twinkled, and she patted her husband's hand. "Did you hear that, dear? The Baba Yaga is staying."

Belinda's brow wrinkled. "Baba Yaga. You called her that before, when she first got here. Is that some kind of Russian nickname I'm not familiar with? The only Baba Yaga I've ever heard of is the witch from the stories you used to tell me when I was a child. Some of them scared the heck out of me."

"Don't worry," Barbara said, a tiny smile tugging at the corner of her mouth. "It isn't an insult." She swiveled so she could face Liam, trying not to seem as though she was holding her breath. "So, are you available to do some work on my house?"

"I'd be delighted," Liam said. "I've always liked that old place."

Me too, Barbara thought. *Especially when you're in it.*

CHAPTER NINE

AFTER DINNER, BARBARA LEFT BABS HELPING WITH THE DISHES, a chore the girl enjoyed immensely for some reason, and walked out into the back yard with Mariska. They took their cups of strong tea and sat under a giant old oak on a couple of sturdy benches set in front of an unlit fire pit.

"So," Mariska said after a few minutes of companionable silence. "You truly are the Baba Yaga? The witch I told my daughter stories about when she was about the same age as your little girl?"

"I am," Barbara said. Then added, "At least, I am one of them. It is a job title, you know, not an actual person. There are two others here in America, Beka and Bella, but they usually deal with issues in the western third or the middle of the country, respectively."

"The Baba Yaga," Mariska said with a satisfied sigh. "I always knew you were real." She smiled shyly at Barbara. "When I was growing up in the Old County, my grandmother told me the stories, as her grandmother had passed them on to her. She always swore, my Babushka, that she had met the Baba Yaga once, as a child lost in the woods near where she grew up.

"But she described the witch as an old crone with hair as white as mine, and a great beaky nose, and iron teeth. Terrifying, my Babushka said, although the witch guided her back to the path, and only took her basket of berries as the price for helping her."

Barbara touched her own nose a trifle self-consciously. "Well, I don't have white hair or iron teeth, so that's something." She winked at Mariska and for a moment, there were two old women sitting on the benches. Then only one, with an astonished look on her face, and a tall woman with a cloud of long dark hair and a nose that was a little long, but fit well with her strong face.

"The old woman my grandmother met? She was an illusion? A masquerade?" Mariska took a gulp of her tea.

Barbara shrugged. "Perhaps. It was traditional, after all, especially in those days. We do grow old, eventually, though, so the one your Babushka met might have been genuinely ancient. It is hard to say. But your grandmother must have been polite, if the Baba helped her. We may not be the evil witches of the old tales, but it is also tradition that we only help the worthy seeker, who approaches us correctly."

"Neither good nor bad witches," Mariska said. "But with the potential for either, depending on the actions of those who deal with them."

"Something like that, yes," Barbara said. "Although some of us are softer-hearted than others. You should meet my sister Beka. She is actually quite kind."

"And you are not?" Mariska gave a tiny shake of the head. "You are remarkably gentle with my daughter, and you came to visit an old woman simply because you were asked. These do not seem like the acts of an unkind person to me."

Barbara lifted the corner of her mouth in her barely there hint of a smile. "You happen to have caught me on a good day. I have many, many bad days."

"Oh?" Mariska raised a feathery white eyebrow.

"I once turned a man into a toad after he asked me for directions."

Mariska choked on her tea. "You did?"

"Well, he patted my ass and called me sweetie," Barbara said, by way of explanation. "And I turned him back later. Not that there was much difference, really. A toad in either form, that one."

"Ah," the older woman said. "There was many a day in my youth when I would have done the same if I had your power. It must be nice."

Barbara cast a longing look back toward the house, where she could hear the deep rumble of Liam's voice, mixed with Babs' higher pitched tones. "Sometimes," she said. "But there are problems even my power can't fix. Or at least, not rapidly or easily. I suppose it remains to be seen if they can be fixed at all."

Mariska glanced from Barbara to the kitchen windows that sent a warm glow of light out into the darkness, but said nothing. She only pressed her thin lips together as if wondering whether or not to speak.

Finally, she said, "I have no wish to be turned into a toad, but I need to ask a boon of you, Baba Yaga. I will gladly give you anything you wish in payment, including my own life, although it is worth little, considering how few years there are left in this worn out body of mine."

Barbara sighed. She had known this was coming since Belinda had told her that her mother wished to meet the mysterious herbalist she had missed the first time around.

"Mary Elizabeth," she said. It wasn't a question.

"My granddaughter," Mariska agreed. "And the other children who went missing, whose families pine as much as we do. Can your powers find them and return them to us, Baba Yaga? And if so, would you be willing to undertake the task?"

"This is a formal request for the aid of the Baba Yaga," Barbara said carefully. "Is that correct?" There were, after all, rules to be followed, even for her.

Mariska bowed her white head. "It is. I ask for your help in finding my granddaughter and the other children who disappeared, and for the gift of their safe return. I will pay whatever price is required."

The air and ground around them shivered, and the night birds fell silent as the universe shifted to accommodate the magical bargain. Such compacts were sacred, and they changed things even by their very existence.

Barbara was counting on it.

"I accept your request," she said in a formal tone. "The price will be three tasks, which you will perform whenever I demand them." *Or figure out what the heck they would be—something important enough to fulfill the agreement but not so onerous that they would strain an old woman with a bad heart. I wonder if baking me cookies would count. If they were really big cookies.*

"Very well," Mariska said. She wiped away a tear unobtrusively and took a deep breath. "Can you find her, Baba Yaga?"

Barbara pondered how to answer that question. It had been one thing not to tell Belinda, who didn't understand what or who she was dealing with. Mariska, on the other hand, was a different matter. What Mariska chose to share with her daughter was her choice.

"I have already found her," Barbara said slowly. "And the other children too."

Mariska gasped, a hopeful look lifting the sadness from her face, but Barbara held up one hand in caution.

"This is not exactly the good news it sounds like," Barbara said. "They were taken to the Otherworld. You must know what this means."

The older woman's face fell. "They can never come home?" she whispered.

"It is too soon to say," Barbara said. "Mary Elizabeth and the other girl have aged more than they would have in a year on this side of the doorway. The small boy who was taken hasn't aged a day. There would be no way to explain this if I were to bring them back now. Moreover, they have been changed by their time in the enchanted lands."

She patted Mariska lightly on the hand, something she would probably never have done before living with Babs. "But they are alive and well, and being treated with kindness, and I hope that is some kind of comfort."

"Time has gone awry and must be returned to its correct path. I am not even sure that such a thing is possible." She poured the rest of her tea out on the ground and then snapped her fingers, so that it streamed backward into the cup—a simplified demonstration. "I can make you no promises but this: I will do my utmost to do whatever is necessary to make it possible for them all to be back home with those who love them. You have my word on it."

Mariska gave her a watery smile. "I have absolute faith in you, Baba Yaga. I know that you will not fail."

Barbara tipped the cup again, watching the cool tea sinking away into the dirt below. She wished she shared the other woman's certainty. It helped to have this be an official task: the universe often seemed to line up so that things fell into place when a Baba Yaga was on a mission. But nothing was guaranteed, and Barbara still had no idea how to mend the unraveled threads of time.

The next morning, they moved the Airstream to its regular spot out behind the barn at the yellow house. It felt good to be home again, even if home was currently a dusty, dirty long-uninhabited wreck with broken windows and several generations of mice families living in the walls.

"I somehow thought that buying a house took a lot longer than an afternoon," Chudo-Yudo said after giving the mice a strong suggestion that it might be healthier to relocate to the great outdoors. Or the neighbor's house. Their choice.

Barbara snorted down her long nose. "Well, it helps to have a bag of gold and the ability to magically alter documents. Plus, I'd already bought the house before, which made it easier. I knew who to talk to without having to go through all the official channels. The thing has sat derelict so long, they practically begged me to take it off their hands."

She looked sadly at the house on which she and Liam had worked together to make into a warm and comfortable home. Just like the first time she'd acquired it, it was nowhere near ready for anyone to move in. There were broken windows and many of the shutters were barely hanging on. Bits of broken shingles littered the ground amid the overgrown shrubbery that had crept up to cover much of the lower story, making it dim inside even on this sunny day. The floors and surfaces were covered with dust, and cobwebs hung in swaths from corner to corner.

"Déjà vu all over again," Barbara said softly. She glanced over at Chudo-Yudo. "I've been meaning to ask you. Can you tell me what happened during the time we were here last year? From what I can tell, we hung around for a week, but since I wasn't involved in searching for the lost children, what the heck did I do all that time? And why did we come here in the first place, if I wasn't *Called* by Mariska Ivanov?"

"The 'why' we came here was simple," he said. "There was some sort of imbalance between our world and the Otherworld that was creating chaos over there. The Queen summoned you to see if you could figure out if something on our side of the doorway was causing it. That led you to this area, and then it took you a couple of days to find an unauthorized portal that had been opened up by the local fracking operation."

He shook his massive head. "Why we stayed after that, I'm not sure. Once you'd closed the portal, we could have left, but after that sheriff showed up on the first day with some nonsense about needing a permit to park the Airstream in an empty meadow, you started acting goofy." The other penny dropped. "Wait a minute. *That* guy, that sheriff, he's your Liam? The one you say you ended up married to? Holy crap. And he was at that dinner you went to last night? Man, that must have been interesting."

That was one word for it. Agonizing was another. "So what did I do for the rest of the time we were here, once I'd done what I'd come here to do?"

"Mostly you hung around someplace called Bertie's, and a couple of times that sheriff guy came out here for barbeque and a beer after his shift was over. To be honest, I didn't pay much attention. Nothing ever happened. You just sat there and neither of you talked much, and he got more and more stressed about whatever case he was working on. Then one day you just woke up and said, 'This is crazy. What was I thinking, me and a Human? We have nothing in common.' And you hooked the Airstream up to the truck, and we left. I think it was not long after that you went to the Otherworld and came back with Babs, after you went to check that the imbalance had been righted."

Well, that explained that. Without the common goal of finding the missing children to bring them together, not to mention common adversaries to fight, she and Liam had never fallen in love. Or if they had, she hadn't stuck around long enough for them to act on it. Not surprising, really. Before she met Liam, she never even considered trying to have anything resembling a normal relationship. It just wasn't something Baba Yagas did. At least not before her. And in this timeline, apparently not after, without her example to lead the way for Beka. She still had to check in with Bella. Perhaps the middle Baba had had more luck with her love life than the other two.

She looked back at her poor neglected house with a sigh. Back to the beginning again.

Babs didn't seem to mind, thankfully. She was clearly just happy to be back on familiar ground. Since they'd pulled in, she had been walking around talking to everything from the trees to the fading yellow paint, giving them all her familiar *pat*

pat pat as if to reassure them. Barbara suspected it was comforting for the girl as well, although being a Baba Yaga in training, she was also spreading little bits of her energy around as she went. Barbara intended to do the same thing soon, kind of like an animal marking its territory. Only with less peeing.

Chudo-Yudo had already taken care of that part, immediately anointing a favorite tree. Sometimes she thought he took the "dog" portion of his dragon-dog disguise a smidge too far.

"I'm not saying it isn't nice to have a house," he said. "But I don't quite understand why you bought it. I mean, if we somehow figure out how to fix this mess, we'll be back in the right timeline, and you'll already own it. If you can't fix it, won't we just get back into the Airstream and hit the road again?"

Barbara watched a beat-up brown pickup truck roll into the driveway and felt her heart thump in her chest as the tall man in need of a haircut hauled himself out from behind the wheel.

"No," she said firmly. "We're not going anywhere. I have a mission to accomplish—two of them, now that I have been officially *Called* by Mariska—and I fully intend to succeed. But I needed a back-up plan in case I don't, and this is it.

"The first time around in this timeline, I let Liam McClellan slip through my fingers. I thought there was no way to make a relationship with a Human work. Now I know differently, and I intend to pursue him until I get him back."

Chudo-Yudo stared up at her, his red tongue lolling in amazement. "You're going to woo the ex-sheriff? Who are you, and what have you done with my Baba Yaga?"

"Ha," she said. "You know the answer to that already. And yes, yes I am. The man isn't going to know what hit him."

"It's got great bones, but it is going to take a lot of work," Liam said. "A *lot* of work."

"Oh, I don't think there are any actual bones here," Barbara said. "Just one ghost, and she's perfectly harmless."

Liam blinked. "Uh, no. I didn't mean real bones. That's just a way of saying that the structure of a house is sound." He clearly wasn't quite sure if she was pulling his leg or not. "Do you really believe the house is haunted?"

At her feet, Chudo-Yudo was doing his barking-laugh thing. Barbara's booted foot twitched in his direction, but she stopped herself before she stubbed her toes again.

"We're all haunted by something, sheriff," she said.

"I'm not the sheriff anymore, Ms. Yager," he said. "But point taken."

"And you were calling me Barbara last night. Not to mention when I was here a year ago," she said. "If you're going to be playing with the bones of my house, we might as well be on a first name basis."

Liam laughed. "There is that. So what did you want me to

work on first? We need to walk through the whole building and make some notes," he looked at the house and shook his head. "Extensive notes. But it would help to know where you wanted me to start."

"I'm not too worried about the cosmetics," Barbara said. Truth was, she could use her magic to fix almost anything that was wrong with it, but that would defeat the purpose of buying a house that needed a handyman. "I'd like to move into it as soon as we can, so all the functional stuff, like making sure the bathrooms work and the kitchen is useable, that comes first."

"Practical," Liam said with a small smile. "I like that in a woman."

I know. Barbara just nodded. "Shall we go inside?"

They walked in through the back door into the kitchen. The mice were gone, but the sink still dripped and the linoleum floor was bubbled and warped, a trap to catch the feet of the unwary. The once white walls were dingy and gray.

Liam bent down and pulled up the edge of one of the floor tiles. "You know, I think there is decent wood under here. You'd be amazed at the number of people who covered up perfectly good pine floors with manmade crap during the sixties and seventies."

"Oak," Barbara said without thinking. "It's oak."

He got onto his hands and knees for a closer look. "So it is. I guess you did a pretty thorough walk-through before you bought the place."

She actually hadn't set one foot in the door, but she thought it was probably best not to mention that. After all, she'd walked through it nearly every day for over three years. That was practically the same thing.

Liam was checking out the sink and scribbling something in a notebook when Babs wandered through the room. *Pat pat pat.* "Hello, kitchen," she said, running her hand along the walls. "Hello refrigerator. You'll feel much better when we turn you back on." *Pat pat pat.* "Hello stove. Don't worry, we'll fix that back burner."

Barbara bit back a laugh at the look on Liam's face. He'd probably never seen a small pixie-haired child greeting a house before. Thankfully, Babs didn't pat him too, merely gazed at him with those wide, too-wise eyes and said, "Hello Liam. Barbara says you are going to make our house look pretty again. I would like that."

"I like making things look pretty and work better," Liam said. "Maybe you could help me with some of the simpler parts. If it is okay with your mother."

Babs mouthed the word mother, as if tasting its flavor to see how it sat in her mouth. Barbara realized that no one had ever used it to describe her before. She often referred to Babs as her adopted daughter, since that was the simplest way to explain the girl's presence, but she mostly thought of their relationship as mentor and apprentice. That was the way things always were between Baba Yagas and the girls they raised to eventually take up their roles when the time came.

Liam had definitely been Babs' father, but Barbara had never thought of herself as a mother. Certainly her own Baba mentor, a cranky and antisocial woman at the end of her career, had nothing motherly about her, either treating Barbara like a handy servant or an annoying and inconvenient encumbrance, depending on her mood.

It wasn't traditional, but hell, very little about her existence in the last few years had been. "Her mother thinks that would be a very good idea," Barbara said firmly. "You should always take advantage of an opportunity to learn a useful skill."

She was rewarded by one of Babs' rare smiles, which lit up her normally solemn face and rendered it radiant.

"Yes," Babs agreed. "That would be good. You will have to be here a lot to fix things. That is good too." She gave a decisive nod and continued on her way through the room, still patting things and chatting to inanimate objects.

"She's adorable," Liam said. "A little unusual, but adorable."

"Odd, you mean, and yes, I suppose she is. She had a difficult start in life, and she's still trying to figure out how to act around normal people." She gave a brief laugh. "I'm not a particularly stellar example of normal, either, I'm afraid. But she is very smart and fascinated by pretty much everything, so I hope you meant it when you said you'd let her help."

"I did," he said. "I like kids." Only someone who knew him as well as Barbara did would have seen the shadow pass over his eyes. Long before she'd met him, he and his then wife had lost a child to Sudden Infant Death Syndrome—it had destroyed his wife and their marriage and the thought of that lost child still made him sad. Having Babs in his life had almost wiped that shadow away, but of course, in this timeline, that hadn't happened, so the darkness was still there.

"You know," he said, breaking away from his own bleak thoughts, "I don't remember you mentioning you intended to adopt." There was a suspicious undertone to the question, no doubt the old lawman's habit of questioning anything that seemed strange.

Barbara shook her head. "It was kind of unexpected."

"Ah," Liam said. "Hence the sudden desire to buy a house and settle down. I understand now."

Not exactly, Barbara thought. But close enough. "So can you start work right away?"

"Absolutely," he said. "I have to warn you, though, it isn't going to be cheap."

"Not to worry," she said. "I have a fairy godmother." Or at least, the Queen of all the fairy godmothers

"That must be handy," Liam said. "Know where I can get one?"

Barbara gave him a smile so warm, it heated up the room ten degrees and charred the paper of his notebook along one edge. Liam looked a little shell-shocked. "You never know," she said. "Anything is possible."

CHAPTER TEN

AFTER LIAM HAD MADE ENDLESS NOTES IN HIS NEAT BLOCK writing, he drove off to get supplies, promising to be back in the morning. Barbara's chest tightened as he pulled out of the driveway, and she had to remind herself that her plan was working and she would see him again. Even if he had no idea that she was anything more important than a new client. *Breathe,* she reminded her lungs. *It's going to be okay. Breathe.*

Then she took her own turn around the house, walking from room to room with a sage smudge stick and a carved jade bowl full of salt, cleansing away any old negative energy and making the space her own at the same time. Not Babs' *pat pat pat,* but close. She greeted the resident ghost politely and opened all the windows—at least the ones that still would open.

When she was done, she glanced around the dingy living room with distaste. She liked a clean house, so this just wouldn't do. Even if they weren't going to be moving inside for a while. She waved one hand, flicking her fingers to draw a few arcane symbols, and the layers of dust and dirt lifted up and wafted gracefully out the windows.

"That's better," she said decisively. From a shadowed corner, Anna, the ghost, nodded in agreement.

"It is like that movie Liam showed me once," Babs said, peering in from the doorway between the living room and the hallway. "*Mary Poppins*. It was silly, but I liked it. There was singing and dancing."

Barbara grimaced. "Well, if you think I am going to start singing and dancing about like a ninny while I clean, you are very much mistaken. But feel free to do it yourself if you are so inclined." That she'd like to see.

Babs scrunched up her button nose. "I do not think the dancing actually has any effect on the end result, do you?" Instead she concentrated and then snapped her fingers once, twice, three times.

Lacy filaments of cobweb sailed in long strands out the windows, an eerie sight if you weren't prepared for it. The room looked better already.

"Nicely done," Barbara said, going over to give the girl's hair a gentle tug. "You've been practicing." Barbara's own mentor had rarely wasted time or energy on praise, and she was determined to do better at raising her own little Baba. It had helped that Liam had been such a good example, since Barbara had very little experience with the more Human (or kind) aspects of childrearing.

They went through each room, cleaning the superficial dirt and dust in much the same way (there might not have been dancing, but Barbara was pretty sure she heard Babs humming under her breath). It wasn't an activity that took much concentration, so Barbara used the time to think, mostly about what to do next.

In the long run, she had to figure out a way to knit together the unraveled pieces of the timeline. But to do that, she first had to identify the individual threads that were no longer where they belonged. Perhaps if she could put enough things back the way they were supposed to be—like having Mariska Ivanov ask her to find the children—that would help.

Of course, nothing would be exactly the same. For instance, the first time around, Mariska had sent Belinda to ask for the Baba Yaga's aid, but the older woman had been the one to send out the initial *Call* that brought Barbara to the area. It would have to do. Barbara was pretty sure that the final solution would require a spell and some massively powerful magic, but anything she could do to make the task seem less completely impossible could only be a good thing.

Getting Liam back in her life was part of that, although she would have done it anyway. But now she needed to decide which unraveled bit to tackle next. There were two big ones that immediately came to mind: Brenna and Maya.

The Queen would already have her own people searching for Maya in the Otherworld, but Barbara had a feeling they wouldn't find her there.

Rusalkas were water creatures who once lived in the rivers and lakes of Russia. They tended to be dangerous and bloodthirsty at the best of times, and it was probably a good thing for Humans when they were relocated to the Otherworld with most of the other Paranormals.

Maya had stumbled onto the unguarded portal and come through the doorway with two goals in mind. The first was to steal Human children to trade for power. The pollution of the waters on this side of the doorway had affected the waters in the Otherworld, eventually diminishing the magic of those whose essence was closely entwined with that element. In Maya's twisted mind, the exchange was only fair. Her second goal, no less important than the first, was to exact revenge on the Humans who caused that desecration out of greed and carelessness.

When Barbara had closed the portal, she would have ended Maya's ability to carry out her first task, but that didn't mean Maya would have given up on her second goal. If Maya had been trapped in the Human world when the doorway was shut, it was almost certain that she was still up to no good. The question was, how to track her down?

When they were done with the bulk of the superficial cleaning at the house, Barbara returned to the Airstream and pulled her laptop out from the cabinet that also held some old books and Chudo-Yudo's spare water bowl. She placed it carefully on the counter but didn't lift the cover.

"You know, it works better if you turn it on," Chudo-Yudo said from where he was curled up in a spot of sunlight near the sofa.

Barbara grimaced. "Not for me, it doesn't." She had reluctantly succumbed to using a computer because of the benefits of being able to look up information with ease wherever she was. (Baba Yagas didn't need anything as frivolous as a WiFi signal.) But she'd never really gotten comfortable with technology and tended to look at her laptop as though it were an intermittently helpful gremlin who might at any moment decide to turn around and bite her.

Sadly, Babs was even less at ease with most modern tools after being raised in the Otherworld, and the ones she did like tended to become a bit more animated than was normal. Liam's last coffee maker had developed the unsettling habit of asking whether you wanted cream or sugar until he'd finally begged Babs to stop chatting to it.

"I need Beka and Bella," Barbara said, shoving the laptop away. "They're much better than I am at this kind of thing, and besides, I need to let them know what's going on."

"You tried telling Beka," Chudo-Yudo reminded her. "It didn't go very well."

Barbara gritted her teeth. "I haven't forgotten," she said. "But now that the Queen has agreed there is something wrong, and I have an official mission, they'll have to believe me." She thought about it for a moment. "Or at least they have to listen, and hopefully they'll agree to help."

She pulled out the despised cell phone. "Besides, I have to warn them about Brenna. The woman is clearly up to something, and Beka is right in the line of fire."

Chudo-Yudo growled under his breath and said something rude in dragon.

"I couldn't agree more, old friend," Barbara said. "I don't care if the Queen doesn't believe me. That witch is going down."

Barbara breathed a huge sigh of relief when Bella come through the cabinet with the wonky handle, trailed by a teenaged Jazz. To begin with, Barbara hadn't been at all sure if Jazz and Bella would have found each other, since most of the events that led up to their meeting probably never occurred. But apparently Jazz becoming Bella's apprentice was another one of those immutable things that hadn't changed no matter how much everything else had.

Maybe some parts of reality were destiny and would have happened in any timeline? Or perhaps they were simply strands that hadn't unwound. Barbara had no idea.

There was one change, though. Jazz was still a teen of about fifteen or sixteen, rather than the seeming adult nearly ten years older that she'd become after working a powerful spell in a futile effort to give the Riders back their immortality. That made sense, since if Brenna never stole their immortality in this timeline, there was no reason for Jazz to attempt such an insanely impossible magical working. In some ways that was also a relief, although it was yet another difference, and Barbara had had a glimmer of an idea about that spell…

"So what's all the urgency?" Bella asked as they closed the

closet behind them. "I was in the middle of painting a particularly nice patch of woods and the sunlight was just perfect."

When she wasn't on a Baba Yaga mission (and sometimes when she was), Bella presented herself as a traveling artist, moving about the more deserted parts of the middle of the country in a modern caravan on wheels, just as Barbara used the guise of an herbalist doing research in her Airstream.

"I was doing homework," Jazz said with a grimace. "Personally, I appreciate the interruption." She looked much the same, although her brown hair was cropped short and sported a purple stripe along one side, and at some point she'd had her ears pierced and wore small dangling silver pentacles along with her blue jeans and a tee shirt bearing the name of some band Barbara had never heard of. Mind you, that was almost all of them.

Barbara crossed her fingers behind her back hopefully and asked Bella, "So, did Sam mind you coming? You guys didn't have plans or anything, did you?"

The pretty redhead squinted at Barbara. "Sam who? What are you talking about?"

"Damn," Chudo-Yudo said.

Barbara had been afraid of that. "I'll explain in a minute, as soon as Beka gets here. No point in going through it twice, although I've told Beka a little bit already. Not that she believed me."

She stared at the closet. "What's taking her so long, anyway? All she has to do is step through the hidden doorway in the bus, dart through the Otherworld, and come out here. I called her before I called you. She should have been here already."

Bella sighed and helped herself to a beer from the fridge. Jazz held her hand out but Bella just shook her head and gave Jazz a bottle of ginger ale instead, getting a classic teen eye roll in return.

"You know how it is," Bella said. "Any time Beka wants to come see either of us, Brenna finds some kind of last minute chore that Beka just *has* to finish first. Passive-aggressive old bag."

"Yeah, well that old bag is part of what I wanted to talk to the two of you about," Barbara started to say, when the closet door was flung open and a gorgeous long-legged blonde rushed through.

"Sorry, sorry," she said, gasping as if she'd run the whole way. From the look of her tousled long hair and bright pink cheeks, she probably had. Her multicolored patchwork skirt had a couple of greenish-blue leaves stuck to it, no doubt picked up in the Otherworld, and her light blue tank top bore an odd stain near the hem that was still smoking lightly. "Brenna had a potion that needed to be stirred without stopping for ten minutes, and she didn't have time to do it."

"Uh huh," Bella said with a glower. "What a surprise. Really, Beka. You are a grown woman who spent a couple years being Baba Yaga on your own. I don't know why you let that frizzy-haired tyrant boss you around as if you were Jazz's age."

"Maybe because I failed so miserably as a Baba Yaga," Beka muttered, looking at the floor. A tiny embroidered newt in the rug wiggled its tail and gazed back." "Brenna was right about me not being ready, and she was nice enough to come out of retirement and keep training me, so it really isn't too much for her to ask me to do a little task now and then."

"ARGH," Bella said, and tiny flames sputtered out of her fingertips. "Oops. Sorry. It just makes me so mad, the way that woman takes advantage of you."

Barbara blinked and snapped her fingers, extinguishing the sparks before they could do any damage. She'd forgotten how much difficulty her sister Baba had had containing her fiery nature when she got angry. In the other timeline, Bella had gotten a much better handle on her emotions after settling down with her ex-Hotshots firefighter husband Sam.

But in this case, Barbara felt a little bit like shooting fire out of her own fingers. "You were *not* a failure," she said to Beka in her "don't you dare argue with me" voice. "You were sabotaged, and some things that should have happened didn't, but you were a great Baba Yaga. And as for Brenna doing you a favor, I assure you, it is quite the opposite."

Beka was both thinner and paler than the version Barbara was used to. She had lost the deep tan that came from spending most of her time either surfing or out on her husband Marcus's fishing boat. She sighed and shook her head.

"You don't understand," she said.

"No *you* don't understand. Neither of you do." Barbara gestured them over to sit in the small living room area. "But it is time you did. Sit down, please. This might take a while."

"And that's why I need your help finding Maya, this rusalka." Barbara said, finishing up her story. Her audience stared back at her with varying expressions: disbelief (Beka), doubt (Bella), and stunned excitement (Jazz). Babs and Chudo-Yudo were curled up together on the edges of the circle, having remained mostly silent throughout Barbara's recitation of the explosion, the changed timeline, the Queen's reaction, and her tentative plans to try and fix it all.

"That's just crazy," Beka said. "I thought the part of the story you'd already told me sounded bizarre, but the whole thing… that's even harder to believe. I saved the Selkies and the Merpeople? Married a hunky former Marine who knows I'm a Baba Yaga and doesn't mind? You have to realize how insane that all sounds."

Bella looked thoughtful, twirling a piece of her long curly hair around the tip of one paint-stained finger. "Oh, I don't know. The part about Brenna is pretty believable, if you ask me. I'm not so sure about me getting married either, though. It doesn't seem likely." She gazed at Barbara and bit her lip, trying not to laugh. "As for you falling in love with a Human sheriff…I think that's the most far-fetched part of the whole thing."

Wordlessly, Barbara held out her ring. The other two took turns holding it and staring at her.

"Hmmm," Bella said in a quiet voice. "There's definitely something there. And you say the Queen believed you?"

"Enough to make fixing the unraveled timeline an official

assignment," Barbara said. "Although I couldn't convince her about Brenna's actions in my reality, or that she was still actively working against Beka in this one."

"I don't have any problem with that part," Bella said with a grimace. "I never liked that woman, and ever since she came back, it's as though she's determined to make Beka feel smaller and smaller." She turned to look at the blonde sitting next to her. "I can't even remember the last time I saw you smile."

"I smile," Beka protested. "I'm fine. Just a little discouraged about my own lack of progress, that's all. And I can't imagine Brenna doing everything you said she did. Torturing the Riders. That's ridiculous. How on earth would one old woman —even one with magic—overpower Mikhail and Gregori, not to mention a giant like Alexei?"

"Trickery, guile, and threats," Barbara said, but she could tell she wasn't going to change Beka's mind. "Look, all I ask is that you be on your guard, okay? And in the meanwhile, can you help me to track down the rusalka who calls herself Maya Freeman?"

Jazz sat up straight and hand out one hand in demand. "Finally, something I can do. And by the way, I know that nobody is asking me, but I believe Barbara."

She gave Beka a hard look, memories of the hellish years spent growing up in the foster system suddenly wiping away any vestiges of teenage innocence in her deep brown eyes.

"I know you think the best of everyone. Hell, that's one of the things I like about you, Beka. But I can tell you from experience that there are plenty of people who will do anything to get what they want. *Anything*. Brenna's sweet aging hippie act might fool you, but it never fooled me. That woman is cold, through and through."

Beka opened her mouth, then shut it again, shaking her head stubbornly.

Jazz just rolled her eyes and opened up the laptop. She tapped some keys, hummed, and tapped some more.

"Huh," she said finally. "That's interesting."

Bella sat up straighter. "You found something to prove Barbara's story?"

"Yes and no," Jazz said. "I found nothing at all, which is *way* more suspicious than finding something."

"I, uh, excuse me?" Barbara said. She liked Jazz, but sometimes she felt as though the girl was talking a foreign language. And not a nice, easy to understand one like Russian.

"Okay, assuming we believe the basics of your story, and I for one definitely do, this Maya should show up somewhere online. Even if she doesn't have a social security number," Jazz grinned, "and I'm assuming that rusalkas don't, there should be some trace of her. For instance, in some local newspaper article about this Peter Callahan and his company. Somewhere in the company records. Or a photo of her with him at some public event."

"But you didn't find any of those?" Beka said, leaning forward. "Not even one mention?"

"Not one," Jazz said. She turned to Barbara. "You said you've talked to people in this timeline who remember her, right?"

"Of course," Barbara said, trying not to sound defensive. "Both Liam and Belinda, the deputy whose little girl went missing. They knew exactly who I was talking about when I asked about Peter Callahan's assistant."

Jazz held up one hand. "Jeez, don't jump down my throat. I'm not doubting you. Just double checking that you're sure she was out in the open in our timeline too. Because if she was, she's done a damned good job of either staying out of the public view or covering her tracks, or both."

"What are you saying?" Bella asked. She'd lived with Jazz for long enough to know not to underestimate her intelligence, not to mention her ability to think outside the box. Not having been raised to be a Baba Yaga might handicap her in some ways, but it also meant that she often looked at things completely differently than more traditional Baba Yagas did. That wasn't necessarily a bad thing, especially in a situation like this.

"I'm saying that if she had gone back to the Otherworld, she would have had no reason to make sure people didn't realize she'd been here. And if she was stuck here and decided to make the best of it by trying to blend in with Humans, she would probably have tried to appear as normal as possible. The only reason I can think of for her wanting to keep her presence quiet is if she is still here and still bent on causing some kind of trouble."

Jazz gestured at the laptop triumphantly. "Thus the complete lack of any reference to anyone named Maya Freeman who matches her description is *very* suspicious, and in fact supports Barbara's story." The *ta da* was left unsaid, but rang in the air nonetheless.

"Well, that's encouraging," Barbara said, feeling the complete opposite. "But how do we find her if she has gone to all that effort to stay under the radar? She's too clever to have left anything around this area that would allow me to trace her magically."

Bella nodded. "Yeah, you'd better believe that if she has gone to the trouble to hide her tracks, she will have wiped out any literal tracks she made here."

"Do you think she will still be with Peter Callahan?" Jazz asked. "Because with a little digging, I can probably find out where his company is active now, and figure out which one of their sites they sent him to."

Beka had perked up a little, once they'd stopped talking about her. Or Brenna. "You said she might still be pursuing vengeance on the Humans who are destroying the waters, right?"

"Sadly, that doesn't narrow things down much," Bella said glumly. It was part of a Baba Yaga's job to help maintain the balance of the elements, but lately, that had become nearly impossible, with all the damage that Humans were doing to the environment.

"It does, actually," Barbara said. She thought for a moment. "After all, Maya attached herself to Peter Callahan because of his connection to a company that made their money by fracking, also known as hydraulic fracturing, which is seriously detrimental to water. Not only can it contaminate the water table for miles around—an ecological disaster that can never be reversed—there have also been incidences of spills of the highly toxic chemicals used in the process."

Bella snapped her fingers. "I get it! You think that wherever she is, whether or not she is still with this Peter guy, she'll still be trying to attack those who are threatening water in a big way. Not just some guy who dumps the sewage from his summer camp into a lake because he's too lazy or cheap to have it dealt with properly, but some company or organization that is causing widespread or intense damage."

"I'd like to sic her on some of the people who dump garbage into the ocean," Beka said, her eyes narrowed. "Did you realize that there are garbage patches—floating islands made up predominantly of pieces of plastic—that are hundreds of miles across?"

"In the ocean?" Babs asked from where she was leaning against Chudo-Yudo as if he were a large cushion. "This is a very bad idea."

"No kidding," Chudo-Yudo muttered. "Humans are full of bad ideas."

"Now, now," Beka said. "Most Humans are really very nice. They just don't always see the big picture."

"I could draw them one," Babs said seriously. "If you think that would help."

"Probably not, sweetie," Barbara said. "But it is kind of you to offer."

Jazz rolled her eyes. "Can we get back to the subject at hand, please? My homework isn't going to do itself." She glanced at Bella. "Unless I could do a spell for—"

"Forget it," Bella said. She shook a lightly sparking finger at her foster daughter.

"Fine. Whatever." Jazz shrugged. "In that case, I can do an online search for any mention of suspicious catastrophes involving water. Especially anything that smells like it might have supernatural causes." She got a faraway look in her eyes. "I'll bet if I cross-search for water, disaster, and mysterious or unexplained…"

"That would be great," Barbara said. "And maybe Bella and Beka, you could just keep your eyes open in your travels for anything that seems like it might be connected."

"Happy to," Bella said. "Although where we are in the northern central states, it is less populated and we're not likely to be as good a target as either the west coast or the east coast."

"I'll do what I can," Beka said. "But I probably wouldn't be much help. Brenna says I couldn't find a shell on the seashore most days."

Barbara and Chudo-Yudo made almost identical growling noises.

"That witch is a bitch," Jazz observed in a casual tone.

Barbara noticed that Bella didn't bother to scold her for rudeness.

She might have added something even ruder, but there was a knock at the Airstream door. Chudo-Yudo picked his head up, but didn't look at all alarmed.

"Someone coming for an herbal remedy?" Bella asked.

"No idea," Barbara said, walking over to open the door. She felt her heart skip a beat. "Oh, hi, Liam. I thought you were over at the house."

"I was," he said, sweeping his too-long hair out of his eyes. "But I've finished fixing the sink in the kitchen, and I've repainted all the cabinets, so I was looking at that wonky burner on the stove. I have to tell you, I think you're a lot better off just buying a new stove, if you can afford it. Turns out the oven doesn't work either." He made a face. "Not to mention that olive green color is just butt ugly. I think the seventies have a lot to answer for."

Beka tittered and he peered around Barbara's shoulder. "Oh, I'm sorry, I didn't realize I was interrupting something." His brow wrinkled. "I didn't see any cars outside, or I would have realized you had company."

"Oh, we walked," Bella said casually, getting up to shake his hand. "Hi, I'm Barbara's sister Bella. This is Beka," she gestured at the blonde, "our other sister, and my foster daughter Jazz. I think you already know Babs and the giant white monstrosity she is leaning against."

Barbara glared at Bella, since she hadn't been intending to

introduce them all. Of course, Bella knew that, and ignored her. As usual. What was the point of being the oldest and most powerful if no one paid attention to you?

"And you are?" Bella asked.

"I'm Liam McClellan. I'm doing some work on the house for Barbara. I mean, Professor Yager," he said. He looked from one to the other. "You don't look like sisters."

Barbara scowled. "It's complicated. We're not actually related by blood. Although there might be some blood involved before we're done here." She muttered that last sentence in Bella's direction.

Then she turned back and gave him a crooked smile. "I agree, though. A new stove is definitely a good idea. That color really is ghastly. In fact, you should probably get all new appliances. I think that refrigerator is older than I am."

"And that's *really* old," Bella said helpfully.

"Bite me," Barbara said without bothering to turn around.

Liam chuckled. "Now I believe you're sisters." He pulled out his ever-present notebook and jotted down a couple of things. "Do you want me to start a line of credit for you at the local hardware store? They sell appliances there too, out back. They usually want to have a credit card on file, though."

Barbara shook her head. "There's no need for that," she said. "Hang on a minute. Now where did I put…" She started rooting around in the cupboards and pulling out drawers.

"Chudo-Yudo, do you have any idea where I put that stash of money?"

The dragon-dog lifted his head. "Did you try looking in the cookie jar?"

"There are cookies in there," Babs said. "I ate one for breakfast. This is how I know."

"What about the cabinet with the tools?" Chudo-Yudo suggested. "I think I remember you making some comment about how money was just a tool, and your mind does work in strange ways."

Liam looked a little baffled by the conversation, no doubt because he would only hear Chudo-Yudo's part of it as barking.

Barbara pulled out a drawer and placed a screwdriver on the counter, followed by a heavy red pipe wrench (that was actually too large to fit in that drawer, which she hoped Liam didn't notice), and a large roll of hundred dollar bills. "Brilliant! Here it is." There were times when money came in handy, so she always tried to have some around.

"This should probably cover anything you need right away," she said, handing it to Liam. "Let me know when it runs out."

Liam's mouth gaped open. "Do you always carry this much cash around with you?" He gave her the kind of look he'd used quite a bit when they'd first met in the other timeline. She called it his professional sheriff's "I'm pretty sure you've done something illegal, I just haven't figured out what yet" look. "It's not safe."

He removed the black leather thong holding it all together and checked to see that it was all large bills. "There must be ten thousand dollars here! What do you do, rob a banks on the side?"

"Not at all," she said in a bland tone. "I just don't believe in credit cards. Little pieces of plastic never seem like real money to me."

"Uh, huh." It was clear he still thought there was something funky going on, but couldn't think of any way of refusing to take the roll. "They must pay professors better than I thought. Do you want me to give you a receipt for this?"

"No, that's not necessary. I trust you." She gave him the full-on smile again, the one she hardly ever used, and he almost fell down the stairs on his way out.

"So that's your Liam," Bella said, looking intrigued. "He's damned cute. Kind of suspicious, but cute."

"That's the sheriff in him," Barbara said. "I think it is still his default setting, even though he lost his job."

"You really do like him," Beka said with amazement. "I saw you. You *smiled* at him. And he likes you back, I can tell. My goddess, maybe you really are under some kind of spell."

CHAPTER ELEVEN

"Speaking of spells, Jazz," Barbara said, deciding that a change in subject was a good idea. "I think the one you wrote in the other timeline might be useful in coming up with a solution to repairing the current mess. Unfortunately, I only remember bits and pieces of what Bella told me was involved. To be honest, at the time, we were all just in shock that you'd somehow managed to age yourself ten years, which took more power than anyone knew you had, even Bella."

"Cool," Jazz said.

"Not terribly," Barbara said in a dry tone. "You nearly died. And then the Queen made Bella take you into the Otherworld for a year of intensive training. Since Bella was still a newlywed at the time, she wasn't all that thrilled to have to leave home and Sam behind."

Bella raised an eyebrow. "I'd like to meet this Sam," she said. "From your description, he sounds hot."

"Oh, I don't know," Beka said. "I think my imaginary husband sounds hotter. Almost as hot as that nice Liam." She hid a laugh behind her hand.

"Focus, ladies," Barbara said. "One predicament at a time."

She turned back to Jazz. "I realize that in this timeline, you never wrote the spell. But I wonder if you could put your mind to how you would create such a thing if you had been in alternative-Jazz's position. If the Riders' immortality had been stolen away and you were determined to come up with a magical way to return it to them."

"You said she used my Book, the one that all the Baba Yagas in my line had handed down over the years, which I added to after I took over," Bella said. "I'm not sure how I feel about letting her have unlimited access to all that magical information."

Barbara gave Bella a rare, pleading look. "You would supervise her, of course, but there is no way she could come up with the spell without everything she read in there. You could use it as a teaching opportunity."

"Please? I want to help," Jazz said. "I wouldn't actually *do* the spell. I mean, now that I know it could, like, kill me. You and Koshka could be with me the whole time I'm working on it." Koshka was Bella's Chudo-Yudo, although in this case, her dragon was disguised as a gigantic Norwegian Forest cat, instead of a dog.

Bella sighed. "Okay, okay. We'll work on it and see what you can come up with. But it seems like a long shot to me. I'm not sure how a spell that was supposed to give the Riders' back their immortality but instead made Jazz ten years older in an hour is going to help you knit time back together."

"To be honest," Barbara said with a grimace, "I'm not sure either. It's not that I think it would work as is, even if Jazz could reproduce what she came up with in the first place. But I am hoping that there is something in the elements she chooses that will give me ideas. If for no other reason than it is the only spell I've ever heard of that actually altered time in any concrete way."

"Don't worry, Bella," Jazz said. "I can work on the spell and still do the more practical online search stuff, too." She gave her mentor a guileless look. "I just might not be able to help quite as much with the housework if I am going to have time to do my homework on top of all that."

Bella snorted. "Nice try, brat. Speaking of which, we should get back." She stood up and gave Barbara a quick hug. "I honestly don't know how much of this I can wrap my brain around, although I do believe that *you* believe it. But if the Queen says to fix it, that's good enough for me. We'll do whatever we can."

She and Jazz walked over to the closet, wiggled the wonky handle, and opened it up to look at a lot of black clothes. Bella shut the door again with a sigh.

"You are so freaking annoying," Jazz muttered to the door. "Like should-be-turned-into -kindling annoying."

The door made a barely audible whimpering noise, and the next time they tried it, the glittering fog that marked the passageway to the Otherworld swirled into view. Jazz turned and winked at Barbara as they walked through.

Beka stood up slowly. "I should be going too. I've got a spell to practice that hasn't been working for me consistently, and I haven't been able to figure out why. It used to be one of my favorites. Brenna says I just need to focus more, but I swear, I really am."

"Maybe you just need a little less pressure, and a little more fun," Barbara suggested. It broke her heart to see Beka so beaten down. The youngest of the Baba Yagas had always had issues with self-doubt and feeling as though she wasn't quite good enough for the job—a state of affairs due entirely to Brenna's subtle undermining. But in this timeline, it was so much worse.

"Maybe you should go surf. You know, commune with the ocean and the waves and such. You are as strongly connected to the element of water as I am to the element of earth. I always find if my powers need a little boost, the best thing I can do is spend time with plants, play with my herbs, sit under a tree, that kind of thing."

"Oh, I don't surf much these days. Brenna says it is just a waste of time, and I should have outgrown such childish activities. Besides, the bus is parked further inland now, so it isn't as though I can just walk across the street to the ocean like I used to." A tiny smile flitted across her face. "It does sound like a wonderful idea, though. Maybe I'll go during the next mission that takes Brenna out of town without me."

"You do that," Barbara said. *I wonder if that is why she never met up with Marcus, since she was out surfing the first time they came into contact.* More evidence of unraveling, but she wasn't sure how knowing that helped her, if it even did.

She gave Beka an unusually gentle hug before letting the blonde head toward the closet. Which behaved itself perfectly for a change. "Don't forget what I said about watching your back, Beka," Barbara reminded her.

All she got was a wave as Beka disappeared through the door.

"What a mess," she said to Chudo-Yudo and Babs. Chudo-Yudo growled agreement, and Babs padded over to the cookie jar and brought it to Barbara. It did, in fact, have cookies in it, although Barbara didn't remember either buying the treats or putting them in there.

She gave Babs a suspicious look, but the pixie-like child just gazed back with her usual deadpan expression. Barbara shrugged. It had been a long day, and she definitely deserved a cookie. Sometimes it was better not to ask.

The sun was getting low in the sky and Barbara was starting to think about what to make for dinner, and whether or not it would be pushing her luck to ask Liam if he wanted to join them. He was still over at the house, banging away at something or other. She'd had the electricity turned back on, but she wasn't sure if many of the bulbs in the ceiling fixtures worked, so she was on the verge of going over to check—and not just so she could see Liam again—when there was a noise from the closet that led to the Otherworld.

Maybe Bella had come back to talk to her about Beka, or tell Barbara that Jazz had already found something?

But no, it turned out her long day was about to get longer.

The distinctive odor of patchouli wafted through, followed a moment later by a woman of indeterminate years with long frizzy gray hair, wearing a funky purple, blue, and red crinkled skirt and tunic top with tiny silver mirrors sewn on in random spots. Her ample bosom was adorned by multiple strands of long colorful beads that jangled together when she walked. Her face was wrinkled and brown like an apple that had been sitting out too long, but sharp black eyes belied any illusion of decrepitude.

Given that she could have looked like anything she wanted, Barbara was always amazed that *this* was the appearance the former-and-returned Baba Yaga chose. Still, it did have a tendency to encourage people not to take her seriously or see her as a threat, so perhaps that was its purpose. The modern version of a witch with a house made out of candy. Only more dangerous.

Out of the corner of her eye, Barbara saw Babs make a face and duck out of sight. Chudo-Yudo, who had been napping in a stray sunbeam, went from resting to alert faster than you could say treasure trove.

"Brenna." If Barbara's greeting had been any cooler, it would have had icicles on it. As it was, a tiny film of frost formed on the inside of the nearest window. "I wasn't expecting you."

"I hope this isn't a bad time, dear," Brenna said, gazing around with open curiosity. "I heard you finally got yourself a permanent home and I just had to come see for myself. And congratulate you, of course." She walked over and peeked out of a window, fingers like brown twigs twitching the curtains out of the way.

"Hmph," she said. "It doesn't look like much, does it? And it is so very *yellow*. I've always found yellow to be rather bright for a house color. Not that anyone could call that shade bright." She made a tutting noise. "That poor building has seen better days, hasn't it?"

"Look who's talking," Chudo-Yudo muttered.

"It's a work in progress," Barbara said. "If you don't like the color, feel free not to look at it. If you switch windows, you have your choice of a faded red barn on one side or a bunch of lovely green trees on the other. Or you could go back through the doorway and stroll through the Queen's garden. I hear her flowers are looking quite spectacular this millennium."

"Oh, I have seen Her Majesty's garden quite recently," Brenna said. "She summoned me for a visit and we had a very interesting chat. Did you know that one of the moons is crooked now? It was very odd." She sat down on the couch with an unmusical clatter of beads and fluffed her skirts. "Aren't you going to offer me a cup of tea? My goodness, your manners are dreadful. Your mentor would have been appalled."

Barbara sighed and eyed the kettle, then decided she couldn't be bothered, under the circumstances. Instead, she snapped her fingers and two steaming glass mugs of tea appeared on the table between the couch and the chair across from it. A tiny white jug of milk, a plate with a few slices of lemon, and a footed bowl with lumps of sugar and a pair of silver tongs appeared next to them.

"Help yourself," she said.

Brenna plucked out a cube of sugar with her fingers, ignoring the tongs, and placed it between her teeth, then slurped her tea around it. Barbara hadn't seen anyone do this since she was a child, back in Russia.

Barbara ignored her own tea, sitting upright with her hands folded in her lap. She had a feeling Brenna would get to the point of her visit eventually. In the meanwhile, Barbara sure as hell wasn't going to make small talk. It wasn't her strong suit to begin with, and definitely not when it was taking all of her willpower not to simply leap across the table and strangle her unexpected guest. Only the thought of the Queen's reaction stopped her. For now.

After a few moments of silence, Brenna crunched the rest of her sugar viciously and set down her mug with a thump that cracked the glass. Barbara didn't bother to mend it. Some things were beyond fixing.

"Very well, dear. Shall I tell you about my conversation with the Queen and King? It was most peculiar, I must say." She stared across the table at Barbara, her lips pursed so that the wrinkles spread outward in like corrugated tissue paper.

"Her Majesty asked me some highly offensive questions about my activities and intentions. *Highly* offensive. And then she and her consort proceeded to inform me that you had accused me of various heinous crimes." Brenna fanned herself with her hand, as if overcome. "Crimes that I apparently committed in some imaginary alternative timeline, of all things."

"Is that so?" Barbara said in a mild tone. "It's nice to know that the Queen is taking me so seriously."

The benign expression dropped away from Brenna's face and she rose to her feet with an indignant screech. "Seriously?" she said, her cheeks turning pink. "No one is taking you seriously, Baba Yaga. I don't know what game you're playing, but you are playing it with the wrong person."

"No games, Brenna," Barbara said, standing up too. "In the timeline I came from, you did some horrible things to people I love. I don't know what you're up to here, but I damn well know that whatever it is, it isn't going to end well. Take my advice and go back into retirement while you still can."

Chudo-Yudo bared his teeth and nodded his huge head in agreement.

Brenna dropped the polite old lady act as if it were a flaming bag of poo. "I will give you some advice instead, you interfering pest. You are out of your league. You may be the oldest of the current Baba Yagas, but I have lived centuries longer than you, and I know tricks you haven't even dreamt of. You do *not* want to mess with me."

"Oh no?" Barbara said. "I rather think I do. Unless you promise to go away and leave Beka alone, and stop plotting whatever the hell it is you're plotting."

"I will go where I want, when I want, and you will shut up and stay out of my way," Brenna spat. A pair of doves woven into a wall hanging pulled themselves away from the rest of the picture and flew out the window, tiny threads dangling from their feet and wings.

"Dammit, I liked that piece," Barbara said under her breath. Then to Brenna, "And if I choose not to? I mean, you've met me. Shutting up and staying out of the way has never been my best thing."

"Well, you might wish to reconsider your approach, dear," Brenna said. Her black eyes glinted. "Or I will be forced to convince the Queen that you are suffering from delusions brought on by The Water Sickness, and suggest that she have you confined to some dank, dark corner of the Otherworld. For your own protection, of course."

Barbara snorted. That was rich, coming from Brenna, who had actually succumbed to the rare but terrifying madness that sometimes affected Baba Yagas who had spent too many years drinking the Water of Life and Death. "Why would she believe you over me?" Barbara asked.

"I can be very persuasive," Brenna said, twirling her beads. "The King is not nearly as certain of your story as the Queen is, and they both find your accusations against me to be ludicrous. Beka is already half certain that you are either crazy or under some kind of evil spell, and I am quite sure she will take my side, the darling girl. I did raise her, after all."

"The Queen would never believe you," Barbara said. But in her heart, she wasn't so sure. As mercurial as she was beautiful, it was always difficult to predict which way the Queen might swing on any given day.

"Oh, I think she will," Brenna said. "But if you aren't concerned enough about your own welfare, you might wish to consider the possibility for collateral damage. Beka is a powerful witch, but she is also trusting and naïve. And Human sheriffs—even former sheriffs—are vulnerable to attack from all sorts of things."

Barbara growled low in her throat, her hands clenched into fists. Beka must have told Brenna everything they'd talked about. Or perhaps the Queen had mentioned Liam, when telling Brenna whatever part of the story she'd shared during their "chat."

"Let me eat her, Baba Yaga," Chudo-Yudo said, taking a step closer, his form starting to waver between dog and dragon. "I'd get indigestion, but it would be worth it."

Brenna backed rapidly toward the doorway, although she never took her eyes off of Barbara's. "You just think about what I've said. I have big plans, and I have no intention of letting you ruin them. Go ahead and play with your run-down house and your pathetic Human lover. But stay out of my way, or you'll be sorry."

She reached behind her for the wonky handle, which opened under her touch as if it were as happy to see the last of her as Barbara was. Then she was gone, with only the echo of a slamming door and the lingering smell of patchouli to mark her passing.

"You should have let me eat her," Chudo-Yudo said in a grumpy tone. He pulled a fresh bone out from underneath a cabinet that, strictly speaking, didn't have an underneath, and started crunching on it morosely.

Another cabinet door swung open and Babs crawled out, her short dark hair more disheveled than usual. Barbara wasn't sure how the girl had even fit into that space, not to mention where all the things that had been stored in it had disappeared to, but she figured this wasn't the time to ask. She had bigger things to worry about.

Apparently Babs shared her concern. "I think you should have let Chudo-Yudo eat her too," the girl said flatly. "She is a very bad woman. She wants to hurt Liam." The normally mild-mannered child suddenly looked surprisingly fierce. "I will not let her."

Barbara reached down and gave Babs a quick hug. She couldn't have said which one of them it was intended to comfort. "No, we will not let her hurt Liam."

But if she was being completely honest, at least with herself, she had no idea how she was going to keep him safe, short of shadowing him night and day, which might be a bit difficult to explain. As tempting as it was. As for Beka, Barbara felt completely helpless to protect the younger Baba Yaga. And helpless was *not* a feeling Barbara enjoyed.

"The Queen would have been very angry with Chudo-Yudo if he had eaten a Baba Yaga," she explained. "It isn't a good thing to have the Queen mad at you, even if you are a dragon."

Babs thought for a minute. "I think we need to make more cookies," she said.

"O-kay," Barbara agreed, a little confused. "But I don't see how that is going to keep Brenna from hurting people."

"The cookies are not to keep Brenna from hurting people," Babs said, looking very serious. "The cookies are for the Riders. They like cookies. Especially Alexei. You said before that we should not call them because we needed magic help, not brute force help. Do we need brute force help now?"

"Yes," Barbara said, thoughtfully. "Yes, I think we do." She had no idea how she was going to convince them to believe her, but it was worth a try. If nothing else, it would be wonderful to see them with their immortality intact, the way they were before Brenna broke them with torture and black magic. That might be the one bright spot in the middle of all the changes for the worse. The Riders were still themselves, whole and unbroken.

Of course, if she managed to fix the timeline, she would be taking that away from them again.

Crap.

CHAPTER TWELVE

TWO DAYS LATER, BARBARA AND BABS WERE HELPING LIAM to repaint the living room walls a soothing cream color when the sound of roaring engines made them drop their brushes and run outside.

A huge black Harley was just pulling into the yard, followed closely by a low-slung red Ducati and a shining white Yamaha. The three motorcycles fell silent as their riders dismounted. Or more properly, their Riders, since that was who rode them.

Back in the old days, the Black Rider, the Red Rider, and the White Rider, whose job it was to assist the Baba Yagas in whatever they might need, rode magical steeds whose speed and stamina far exceeded that of any ordinary horse. Like the Baba's huts, which had transformed themselves to better suit the modern era, the Rider's steeds had morphed into equally enchanted motorcycles. The Riders themselves, however, had remained largely unchanged.

Or in the case of Alexei, simply large.

The middle of the three half-brothers, sons of a Russian god and different mothers, Alexei was a giant bear of a man with coarse brown hair and a braided beard. He wore black leather that jangled with silver chains, and he grinned wildly as he picked Barbara up and swung her around as if she were Babs' size.

When he finally put her down, the oldest brother, Gregori, gave her a dignified bow, his hands pressed together in front of his chest. As serene as Alexei was rowdy, Gregori had the slim build and easy gait of a martial arts master, and the long black hair and Fu Manchu mustache of the Russian steppes where he had been born. He wore a red leather jumpsuit that fit him like a second skin, and his hair was pulled back with a red leather thong.

Mikhail, the youngest of the three, bowed more deeply than Gregori had and then leaned forward to kiss Barbara's hand, repeating the gallant gesture with little Babs. Tall, slim, and classically handsome, Mikhail's blonde hair reached down to touch the shoulders of his pristine white silk shirt. "How wonderful it is to see you, Baba Yaga," he said. "It has been too long."

Barbara felt unaccustomed tears prick at her eyes. They all looked as attractive, confident, and dangerous as always, but with a subtle difference that marked the lack of the traumas that had beset them in her own timeline. Seeing them like this made her heart feel ten pounds lighter, despite the worries she still bore.

"It is good to see you all too," she said in a quiet voice. "You have no idea how good."

The sound of a throat being cleared reminded her that they had company. Liam had followed her and Babs out the door and was staring at the visitors with an expression that seemed to hold warring elements of awe, suspicion, and maybe even jealousy. Of course, she told herself, that might have been for the motorcycles.

"Ah, right. Liam, these are my friends Alexei, Mikhail, and Gregori. Boys, this is Liam. He's helping me to fix up this house I just bought."

Alexei marched up and shook Liam's hand with his usual enthusiasm. Barbara hoped all Liam's fingers still worked afterwards, since she needed him to finish the painting.

"Hello," Alexei said, his Russian accent still the thickest of them all. "I don't suppose you have beer?"

"Alexei, you oaf, where are your manners?" Mikhail said, reaching up to smack his brother on the head as he walked by. "Any friend of Baba—I mean, Barbara's, is a friend of ours."

"Of course, most of our friends usually have beer," Alexei added helpfully.

"Please excuse him," Gregori said, bowing to Liam as he had to Barbara. "He was raised in the woods by bears. It is a pleasure to meet you. Don't let us keep you from your work."

He walked back to Barbara. "You bought a house?" One

feathery black eyebrow rose as he assessed the structure more thoroughly. "To be specific, you bought *this* house?"

"It is a long story," she said, gesturing him and the other two toward the Airstream. "One of several. Why don't you come in. I'm pretty sure I have some vodka in the freezer."

"That is more like it," Alexei said cheerfully as he stomped toward the trailer. "A story and a glass of vodka—this is going to be good."

There was silence as she finished yet another rendition of her saga. She braced herself to try and convince the Riders to believe her, no matter how implausible her story. They had no innate magic, so handing them her wedding ring wouldn't help. Not that it had convinced Beka anyway.

She held her breath, looking from one unreadable face to another. The Riders had been her lifeline for years; she didn't know what she would do if they decided she was crazy and just walked away.

Their responses to her story weren't exactly what she'd been expecting.

Gregori, as usual, was the most stoic of them all. He poured himself another shot of vodka, drank it down, and said in a thoughtful tone, "I run a shelter for troubled teens?"

Not knowing what to say, she just nodded.

"And I fall in love with a woman who has a baby?" Mikhail said, sounding both bemused and intrigued.

Alexei threw back his next shot and said happily, "I own a BAR?" He pumped his fists in the air. "I marry a woman who owns a bar. I definitely win."

Barbara just stared at them. "Uh, guys? I think you are missing the point. All those things are in my timeline. If I put the universe back the way it is supposed to be, you will all lose your immortality again. You will have lived through torture, and a year in which you don't speak to each other at all, and take these impossibly difficult journeys to figure out who you are once you can't be the Riders anymore. It was terrible."

The three brothers exchanged glances, communicating with each other in that silent way they had after spending centuries in each other's company. Finally, Alexei gave a characteristically Russian shrug.

"We will take our chances," he said. "What is meant to be is meant to be. Of course we will help."

Barbara was overwhelmed with a combination of gratitude and guilt. "You guys are the best," she said.

"Of course we are," Mikhail agreed. "Now, tell us what you need us to do."

After a meal and some more conversation, Gregori accepted a container full of cookies from Babs and rode off to keep an eye on Brenna. Surprisingly, Barbara had had no trouble convincing the Riders that Brenna was up to no good. As Alexei said in his typical blunt fashion, they'd seen the crazy handwriting on the wall a long time ago.

They had been pleased when the Queen forced Brenna to retire and hadn't been in favor of her coming back—although, of course, the Queen didn't consult them on that kind of decision. Plus, they'd seen the way that the old witch had chipped away at Beka's confidence. Gregori was quietly delighted to be given the chance to help bring the old witch down.

Luckily, the trip out to California, which would have been lengthy on any normal motorcycle, would only take him a couple of days on one which could magically go faster and find shortcuts where none existed on any Human map.

A few minutes later, Alexei heaved his bulk up onto his Harley, having tucked his own cookies into his fringed black saddlebags, and headed toward southern Ohio. Jazz had been able to track down Peter Callahan's location there, apparently using a combination of magic and computer skills that had Bella both impressed and slightly worried about the fate of the world. Alexei was going to see if there was any sign of Maya, and report back to Barbara if he found the rusalka.

Mikhail had chosen to stick around the area for now, although he'd promised to keep a low profile. As he drove away in search of a local bed and breakfast, the sun gleaming off his blonde hair and snug white jeans, Barbara thought that might be easier said than done. Still, the Riders had all been hiding in plain sight for much longer than she'd been alive, so she would try tp have a little faith. As it was, just knowing they were unreservedly on her side made her feel better than she had since the moment she'd realized that her universe had been turned upside down.

"So, your friends not staying the night?" Liam asked as he put the paint away in his truck.

"Nope," Barbara said.

"I don't remember seeing them in the area before. They're not from around here?"

Barbara scanned his face. She'd never been all that good at reading Human emotions, but she'd gotten a little better at it during the last few years married to the man standing before her. She was almost completely certain she was detecting a note of jealousy in his voice, which made her absurdly happy, although she was careful not to let it show.

"Nope," she said. She could practically hear Liam grinding his teeth.

"I noticed they all had Russian accents, although not to the same degree. You have a tiny bit of one too, don't you?" Liam tossed his tool belt onto the passenger seat and turned around to meet her eyes. "Is that where you met them?"

"You ask a lot of questions for someone who isn't a lawman anymore," she said. "Why would a handyman care where someone is from?" Then she took pity on him. "They're just old friends who were passing through the area, so they came by to check out the house."

"What did they think?" Liam asked, the hint of a smile playing around his lips.

Barbara sighed. "They thought I'd lost my mind, like most everyone else. But I still think the house is going to look great when we're done. I can see it in my head." Plus, of course, she'd seen it when it was finished the first time, which helped.

"Oh, I agree," Liam said, to her surprise. "The house is solid. All the stuff that needs to be fixed is superficial. It's going to be a beauty in the end."

Barbara had no idea if she would be around to see it or not, which made the whole effort somewhat bittersweet. Still, the point had been to spend time with Liam, just in case she couldn't solve the timeline issue.

"If you're taking a break, would you like to come in for a cup of coffee?" she asked.

He hesitated, possibly questioning the wisdom of having coffee with a woman who, in another lifetime, he had referred to as odd, mysterious, and infuriating.

"I don't know if you want me in your trailer," he said. "I'm kind of a mess."

"I live with a huge white dog and a small inquisitive child," Barbara said. "I stopped worrying about messes a long time ago."

His sudden flash of smile caught her by surprise, practically rocking her back on her heels. "Then thank you, I'd love a cup of coffee. I brought a thermos, but it's pretty cold now."

They walked into the Airstream, where Babs was sitting at the kitchen table working intently on something—it could have been her homeschooling, or a list of names for her new stuffed bear. She approached almost everything with that kind of concentration. At her feet, Chudo-Yudo was gnawing on a bone almost bigger than his head, which was really saying something, given that his head was the size of your average microwave oven.

"This is really cool," Liam said, looking around. "I've been in a few RVs in my life, but I've never seen one like this."

"What is an RV?" Babs asked, lifting her eyes from her paper. "Hello Liam. Would you like a cookie?" Her gaze darted to Barbara, who nodded reassuringly. She felt sorry for Babs, who had to pretend to barely know the man she considered to be her father. It was tough enough for Barbara, nearly impossible, really, but she had a lot more years of practice with accommodating the impossible. She thought Babs was doing remarkably well, all things considered. Of course, that was Babs for you.

"It's short for recreational vehicle," Liam said. "This Airstream is one kind of RV. There are lots of different types."

Babs shook her head. "This is not a recreational vehicle. It is our home. It is very special."

Liam smiled at her. "It certainly is. I've never come across one that was so fancy." He pointed at the rich fabrics and Oriental rugs. "And yes, I would love a cookie, thank you."

Babs hopped up to get the cookie jar, which was currently in the shape of a sitting cat. She'd been agitating for a kitten before everything had gone sideways, and had developed a slight tendency to drop less than subtle hints. Of course, given her unconventional upbringing, followed by a few years spent in Barbara's company, it was no wonder that subtle wasn't in her repertoire. It wasn't usually in Barbara's either.

"Chocolate chip," Liam said. "That's my favorite."

"I know," Babs said.

Oops. "Chocolate chip is everyone's favorite," Barbara said smoothly, putting a cup of coffee down in front of Liam. He'd taken a seat opposite Babs and was reading her piece of paper upside down. No doubt another sheriff-acquired skill set.

"This is great," Liam said, after taking a sip from his cup. "Two sugars and just a splash of milk, just the way I like it. How did you know?"

Oops again. Apparently Babs wasn't the only one who needed to be more careful.

"Is it? That's the way I take mine. I guess I just made them both that way out of habit." She twitched her fingers, adding milk to her own normally black coffee. She hoped he wouldn't notice the faint aroma of blue roses from the enchanted coffeemaker.

Luckily, he was more focused on the adorable urchin on the other side of the table. "That's an interesting list," he said. "Pooh. Pooka. Grizzly?"

"They are traditional names for bears," Babs explained gravely. She held up the stuffed animal Barbara had picked up for her in town the other day in the hope that it would be some kind of comfort. "I have a new bear and I need to name him."

"Ah, I see," Liam said. "You know, you don't have to give him a traditional name. You can name him anything you want."

Babs paused with a cookie halfway to her mouth, considering this. "Anything?"

Liam shrugged. "I guess so. Why, what do you want to call him?"

"Kitty," Babs said.

Barbara bit back a laugh as Liam nearly choked on his coffee. "I should have seen that one coming," she said. "She'd been trying to convince me to get her a cat for a while now."

"That explains it," Liam said. "A stuffed bear named Kitty. Sure, why not? It's no odder than anything else around here."

Barbara gave him her best innocent look, well aware that is wasn't her best talent. "We're not odd. We're just not ordinary, exactly."

"Ordinary is boring," Babs said with assurance. "Barbara always says so."

"I see," Liam said. "And yet you bought an ordinary house in an ordinary town."

"The house isn't ordinary," Babs explained. "It has a ghost."

Barbara finished her mouthful of cookie rapidly and added, "Dunville isn't an ordinary town. It's charming and just a little bit quirky."

"So it is," Liam said. "Not everyone appreciates that. But I guess it must have made quite the impression on you when you were here a year ago if you came back to stay."

"Lots of things about the area made an impression on me," Barbara said, gazing directly at him. She was rewarded by a hint of a blush. "The land is quite beautiful, and there are some interesting herbs that grow around here. But to be honest, it was the people who made the biggest impression on me."

She wasn't lying, either. For a woman who mostly professed not to like people, she had become very attached to those she had met when she'd come to Clearwater County: Liam, of course, but also Belinda and her parents, Bertie who ran the dinner and lived to make sure that everyone had as much comfort food as they needed, and Nina the dispatcher, and so many more. Mind you, there had been plenty who hadn't welcomed her at first, but even those had mostly come around in the end.

The sad look crept back into Liam's eyes. "They're why I stay," he said. "Even though in many ways it might be easier to leave."

Barbara's heart cracked a little bit more, but there was nothing she could do at the moment that would make him feel better. If only buying him a stuffed bear would help.

Reminding herself that the best thing she could do would be to fix the whole damned screwed up situation, she tried to put her focus back on her mission.

"Speaking of people, I remember meeting a man named Peter Callahan when I was here the last time. He worked for an energy company and had an assistant named Maya. I chatted with her a few times," if head-on confrontations and death threats could be considered chatting, "and I promised I would look her up if I were ever back in the area. Do you happen to know if she is still around?"

Liam took another sip of coffee. "No neither of them is. They left not too long after you did, when the fracking moratorium was passed by the state. There was a bit of drama surrounding their departure, actually. I've never been clear on what exactly happened, but Peter's son disappeared right around the time the company pulled out."

"Oh?"

"Initially we thought it had something to do with the other children who went missing, but then it appeared more likely to be some kind of custody dispute, since he and his wife apparently had a very public falling out, and not long after that he was seen leaving town with Maya. Of course, she was his assistant, so maybe one had nothing to do with the other."

"Did you ever investigate Peter's son's disappearance?" Barbara asked, curious. In her timeline, Maya had stolen Peter's son and taken him to the Otherworld, but there hadn't been any sign that had happened this time around.

Liam gave a half-hearted shrug. "I probably would have, but the town board fired me around then for my failure to find any clues into the whereabouts of the other children who had vanished. My successor said that since all the parties involved had left town, and no one had filed a missing persons report, it wasn't his problem."

"I still can't believe they fired you," Barbara said, probably a tad too fiercely. "So did the new sheriff ever make any headway on the case of the missing children?"

"No," Liam said in a brusque tone, the grooves around his mouth deepening. "And yet somehow he still has his job." He put his cup down with a decisive clunk and stood up. "Thank you for the coffee. That should keep me going for another couple of hours. I'm going to try and rescue those shutters of yours before they fall off the house entirely."

Barbara followed him to the door as he marched over to his truck and grabbed his tool belt. The late afternoon sun had gotten quite warm, and Liam took off his shirt and slung it over the tailgate before attacking the crooked shutters with the fervor of a man being chased by his own demons.

She stood there and watched for a while, admiring the movement of his muscles under his tanned skin. Eventually Babs came over and stood next to her, holding Kitty the bear.

"I thought it was not polite to stare," Babs said. "Did I get that wrong?"

"No," Barbara said. "But in this case, because I am technically still married to him, it is allowed."

"Human rules are confusing," Babs said.

"You're not wrong," Barbara said. "You're definitely not wrong.

CHAPTER THIRTEEN

TO BARBARA'S SURPRISE, SHE WAS AWOKEN TWO DAYS LATER BY the muted rumble of a motorcycle coming to a stop in front of the Airstream. She stuck her head out the window to see Alexei, looking as perky as ever despite the early hour. Mind you, she'd seen him look just as energetic after a three day binge of carousing and injury-inducing bar fights. It was more or less his default setting.

"Good morning, Baba Yaga," he said. "I hope I didn't wake you up."

Barbara glanced at the angle of the sun. "Of course you woke me up, you twit. It's only around five am." But she had to fight to keep the smile off her face as she said it.

Alexei squinted at the sky. "Ah, so it is. Well, you go back to sleep then. I'll just sit out here on the hard ground in front of your decrepit new house and wait for you to be awake enough to hear my news. No hurry." He gave a huge yawn and stretched. "Just because I drove all night to get here is no reason to interrupt your beauty sleep."

"You were in Ohio," Barbara said, unimpressed by his melodramatics. "With your enchanted steed, it probably took you less than four hours. That's hardly all night."

"Well, it was part of the night," Alexei said. "And I was awake all the rest of it watching your friend Maya. The least you could do is give a poor Rider a cup of coffee and a piece of pie."

"You found Maya?" Barbara said. "You can have two pieces of pie. If the refrigerator can be persuaded to produce some, that is. Come on in." She would have let him in anyway, of course, but the fact that he had found Maya made her stop playing their games a little sooner than she would have otherwise.

"Of course it will produce pie for me," Alexei said smugly. "Your refrigerator loves me."

It was true. Everything in the Airstream was more likely to cooperate for any of the Riders than it was for her. Traitor. The one time she'd asked it for pie, she'd gotten nothing *but* cherry pies for three days. Magical traveling huts could be a pain in the butt sometimes.

Since there was no way Alexei's bulk would squeeze into one of the banquet seats designed for more average sized people, he perched on a stool and gratefully accepted a large mug of steaming coffee, black with six sugars. Despite the way he ate there was never an extra ounce of fat on him—all that mass was pure muscle—because his metabolism burned calories as if they were twigs in a bonfire.

"Good morning, Alexei," Babs said, climbing down from her bed and then giving it a shove until it folded neatly back up into its spot on the wall. "I named my bear Kitty. Liam said it was okay." She set the bear down on the couch and sat down next to it, seemingly not at all perturbed by the early hour. Her clothing sense was a little unusual at the best of times, and she seemed to have slept in a pair of orange and pink striped shorts and a purple tee shirt with a picture of a grumpy cat on it.

"Did he?" Alexei said. "And did you ask him to get you a real kitten?"

"Not yet," Babs said.

"Not ever," Barbara said, feeling grumpier than the fabric feline. She got her own coffee and a glass of milk for Babs, and set an entire blueberry pie in front of Alexei. "Don't encourage her, please." She and Babs got buttered toast with marmalade.

"Now, are you going to tell me about Maya, or am I going to have to turn you into something that eats flies for breakfast instead of pastry?" she said to Alexei.

He gave his rumbling laugh, as unimpressed with her threats as ever.

"She wasn't very difficult to track down," he said. "Just as you thought, she is still with Peter Callahan, although the balance of power in their relationship has clearly shifted. Any illusion that he was the one in charge is gone now.

"The only reason it took me this long to get back to you was because I thought you'd want me to watch her for a bit, and see if I could figure out what she is up to."

"And what *is* she up to?" Barbara asked.

"Nothing good," Alexei said with a shrug. "I talked with some of the people in town and then backtracked to the last few places Callahan's company sent him. It appears that all of them have experienced mysterious problems. Machinery not working for no obvious reason. Sinkholes swallowing up entire operations. One well site in Pennsylvania apparently had quite a spectacular explosion. You'll have to ask Jazz if she has turned up anything looking at that fancy computer of hers, but I'm guessing his company isn't too happy with him about now."

"Is anyone blaming him for causing the problems? Or looking in Maya's direction?" Barbara was a little concerned about Alexei going around asking pointed questions. He wasn't exactly subtle, and even with his best intentions, he tended to stand out in a crowd. She had hoped to stay off of Maya's radar until they had gathered more facts and had something resembling a plan of action. Oh, well. What was done was done. Maybe Maya hadn't gotten wind of his presence.

"I don't think so," Alexei said. "Most of the folks I talked to were putting it down to bad luck or incompetence, and seem more likely to blame the company."

It was hard for Barbara to feel sorry for a business that made money from destroying the earth and polluting the water, but in this case she almost did. Almost. She definitely felt sorry for the people who lived near the fracking sites. It was unlikely that Maya cared much about collateral damage.

"I've got another interesting tidbit for you," Alexei said, holding out his mug for a refill. "I think you're going to like this one."

"Oh?" Barbara raised an eyebrow.

"You sent me a message asking if Peter's son was with him. Initially I was going to say no, since there are no obvious signs of a child in the house. No toys in any of the bedrooms or children's clothing. No babysitter when Callahan leaves for work, and the school bus doesn't stop there."

"I'm sensing a but," Barbara said, intrigued.

"But I looked in the refrigerator when no one was home, and there is food suitable for a child—nothing fancy, just things like juice boxes and cheese snacks and such. But I've never seen a grownup drink from one of those silly little boxes."

Barbara's eyebrow went higher. "You broke into the house Maya and Callahan are living in?"

Alexei gave her a wide-eyed look. "The back door lock was broken. Well, it is now, anyway. Flimsy things, those locks. They just don't make them like they used to."

Barbara stifled a groan. Just as she'd thought. Not subtle. Still, it was important information. "So you think young Petey is locked up somewhere in the house?"

"Not sure," Alexei said. "I checked the basement and attic and didn't find anything, but I couldn't stay long without risking discovery, so it's possible I missed something."

"Well, the Maya I knew was awfully good at illusions, so she could have him tucked behind a hidden door," Barbara said. She weighed how much she needed to know the answer to Petey's location versus the chances of tipping Maya off to the fact that a Baba Yaga was looking into her activities. Although frankly, giving Alexei's general lack of anything resembling stealth, that ship had probably already sailed.

"The Queen isn't going to be interested in supposition," Barbara finally said reluctantly. "Not to mention that I'm not too happy about leaving any child in the indelicate hands of that rusalka. I guess you're going to have to go back there and see if you can find out for sure. But do try to be a little discreet," she said sharply.

"What do you mean, discreet? I am always discreet." Alexei thumped his chest forcefully, making the entire Airstream rock.

"Uh huh," Barbara said. "If by discreet you mean 'like a bull in a china shop.'"

"I don't even like china shops," Alexei muttered. "Although bull can be quite tasty."

He picked up the rest of the pie, his fork, coffee mug, and the last couple of pieces of toast. "If you don't mind, I think I'll go take a little nap out under your lovely trees before I head back."

"No problem," Barbara said. "Just try not to—"

But he was already gone.

Around eight that night, Barbara tucked Babs into bed and gave Chudo-Yudo a stern look. "I shouldn't be gone long," she said. "I need to meet up with Bella and Beka, and Beka sent a message saying that Brenna was off dealing with some kind of Baba Yaga business without her, so the coast was clear for us to visit her."

"Why does she not come here?" Babs asked, her arm curled around Kitty bear, with a book in her other hand. "Then you could all read to me." For some reason, Babs had fixated on being read to as one of the few forms of affection and attention she was comfortable with, and Liam had done so every night, occasionally assisted by Barbara. Babs was an odd mix of older than her theoretical age, strangely wise and focused, and much younger, since her first few years hadn't born any resemblance to a normal childhood.

"She said she isn't feeling well," Barbara said. "So she'd rather we came to her."

Chudo-Yudo raised his blocky white head and stared at her. "She isn't feeling well."

"Yeah, I know. Baba Yagas don't get sick." Barbara felt a frown wrinkling her forehead and consciously smoothed it out so as not to worry Babs. "I'll talk to you when I get back, okay? No letting Babs stay up until midnight this time. Not that I expect to be gone that long."

"Hey, it's the witching hour, and she's a little witch…"

Worst babysitter ever.

She tugged on Babs' hair. "You're in charge," she said to the child. "Ignore whatever he says. I'll be back soon."

Barbara slipped through the closet portal and took the most direct route she could find through the Otherworld to Beka's location. Sooner or later Barbara would have to face the Queen again, but she was really hoping to have a few more answers before that happened.

A crimson forest by the side of an azure lake gave way to rocky outcrops that looked like they had been there since the age of the dinosaurs and probably had been. Although to the best of her knowledge, there had never been dinosaurs in the Otherworld. It got their less-inclined-to-extinction cousins, the dragons, instead.

The winding path finally led to a foggy spot that called to Barbara's senses on a molecular level—the doorway that led to another Baba Yaga's home. Each doorway had its own particular flavor, for lack of a better term. Beka's tasted like salty air and briny shrimp and carried with it the echo of seagulls crying against the setting sun. Bella's caravan bore the impression of pine-scented woods, and ripe berries hanging on bushes, and the sound of owls hooting in the night. Barbara had no idea what her Airstream felt like to the others; to her, that tugging feeling just meant home.

She met up with Bella right outside the swirling mists that indicated a portal—in theory, one which any denizen of the Otherworld could access, although few would be foolish enough to try unless they had a very good reason.

"She's not feeling well?" Bella said instead of a more polite greeting. "What the heck is up with that?"

Barbara shook her head. "I don't know, but I don't like it." They exchanged a silent look of agreement before walking through the mists.

They came out into the cheerful surroundings of the inside of a refurbished school bus. Pale wood paneled the walls, floor, and ceiling, and maple shelves covered all the wall space that wasn't windows. Nautical-themed decorations made from shells, driftwood, and brightly blown glass balls hung here and there, and the futon that served as both bed and couch was covered in a blue-green cloth in ocean shades.

The only slightly jarring note was the collection of knives and swords that ran along the top of the walls, but since Barbara had an affection for sharp objects, they made her feel right at home.

The time difference meant that the late afternoon California sun still shone through the bus windows, but there was no sign of Beka. Bella and Barbara walked outside, pausing as always to admire the brightly painted mural of a seascape—complete with a scantily-clad mermaid—that adorned the exterior of the bus. Then they turned around to look for their friend.

"What the *hell* is that?" Bella asked, appalled and taken aback.

Barbara gazed in the direction Bella was pointing and felt the bottom fall out of her stomach. "I'd say it's a damned hut," she answered, staring at the ramshackle house in disbelief. "I know it's traditional, but I think this is going a step too far."

"At least a step," Bella agreed. "Maybe a whole flight of stairs. What on earth are Brenna and Beka thinking? Do you think they're just parked next to it because it was a convenient spot, or are they actually living in it?"

Beka stepped out of the doorway, squinting at the sun as if it hurt her eyes. "Living in it," she said. "Hideous, isn't it? For some reason Brenna took a liking to it, and the bus was getting pretty small with both of us living in it, so she decided we should use it as a home base. I think maybe it is her idea of a Baba Yaga joke."

Barbara didn't think it was a very good one. She'd hoped that Beka would come with them to hang out in the bus, but instead she invited them into the house. Hut. Whatever it was.

Once inside, Barbara felt a shudder running down her spine. The place gave her the creeps. It was dark and dank, the few windows covered with heavy moss-colored curtains, so hardly any light got through. A cauldron bubbled sullenly over a fireplace with a crooked stone chimney, and the air smelled like a combination of smoke and noxious herbs. More herbs, both fresh and dried, hung from the rafters and from hooks on the walls, and jars of disreputable-looking and thankfully not readily identifiable items marched in uneven rows across a line of shelves.

After a minute, she realized the source of her instinctive unease. It reminded her vaguely of the cave in which Brenna had imprisoned and tortured the Riders, although the basic structures was nothing alike. You could take the witch out of the cave, but you couldn't take the cave out of the witch… Barbara almost looked overhead for stalactites.

"Well, it's uh, cozy, I guess," Bella said.

Beka laughed. "It's a pit," she said. "But I'm not in any position to argue. We're on the road in the bus a lot anyway. Brenna took my Karmann Ghia off to do some mysterious errand, so I figured that if you wanted to meet up, now was a good time. She took Chewie with her. Not that I'm worried about him ratting me out." Chewie was her Chudo-Yudo, who took the form of a huge black Newfoundland dog. He'd always preferred Beka to Brenna.

"Plus you said you weren't feeling well," Bella reminded her. "Are you okay now?"

"I'm just tired," Beka said. "And I feel a little flu-y. I might be fighting a bug of some sort. Brenna has had us working some late nights, and I'm a bit run down. No big deal."

"It's kind of a big deal," Barbara said. "Baba Yagas don't get sick. If you really don't feel right, maybe you should have an extra dose of the Water of Life and Death. You are drinking your share, aren't you?"

"Sure," Beka said. "You worry too much."

"Uh huh." Barbara wanted an excuse to get out of the gloomy

shack and away from the reek of unsavory magic. "Let's go sit in the bus. You can get a dose of the Water, and Bella and I will be right by the doorway to the Otherworld if Brenna comes back sooner than expected."

"Good idea," Bella said, heading for the exit with an unseemly haste that made Barbara think she wasn't the only one whose skin was crawling.

Bella shook herself like her dragon-cat when she got back out into the sun. "Whew. I don't know how you stand it, Beka." She turned back to gaze at the youngest Baba Yaga. "Crap," she said. "You look like shit. Nothing personal."

Now that they were outside where the light was better, Barbara could see what Bella was talking about. Beka was even paler than the last time they'd seen her, with bluish-gray circles under her eyes, her shoulders drooping as if it took too much effort to hold them up straight. When Barbara let her vision go slightly out of focus and looked at the younger woman's aura, what she saw looked ragged and uneven, as if tiny psychic mice had been nibbling it.

"Look at her aura," Barbara demanded. "Tell me that seems right."

Bella shrugged at her. "You know aura reading isn't one of my talents," she said. "But I'm not going to argue with you. I can't believe Brenna let you get so run down, Beka."

"Hmph," Barbara snorted. "Let her. Right."

"What are you implying?" Bella asked.

"I'm not implying anything," Barbara said. "I'm coming right out and saying it. I think Brenna is doing this. She's somehow stealing Beka's life energy, just the way she stole the Rider's immortality and vitality. Different timeline, different approach, but I'll bet she's trying to do exactly what she did in my world —extend her life and increase her power by any means possible."

"That's ridiculous," Beka said.

"It kind of is," Bella agreed. "I admit, I think that Brenna is capable of almost anything, and I wouldn't trust her as far as I could throw her, but no Baba Yaga would do such a thing to her apprentice. Not even Brenna."

"You're wrong," Barbara said flatly. She waved her hand in Beka's direction. "Do you really think *this* can be explained by a few nights of missed sleep?"

"Please don't argue," Beka said. "You know I hate it. Brenna and I have both been putting a lot of our own energy into this new potion she's been working on. It's really important—she thinks it can clean the poisons out of the ocean waters—so it will be worth it if we can make it viable. I'm fine, really I am. Can we just go sit down in the bus?"

"Fine," Barbara said, since she clearly wasn't going to get anywhere with either of them. "But I want you to take that extra dose of the Water right now."

Beka shook her head as they walked up the stairs into the bus. "Brenna says it is a bad idea to increase the amount of the Water you drink. She says that can lead to developing the Water Sickness without you even realizing it."

She and Bella both sneaked sideways glances in Barbara's direction.

"Oh, come on," Barbara sputtered. "You're not implying I have Water Sickness, are you? For one thing, I'm only in my eighties. I haven't been drinking it for nearly long enough for that to happen. The few Baba Yagas who have succumbed to it have all been at the end of their careers, and over two hundred years old or older."

"Yes, that's true," Beka said in a quiet voice. "But if someone had been taking extra doses for some reason, even if it seemed at the time like that reason was a good one, she could accelerate the problem. You know, in theory."

"Is that what Brenna has been saying about me?" Barbara could feel her blood pressure rising like the ocean at high tide. She swung her head from side to side, looking at the two women who were closer to her than any sisters, the only friends she'd ever had, other than the Riders. "And you believe her?"

"No, of course we don't," Bella said hastily. "We just thought that it might explain some of the stories you've been telling. I mean, if they weren't true, which of course they are."

Barbara couldn't decide if she wanted to weep or scream. In all the years they'd been working together, there had never been a time when the three of them hadn't been a united front, an unwavering source of support for each other. First Barbara and Bella, and then Beka, when she grew old enough to join their generation of Baba Yagas. They were the ground under her feet. It suddenly felt like quicksand.

"I brought you the notes for the spell Jazz has been working on," Bella said, changing the subject awkwardly. They all settled into seats, Beka and Bella on the futon, and Barbara dragging over a wooden chair from in front of a swing-down desk.

"Great," Barbara said, trying to ignore the most recent part of their conversation. "What has she come up with?" She put out her hand for the papers Bella had pulled out of the leather bag she'd slung over her shoulder, but Bella hung on to them for a moment too long.

"I know you said that Jazz had done this crazy spell in the other timeline after Brenna supposedly stole the Riders' immortality, but that story still seems pretty far out to me." Bella paused, as if weighing her next words carefully. "It's not that I'm doubting you, exactly…but, well, I just wanted to make sure that you aren't contemplating doing some kind of immortality spell for yourself."

Barbara ground her teeth together so hard she was worried she'd cracked a molar. "I wouldn't have eternal life if someone gave it to me gift-wrapped and covered with chocolate," she said. "The extended years we get as Baba Yagas are plenty for me. I have no desire to outlive Liam and everyone else I know, and go on forever. Even the Riders seemed to be getting bored with their unending lives before everything went to hell, although I doubt they would have given up their immortality willingly."

She understood why Bella felt as though she had to ask the question, but it still hurt that the other woman would even have considered such a thing. It sounded like Brenna had been getting into Beka's head, and Beka's doubts had been shared with Bella. Back in her own reality, that never would have happened.

Barbara wasn't sure which was the worst aspect of this altered timeline; having lost Liam, or the feeling that she was losing the bond with her sister Babas, the bond which had always been the best part of her life.

Barbara blinked her eyes rapidly. There must have been something in the dusty hut that made them blurry and moist.

"You either trust me or you don't," she said finally. "It's up to you. If you don't want to give me Jazz's notes, I'll try and find some other way to fix the timeline." She got up to leave.

"I trust you, I trust you," Bella said, standing up too and thrusting the papers into Barbara's hand. "It's just, this is all so strange."

"Believe me, it is a lot stranger for me," Barbara said heavily. "At least you're still living in the world where you belong, where people don't treat you as if you have suddenly lost your mind."

She stumbled toward the doorway, not looking back at the sister who didn't believe her or the one who hadn't yet made up her mind if she did or not. Tried not to worry that she was walking away, leaving Beka vulnerable to Brenna's evil intentions, and doing nothing to stop them. Trying not to think about that hut that felt so much like the cave from hell.

Or that if she were going to use elements from Jazz's spell, she might have to go back to the Otherworld for ingredients that weren't available anywhere outside than that magical land. Barbara really wasn't ready to face the Queen again. Not until she had more answers. If anything, she felt as though she knew less now than when she started. And she felt a lot more alone.

CHAPTER FOURTEEN

THE NEXT MORNING BARBARA WAS BROODING OVER JAZZ'S notes, making lists of the bits she thought might be helpful, when there was a knock on the door.

Her heart skipped a beat, making the wind chimes hanging outside the window jingle even though there wasn't a breeze, but when Babs opened the door it was only Mikhail standing there, his blonde head haloed by the sunlight behind him. Not that Barbara wasn't happy to see a friendly face.

"Hey there," she said. "What brings you around? I thought you were going to try and stay out of sight."

"Oh, I was," Mikhail said, dropping gracefully onto the couch and putting his feet up on the coffee table. "But things are getting a little weird, and I thought you'd want to know."

"Weird how?' Barbara asked, fetching him a cup of coffee and refilling her own. She sat back down on the couch next to him, with Babs perching like some strange exotic bird on the edge of the table.

"Has your friend Liam mentioned anything odd happening to him?" Mikhail asked in an apparent non sequitur.

"No," Barbara said. "But I haven't seen him all that much." *Not nearly enough, anyway.* "Why?"

"Well, I decided I would keep an eye on him, since he seemed to be so important to you," Mikhail said. "I mean, it's not like I'm stalking him or anything. I'm still checking on other things around town, and all. But I figured it couldn't hurt to check in on him periodically."

Barbara bit back a smile. She was pretty sure that Mikhail had been watching out for her, not for Liam. Making sure the former sheriff wasn't seeing anyone else, for instance. Or doing anything else that might hurt Barbara. She thought either circumstance was unlikely, but it was sweet of Mikhail to worry about her. Considering that she had never expressed interest in a man (at least, a Human one) before, she could understand why he might feel a bit protective of her feelings.

And after the way things had gone with Bella and Beka, she appreciated it more than she might have otherwise, so she refrained from scolding him for interfering.

"So, did you find out anything particularly interesting?" she asked. "Something you thought I needed to know right away?"

"Maybe," Mikhail said. "To be honest, I'm not sure if it is a something or a whole bunch of nothings."

Barbara blinked at him. "You're not making much sense. Do you need breakfast? Maybe you have low blood sugar."

"My blood sugar is just fine, thank you, Baba Yaga," Mikhail said with his usual charming grin. "Although I wouldn't mind a bacon sandwich if you feel like magicking one up. I'm sorry I'm not sounding more coherent. I just meant to say that a lot of odd things have been happening around your Liam, and I wasn't sure if they were just strange coincidences or if they added up to something sinister."

Barbara started assembling his not-breakfast, making extras for her and Babs while she was at it—then adding a couple more portions after a pointed look from Chudo-Yudo. There was no such thing as too much bacon. Under the circumstances, it probably counted as a form of therapy.

"What strange things are happening to Liam?" Babs asked before Barbara could. She could detect a worried note under the usual calm of the girl's voice.

Mikhail shrugged. "He had a tire blow out the other day. That's not so unusual, but I overheard the mechanic say that the rubber had been sliced most of the way through, but not completely, so it wouldn't give until he had been driving for a while. Fortunately, he wasn't going very fast when it blew, and there was no one right behind him, so he was able to steer his truck safely to the shoulder. But if he'd been on the highway, it might have been another story."

"Teenage vandalism?" Barbara said. "Or someone with a grudge against him from his sheriff days?"

"Those seemed to be his two theories," Mikhail agreed. "But I thought it was curious that his mechanic mentioned that it was the third time something had gone wrong with the truck in a week."

"Huh," Barbara said. "You don't happen to know what the other two things were, do you?"

Mikhail grinned. "As it happens, I do. After Liam left, I stopped loitering around the back door of the garage and brought my motorcycle around front to have the guy look at my brakes. Which kindly acted up for a couple of minutes at my request."

"That was very nice of it," Babs said.

"It was." Mikhail took a large bite out of his sandwich and chewed thoughtfully for a minute. "Anyway, we got to talking, and he happened to mention that the guy who was there right before me had his brake line fail on him earlier in the week. We had a good laugh about the brake fairies being on the rampage."

Babs' eyes grew wide. "There are brake fairies? I never met one of those."

Barbara covered a smile with the hand not holding her sandwich. "No, honey. That's just a Human joke. There is no such thing. But it is kind of odd that Liam would have problems with both his brakes and a tire. Is his truck old or in bad shape?" She'd seen it, of course, but she didn't have much interest in non-magical forms of transportation.

"Not particularly," Liam said. "And he also had a window

smashed earlier in the week. Again, it could just be random bad luck or someone with a grudge."

"Huh." Barbara frowned. "Maybe. Never underestimate the universe's ability to screw with you just for the heck of it. Still. You said some other weird things happened to him?"

"He's apparently been getting a lot of hang up calls, some of them at rude hours. Could be telemarketers." Mikhail gave Barbara a wicked look from under blonde eyelashes. "You haven't been calling him up and then losing your nerve to talk to him, have you?"

She rolled her eyes. "I may not have much experience with relationships, but I am not a teenage girl. So no, it wasn't me."

"Okay," he said. "I've also been keeping an eye on him while he's been working around the house. Three days in a row, I saw him searching for his lunch, which seemed to have moved from where he left it. He could be getting absent-minded, I suppose, but he seemed a bit frustrated by the third day."

Barbara sighed. "That's probably the ghost. I'll have a word with her. She doesn't much like men, although she doesn't bother me or Babs. She has never been aggressive, though, so other than playing tricks on him, she's not likely to be a real problem."

"She certainly wouldn't have fiddled with his brakes, then," Mikhail said. "What about leaving random pieces of fruit around the house for him? One day there was an apple in his toolbox. Another day it was a banana on the top of his ladder. I thought that was a bit odd, since he clearly wasn't expecting them."

Babs ducked her head. "That was me," she said in a small voice. "I wanted to make sure he was eating right without us to take care of him."

"That's very considerate of you," Barbara said, tugging on the girl's hair. She and Mikhail exchanged sympathetic glances. "Next time why don't you just walk over there and give him the fruit yourself. It might be less confusing for him."

She put down the rest of her sandwich, appetite suddenly gone. "So we can explain some things, but not others. I know you'll say I have a suspicious mind, but I have to wonder if Brenna isn't somehow behind these 'accidents.' It would be just her style to hurt someone I love, in order to distract me from whatever she is up to."

"You have a suspicious mind," Mikhail said obligingly. "But that doesn't mean you're wrong. I think maybe I'll keep a closer eye on him for the next few days. I'm not learning anything in town that you didn't already know, as far as I can tell. Kids disappeared, no one has a clue where they went, and nothing has happened since Maya left town. Not that anyone else is making that connection. I'd probably be more use trying to figure out if Brenna is actually causing trouble for your man."

"Probably," Barbara agreed. "I'll see if I can spend more time over at the house, too. But I can't figure out how she'd get here from California in order to mess with his truck. She'd have to use the doorway in her bus to get to the doorway in the Airstream, and surely I'd know if she'd been in and out, even if she somehow timed it for when I wasn't home. I'd notice the stink of patchouli, if nothing else."

"Could be she's found some local sprite to do her dirty work for her," Mikhail suggested. "Or even paid a Human criminal type."

"Maybe," Barbara said. She thought about her visit to Beka when Brenna had been off on some mysterious errand. "Or maybe there is another doorway nearby that I don't know about. She could be using the undersea portal that belonged to the Selkies and Merpeople before they were forced to move out of their homes in the Monterey trench, if she doesn't want to go through her own doorway in front of Beka." She shook her head. "Or maybe I am just being paranoid."

"Just because you're paranoid doesn't mean they're not out to get you, as Alexei always says." Mikhail finished off her abandoned sandwich and wiped his hands on his white jeans, which somehow managed to stay pristine regardless of the blatant abuse. "Tell you what. When I'm not watching Liam, I'll scout around to see if I can find anything that looks like it might be a portal. Maybe this fracking nonsense opened up more than the one you already know about."

It was good to have friends. Friends who didn't question your every move. "Thank you, Mikhail," Barbara said with perhaps a bit more force than usual, based on his started expression. "I really appreciate it."

"That's what us Riders are for, silly Baba," he said. He winked at Babs, thumped Chudo-Yudo affectionately on the head, and walked out the door.

Barbara watched him go, filled with mixed feelings that were rare for her; she was usually certain of the path she was on. But Mikhail's loyalty and kind heart just reminded her that if she succeeded on her mission, he and his brothers would no longer be immortal. Or enjoy that same lightness of spirit he had just displayed, which had disappeared during their ordeal and never returned, even when their lives had turned around for the better.

The rest of the day was fairly quiet, thankfully. She spent some more time fiddling with Jazz's spell and some ideas of her own, and then she and Babs went over to the house and helped Liam for a couple of hours, putting down new tiles in the bathroom. Other than occasionally catching Babs using magic instead of grout, it went pretty well. The ghost stayed out of the way, which was just as well for her, considering the mood Barbara was in.

Barbara was still a little grumpy later as she stirred something that resembled dinner on the stove in the Airstream. Her plan to use rehabbing the house as a ploy to hang out with Liam was working, but she missed his presence the rest of the time.

Evenings together as a family had always been her favorite part of the day. Liam would cook—he was much better at it than she was, and, unlike Barbara, actually liked to do it. Her idea of cooking was to throw a bunch of things into a pot and then mix them together until they looked more or less like food. The magic in the Airstream could make almost anything taste good, but that didn't carry over to a regular kitchen.

Babs would usually sit at the kitchen table doing homework or perch on a stool by the counter and study whatever Liam was doing. She rarely said much, but it was remarkable what skills she had picked up simply by watching in her usual intent manner. Maybe Barbara should ask the little girl to do the cooking.

Barbara herself usually helped with prep, cutting up onions or chopping whatever other vegetables were needed. In the nicer weather, she would wander out to the garden and pick fresh herbs to add to whatever Liam was creating. Sometimes she just sat and watched him work, reveling in the feeling of love that permeated the kitchen and feeling like the luckiest woman in the world.

She had never expected to have a family. Never even thought she wanted a man who loved her unconditionally. Or a child to raise as her own, as much for the child herself as for the girl's potential as a future Baba Yaga. And yet somehow she had been blessed with both. She wanted that feeling back. Wanted it with a strength that surprised and overwhelmed her, making her fingers tremble and her knees weak with need and suppressed grief.

She would never have imagined that love could make you so vulnerable. Or that knowing this, she still would do whatever she could to get it back.

Thankfully, these unusually maudlin musings were interrupted by a knock at the door. Or where the door would have been, had it not been playing its usual games. Barbara could hear someone walking around to the other side of the Airstream and sternly ordered the trailer to put the door back.

A minute later, there was another knock, and she opened the door to find a confused Liam standing on the steps, holding an envelope in one hand.

"I think I've been breathing in too many varnish fumes," he said, shaking his head. "I could have sworn this door wasn't here a minute ago."

"It tends to blend in with the rest of the Airstream," Barbara said blandly. "What have you got there?"

"Um, you're not going to believe this," he said, brushing his hair out of his eyes. "But a bird dropped off this invitation to dinner. I'm guessing it is from you?" He didn't sound all that certain. About anything, at the moment, poor guy.

Barbara turned to look at Babs, one dark eyebrow raised in question. Babs gazed back, looking innocent, but Barbara wasn't fooled. Apparently she wasn't the only one missing family time.

"I expect that Babs was working on that and left it outside, and a bird found it and picked it up," Barbara said, motioning him inside. "I guess it's lucky it got to you at all. I hadn't been planning on a guest for tonight, but you're welcome to join us for whatever it is that's on the stove. I'm pretty sure it has chicken in it. There's plenty, whatever it turns out to be." She made a few arcane gestures behind her back in the pot's general direction, in hopes of encouraging it to be edible.

Liam let out a chuckle, clearly not sure if she was joking or not. "You don't know what you're making?" he said. "That sounds…adventurous. I like to cook, actually, and I'm not half bad at it, if I do say so myself. The two of you will have to come over for dinner at my house sometime."

"That sounds wonderful," Barbara said. Babs just nodded, but her brown eyes were sparkling.

Chudo-Yudo grumbled, no doubt because he would have to stay behind to guard the Water of Life and Death. Barbara, not wanting the moment to be ruined by a large pouting dragon-dog, opened the refrigerator and pulled out a gigantic t-bone steak. She tossed it on the stove to char it briefly on both sides, the way he liked it. Usually he took care of the charring part himself, but if Liam was already doubting his own sanity, she couldn't imagine how he'd feel after seeing flames shooting out of a white pit bull's mouth.

"Wow, that's a big steak," Liam said. "I thought you said you weren't sure what dinner was."

"Oh, this isn't for us," Barbara said, sliding the steak onto a large pottery platter decorated with traditional Russian motifs. She hoped that this time Chudo-Yudo would remember not to eat the plate too. She placed it on the floor in front of the dog and dished up the rest of their food and put it on the table. Keeping her fingers crossed, she opened the fridge again and took out two of Liam's favorite *Blue Moon* beers that hadn't been there a minute ago.

"This is delicious," Liam said, digging into the food on his plate. "Is there white wine in it?"

Barbara shrugged. "Probably. I know I tossed in some mushrooms and onions and garlic."

"You can't go wrong with those," Liam agreed. "I think you were teasing me when you said you couldn't cook."

"The stove does most of the work," Barbara said, not explaining that some of that work was magical.

"But the refrigerator makes very good pies," Babs added, trying to be fair as always.

Poor Liam got that slightly glazed look in his eyes again, but clearly decided to humor the cute kid. "I'm sure it does, honey." He took a hurried swallow of his beer and Barbara tried not to laugh.

They were just finishing up, and Barbara was wondering if in fact the fridge could be persuaded to produce a pie, or at least a nice simple cheesecake, when there was another knock at the door.

The place was beginning to feel like Grand Central Station. She'd always hated that place. Only went there when she had to use the official portal hidden deep underground.

She got up and peeked out the window and growled under her breath, "*NOW* you make a door? We don't want one." But it was too late.

Maya simply opened it and stalked in, looking blonde and polished and beautiful (and not at all green and drippy, as her true form had appeared the last time Barbara had seen her in the Otherworld). Behind her, an expensive convertible was parked at an angle, as if its driver had been in a hurry. Or, as it turned out, in a gigantic snit.

"How dare you!" Maya hissed at Barbara, not even bothering to look past her to see if she was interrupting anything. "I don't know what you think you're playing at, Baba Yaga, but I am not one bit amused to have been dragged in front of the Queen to answer a series of ridiculous questions. I have no idea what makes you think it is any of your business what I do, but you had better keep your long nose out of my business if you know what is good for you."

"I don't think so," Barbara said calmly. "First of all, the Queen does what the Queen wants to do. I have no control over her at all, as I'm sure you are aware. I just gave her some information, which happened to be true, as you are also aware."

"Information," Maya spat. Her perfected wound chignon quivered. "I don't know where you got your *information*, or why you thought it would be a good idea to go poking around in matters that don't concern you, but I strongly suggest you cease such ill-advised meddling. I hear you have a young ward now. It would be a shame if something bad happened to her."

Liam suddenly appeared at Barbara's shoulder, as if summoned by Maya's last words.

"Did I just hear you threaten a child?" he asked, quiet fury resonating like a snake's warning rattle under the calmness of his tone.

Barbara thought he was as sexy as hell. Not that she couldn't handle Maya on her own, but he didn't know that.

"Oh, my. I didn't know Barbara had company," Maya said, suddenly all charm and batting eyelashes. "And such lovely company at that. I was just joking, sheriff. Ms. Yager and I know each other from our homeland, and as I was passing through town, I thought I'd just stop by and say hello."

"I'm not the sheriff anymore," Liam said through gritted teeth. "But that doesn't mean that I am going to stand by and allow anyone to harm a child. You didn't sound as if you were joking to me, Ms. Freeman. In fact, you sounded like a very angry woman making some dangerous threats."

Maya's smile lost a bit of its wattage but she kept going gamely. "Dear me. It's a shame you lost your job. I remember you from when I was living here last year and it seemed like you were just terrific at it."

She exchanged the smile for a sad little head shake. "If you're worried about someone causing harm, though, you might be better off looking closer to home. Barbara isn't to be trusted, I'm afraid. She tells lies. Many, many lies." Maya gave Barbara a pointed look, then stalked back out to her car and roared off into the night.

"What the hell was that all about?" Liam asked. "And what did she mean about you telling lies. Have you been lying to me about something?"

Barbara sighed. An honest answer to that question could only get her into more trouble. But she couldn't give him a completely dishonest answer without it coming back to bite her later. She suddenly remembered why she'd avoided relationships for so long.

CHAPTER FIFTEEN

"Not so much lying as not bringing up certain topics of conversation," Barbara said, hoping to cut this particular conversation short. "Sensitive subjects I knew might upset you. I assure you, I really did buy this house, and I really do need you to fix it up and make it habitable for me and Babs. Now, how about dessert?"

Sadly, Liam wasn't going to be that easily distracted. She would have been surprised if he had been. "Which subjects?" he asked. "And why was Ms. Freeman so angry with you? Who is this Queen she was dragged in front of is that a nickname for some woman in power you both know?"

Barbara gave an inward sigh, knowing what was coming. "She's angry with me because she knows I believe she was involved in the disappearances of the children here, and I mentioned that belief to someone fairly high in our mutual social circle."

Wait for it…

"You think what?" Liam said, a vein standing out on his neck. "Do you happen to have any proof? And have you told this to someone official?"

More official than the High Queen of the Otherworld? No.

"If I had mentioned it to your current sheriff, would he have believed me?"

Liam clenched his jaw. "That's not the point."

"I see," Barbara said, as patiently as possible, considering that he was completely and totally in the wrong. "Then what is the point, exactly?"

"The *point*," he repeated through gritted teeth, "is that civilians should stay out of police matters. You are a smart woman. You should know enough to leave these things to the professionals."

"Even when the professionals are incompetent?' she asked sweetly. He could hardly argue, since everyone seemed to agree that the new sheriff was an idiot.

He made a growling noise that reminded her a little of Chudo-Yudo. "Yes," he said. "Even then. Thank you for dinner, Ms. Yager. I'll be back tomorrow to work on the house." He nodded his head less brusquely at Babs and stalked out the door.

Well, at least some things seemed to be consistent, no matter which timeline she was in. She made a quiet growling sound of her own and walked over to the refrigerator. "There better be chocolate fudge cake in here," she said.

Luckily for everyone, there was.

Barbara heard Liam's truck drive in first thing in the morning and made the sudden decision that she wanted to be elsewhere. She couldn't tell him the truth, at least not more than she had already (and look how well that had gone) and she couldn't face his stony silence. Or another argument.

"Grab a bag," she told Babs. "We're going to go collect some magical supplies."

"Are we gathering herbs?" the girl asked, jumping down from her current perch on her bed and pulling her shoes on eagerly. She loved being out in the woods as much as Barbara did.

"Yes and no," Barbara said. "We're going to get some things I need for Jazz's spell. From the Otherworld."

Babs pulled off her sneakers and ran to get changed into something more suitable. Barbara followed more slowly to do the same.

Chudo-Yudo shook his massive head, making white fur fly through the air. He didn't have to shed, but he seemed to enjoy leaving traces of himself everywhere he went. "Are you sure that's wise?" he asked. "You know that if you walk through her world for more than a few minutes the Queen will know, and expect you to show up eventually to report."

"Beats the alternative," Barbara muttered, glancing out the window. "Besides, I am going to have to do that eventually. Might as well get it over with. And I need those ingredients if I am going to experiment. The Otherworld is the only place to find some of them."

"Uh huh." The dragon-dog followed her gaze. "So it's a case of the Lady or the Tiger, eh? Which one is the Queen?"

"We'll find out when we see her," Barbara said. She grabbed a couple of containers she thought they might need and headed toward the wonky closet door, Babs on her heels.

"What if that sheriff comes looking for you?" Chudo-Yudo asked.

"Ex-sheriff, not that he seems capable of remembering that," she said. "I doubt he will. But if he does, you're not allowed to eat him."

"Damn," Chudo-Yudo said, and subsided in a heap in a patch of sunlight on the floor. "I don't get to have any fun."

"A dozen centaur tears," Babs read off the list. "I think I met a centaur at court once. They're the ones who have the head and torso of a man and the body of a horse, right?"

"That's right," Barbara said, leading the way past a series of bright purple bushes with pretty red berries. If the berries hadn't been smoking slightly, they might have been more tempting. Not that it was a good idea to eat anything in the Otherworld unless you knew for certain it was safe. Sometimes not even then. "That was Chiron, the leader of the centaurs. Most of them don't go anywhere near the castle. They're not a very sociable bunch, at least with those outside their own race."

"Oh," Babs said. They walked on for a while as she thought. A transparent bird the size of an eagle whizzed by their heads, only visible as it brushed by some trees that sprinkled it with golden dust.

"Are all centaurs boys, or are there girl centaurs too?" she asked finally. "None of the books show the girls. Are they shy?"

"Not exactly," Barbara said. "I met one many years ago, when I was about your age. She was very pretty. And quite skilled with a bow and arrow. Extremely skilled. I suggest we look for the boys today. They're merely difficult to deal with, not impossible."

They finally ended up at a grove of trees on the edge of a small emerald green lake. Iridescent blue cattails sunned themselves and purred amongst the elegant fronds of tall ferns. Dragonflies that looked like miniature dragons flitted back and forth, playing some kind of complicated game that seemed to involve dropping bit of crystals onto lily pads far below.

A group of male centaurs wearing colorful beads braided into their long hair and manes were idly watching the dragonfly antics as they stood nearby chatting about whatever it was centaurs chatted about when they were at home.

"Good afternoon, gentlemen," Barbara said. "You are looking particularly regal today."

One of the group made a snorting noise that sounded more

horse than man and trotted over to meet them. His companions followed, although they let him take the lead.

"What brings the Baba Yaga to our part of the Otherworld?" the leader asked. "It isn't often we have such an unexpected honor."

Babs tilted her head to the side, considering, then looked up at Barbara. "Is that sarcasm?" she asked. She was still struggling with some of the nuances of conversation.

"I believe it was," Barbara said, fighting back a smile. "Well done."

The centaur stomped one front hoof impatiently. "Who is this little person? Is it not enough we have to deal with you?"

"Manners, Polkan," Barbara admonished him. Not that centaurs cared much about such things. "This is Babs, my apprentice. She wanted to see the greatest races in the Otherworld, so I brought her here. Perhaps I made a mistake." She took Babs' hand. "Let's go visit the ogres instead. They're very large."

"Harrumph," Polkan said. "Very large and very ugly. Why would you want to subject this poor girl to that? Besides, ogres are hardly in the same class as centaurs."

"It is true," Barbara said. "You are much more handsome. But since you clearly aren't in the mood for visitors, I should probably take her to see the griffons. They're beautiful *and* they like children, which you clearly don't."

"Oh, pish tosh," Polkan said. "I like children just fine." He patted Babs clumsily on the head. Centaurs might be antisocial, but they were also very vain. The idea that any other creature might be considered greater than they were was unacceptable. "When you grow up to be a Baba Yaga, little girl, you will remember this day when you met the centaurs in all our glory."

"Glory is all very well," Barbara said. "But kindness and generosity of spirit are also part of what makes any race great. Maybe we should go visit the unicorns. They are always kind to children."

Polkan sputtered. "Kind! Kind! There are no creatures kinder than the centaurs. Everyone knows this."

"I must have forgotten," Barbara said, and then in a thoughtful tone, "You know, Babs is working on a special project for me. It requires twelve magical tears. We were going to get them from the unicorns, but if you wouldn't mind…"

"Of course not," Polkan said, puffing out his massive chest. "Our tears are the most magical of all." He hesitated. "Although we do not cry very often. That is probably what makes them so special, but I'm not sure how we would give them to you."

Barbara whipped a glass vial out of her bag. "Normally I would tell you a very sad story," she said. "But we don't have that much time, so I am afraid we will have to use a considerably cruder method. I apologize, and thank you in advance for your cooperation."

She moved closer and reached up to place the vial under one

large, long-lashed eye. Then she quickly yanked out one of the sensitive hairs from his chin.

"OW!" Polkan yelled, and two tears rolled into the vial. She repeated the maneuver with five of the other centaurs (after Polkan refused to let her do it to him a second time).

"Thank you," she said. "You truly are the greatest, most handsome, kindest creatures in all the Otherworld."

"Go away, Baba Yaga," Polkan said in a grumpy tone. "Sometimes it is too much work to be this great."

Babs and Barbara made their way through a swamp filled with geysers that shot rainbow-colored water into the air, and then past a tiny village made up of miniature houses that only came up to Barbara's knees. Finally, they arrived at a small, neat white cottage with a thatched roof and a shiny brass door knocker set precisely in the middle of the red door. A plaque above the door knocker said "SMYTHE."

Barbara used the knocker briskly and then stood with her arms folded as they listened to someone clumping in their direction. The door swung open to reveal a short man with a long beard, wearing brown leather pants, a green shirt, a pointed green hat, and an extremely unwelcoming expression.

"No," he said. "Whatever it is, no. I've already got one, or I don't want one, or I've never heard of it and couldn't care less. Go away."

Babs gave Barbara a wide-eyed startled look, but Barbara just cleared her throat. The dwarf looked up (way up, in this particular case, in as much as he was only about four feet tall, and Barbara was five foot ten).

"Oh. Baba Yaga. It's you. I thought it was someone trying to sell me something."

"Been getting a lot of that lately?" Barbara asked, looking around at the vast expanse of empty lands that surrounded his house. "I'd hardly think it would be much of a problem for you out here."

"Why do you think I moved here?' Smythe asked.

"Your former neighbors took up a petition?" she said. Then realized that aggravating the person she wanted a favor from probably wasn't a good idea.

"Actually, it is quite the opposite," she said in a less spiky tone. "I want to buy something from you."

The dwarf stomped one wooden clog on the doorstep. "Oh no you don't. I'm not going to be taken advantage of by some smooth-talking witch. Whatever it is, I don't have it. If I did, I probably wouldn't want to sell it. And if I did want to sell it, you couldn't afford it. Go away." He started to close the door.

Barbara pulled a small sack of gold out of her bag and poured the coins into her other palm. "Not even for ten gold pieces?"

"Real gold?" he asked cautiously. "Not faerie gold that will disappear in the morning?"

Barbara nodded. "As real as that bald spot you are hiding under your hat."

Smythe pulled the hat down a little tighter. "What do you want then? I don't do adventures, so if you're thinking of putting together a merry band to go off on one, you can count me right out."

"The thought never crossed my mind," Barbara said honestly. "No, all I need are a few shards from the eggs of a phoenix. I remembered that you had one nesting in your orchard. Is it still there?"

"Still there? Still there? I can't get the dratted thing to leave," Smythe sputtered indignantly. He reached out and grabbed the bag of gold. "Tell you what. You can take all the shells you want. I'll throw in the dratted bird for free. Just because I like you."

He went back into his house and slammed the door behind him.

"Yes, I can tell," Barbara said under her breath. Then she set off across the grass toward an orchard of apple trees that grew in regimented rows, their branches all symmetrical and covered with tiny identical leaves.

One tree stood out from the others. Its trunk was surrounded by flaming red rosebushes, each thorn longer than Barbara's thumb and sharper than the sword she wore buckled around her formal "going to court" tunic. At the base of the tree, inside the flames, there were colorful bits of shell, as though someone had smashed an exotic collection of pottery.

Looking up, Barbara could see a gnarled nest of tightly woven twigs and grasses, all of them smoldering lightly. The bird in the nest was glorious and regal, its bright feathers a splendid array of orange and red, with the occasional hint of gold. Its feathers burned in the crisp morning air like the fire they so resembled.

Babs looked from the flaming rosebushes to the flaming bird, and then at the shells. "How do we get the pieces of shell we need without getting burned, Baba Yaga?" She bit her lip. "I am small and fast. I can run in and get them for you if you need me to."

"That is a very brave offer," Barbara said. "But I don't believe it will be necessary." She lifted two fingers to her lips and let out a loud whistle.

Up in the tree, the inferno flared momentarily, then died down as the nest's occupant peered down toward the ground, its coal-black eyes alight with curiosity.

"Hello there," Barbara said. "I'm the Baba Yaga, Barbara, and this is my apprentice Babs."

The phoenix fluttered its wings and made a melodic chirping sound.

"Do you speak Phoenix?" Babs asked in a whisper.

"I'm afraid not," Barbara said. "It is something of a lost language. Hopefully it understands English. Many of the creatures in the Otherworld do."

She bowed in the direction of the tree, since it was fairly impossible to bow upward. "We have need of some of your beautiful shells, if you have no objection to our taking them," she said.

More chirping.

Barbara cleared her throat. "Also, no offence, but I've been informed that the man who owns these trees would rather you moved your nest elsewhere. I'm afraid he's a bit of a neat freak, and your shells and shrubbery, lovely as they are, have got his tights in a twist."

The phoenix gave an indignant squawk, and a nearby branch burst into flames.

"I have a suggestion, if you don't mind," Barbara said, holding up her hand. "I know a place where your beauty and rarity would be appreciated, and where no doubt you would be admired on a daily basis. If you would like to follow me, I would happily lead you there."

The phoenix chirped quietly for a moment, as if talking to itself, and then rose gracefully from its nest with a flutter of crimson feathers. As soon as it did so, the flames below wavered and died out, leaving a small, fragile-looking pile of egg shards lying in the open. Babs ran over and scooped some into her bag, blowing on her fingers when she was done.

"Still hot," she said. "Now where are we going?"

"We're going to talk to a tree," Barbara said.

"Oh," Babs responded. "Is the phoenix coming with us?"

Barbara glanced overhead, where the mystical bird was flying in figure eights as it waited. "Apparently so," she said. "Let's hope it doesn't set the Kalpataru tree on fire. That wouldn't help us at all."

CHAPTER SIXTEEN

"It looks like a tree," Babs said, sounding puzzled.

"Yes, it does," Barbara agreed.

Babs glanced around them. The rest of the growing things that surrounded them seemed well suited for the Otherworld —that is to say, they were bedecked in odd colors and unusual shapes, and often bore very little resemblance to their counterparts on the other side of the doorway.

The Kalpataru tree, on the other hand, was practically ordinary except for its size. It rose up into the sky higher than any of the surrounding vegetation, and unlike most of the Otherworld plants, its arching branches and gnarled roots were brown and the heart-shaped leaves, larger than Babs' head, were a mundane green. As they drew closer, Barbara could hear a murmuring sound, as if a hundred different voices were talking quietly all at once.

They walked underneath the wide spread of its limbs, which

formed a canopy so dense you could barely see the sky through it. Thankfully, the phoenix seemed content to perch in a less exotic tree a short flight away. Barbara and Babs came to a stop not far from the massive trunk.

"It is very beautiful," Babs whispered.

"Thank you" a voice said. It seemed to issue from one of the knots on the tree, which opened a tiny bit to let out the deep and sonorous tone.

"Did the tree just talk?" Babs asked. "How wonderful. I did not know trees could do that."

"Most trees cannot," the Kalpataru said. "But we are not most trees."

Barbara bent at the waist in a respectful bow. "Greetings, great and noble one. I am the Baba Yaga, and this small person is my apprentice, Babs. We have come to ask a boon."

A sigh seemed to come from many different knots at once. "You want one of our leaves, I suppose. As a Baba Yaga, you know the power they hold. Are you certain this is what you want?"

"I am not sure of anything, these days," Barbara said. It paid to be honest with the Kalpataru. No matter how painful that honesty might be. "But I am working on a very important spell, and while its chances of succeeding are very slim, without one of your leaves I believe I have no chance at all."

"I do not understand," Babs said, reaching up to touch the gnarled bark reverently. "What makes these leaves so special?"

The tree made a raspy noise that might have been laughter. Or not. "You are not a very good teacher if your student does not know the answer to that, Baba Yaga."

"On the contrary," Barbara said crisply. "We are here, and she is asking the question. How else is she to learn?"

"Hmmm," the tree said. "Our leaves grant wishes," it told Babs.

"Any wishes?" the girl asked. "Even small and silly ones? That seems like a waste."

The Kalpataru made an approving noise. "You are very wise for one so young. We do not give our leaves away to just anyone," it said. "We must deem the one who asks worthy, and the request truly deserving of our gift."

"Oh," Babs said. "That makes much more sense." She looked up at the large leaves, all still firmly attached to their branches. "The Baba Yaga is very worthy, you know. All the Baba Yagas are special, but mine is the most wonderful of them all."

Barbara felt an odd pricking sensation behind her eyes. Allergies. That was it. She was probably allergic to the tree.

"Thank you, Babs," she said. "I do not ask this wish for myself, mighty Kalpataru. I am trying to right a great wrong, and knit up the unraveled strands of time itself. I am not completely sure how your leaf will help me in this endeavor, but I assure you, without it, I am doomed to failure. There are so many people depending on me, some of whom mean more to me than my own life. Please help me."

There was a rustling sound, and the murmurs of many quiet voices as the group mind of the tree conferred with its members. Finally, there was silence.

"Very well, Baba Yaga," the tree said. A single leaf floated down to come to rest on her open palm. "Wish carefully. There will be no more after this."

Great. No pressure.

Barbara chose a lengthy path that should have meandered slowly to lead them to the castle late in what passed as the afternoon in the Otherworld. Instead, they came out on the front lawn almost as soon as they had left the forest where the Kalpataru lived. Clearly the Queen had noticed their presence. And decided that they should visit her without further delay.

There was a servitor waiting for them when they arrived—rather abruptly, as if the universe suddenly decided to zig instead of zag—at the entrance to the castle grounds.

"Their Majesties are in the throne room," the servant announced. She was a small brownie with pointed ears, wearing a white frilled apron and a neat white cap. "They are eagerly awaiting your attendance."

In short, hurry up. Babs and Barbara hurried, the phoenix flying lazily behind.

A marbled hallway led from the mammoth wooden front doors

to the vast black onyx ones that stood open to reveal the throne room in all its grandeur. A vaulted ceiling rose so high it dwarfed the slender white birch trees bordering the grassy path that meandered through the space. In the middle of the room, a fountain splashed exuberantly, tossing lavender-scented spray over nearby crystal chairs like some exotic spa. In the basin at the foot of the fountain, rainbow-hued fish swam and played.

Courtiers leaned decoratively against plants that changed their colors to match the nobles' clothing, as ornate and fanciful as the rest of the surroundings. As Barbara's party moved through the room, eyes of every color and shape shifted to follow their movements, without in any way deigning to reveal actual interest.

Eventually, the grass gave way to variegated tiles of green malachite and blue lapis, inlaid with gold patterns whose meanings had been forgotten centuries ago. Barbara and Babs came to a halt before two magnificent thrones fashioned from still-living trees, the roots entwined in complicated designs twisted around large, perfect crystals that seemingly grew out of the ground underneath.

On the thrones, the Queen and King sat in elegant splendor. The Queen wore gossamer-thin silk robes in vivid royal blue, and her consort's velvet tunic and tights were the deep dark blues of a midnight sky. As always, they were impossibly grand and imposing.

"Baba Yaga," the Queen said in her melodious voice. "We had expected you sooner." Disapproval hovered dangerously near the surface, and a few of the wiser courtiers standing too close to the thrones began to edge discreetly away. "It is to be hoped that you finally have some answers for Us."

Barbara bowed so low, her hair touched the floor. "My apologies, Your Majesties. I assure you, I have been working on the assignment you set me without ceasing. I have not made the progress I would have wished, but I hope that the gift I have brought you will is some small measure make up for my tardiness."

The Queen sat up even straighter, if such a thing had been possible in one whose posture was impeccable, and anticipation brought the tiniest hint of a pinkish blush to her pale porcelain complexion. "You brought Us a present, Baba Yaga? How nice. We do hope it is something unusual and interesting. We have been somewhat bored of late."

The King nodded in agreement. A nearly immortal life spent in a perfect world had its downsides. He stroked his pointed black beard. "What have you brought Us, Baba Yaga?"

Barbara pointed upward and the phoenix soared into sight as if on cue. The nearest courtiers murmured in wonderment at its blazing glory.

"My gift is indeed rare and precious, Your Majesties. May I present to you one of the rarest creatures in your land, the magical phoenix, whose beauty is but a shallow reflection of your own, and yet still fabulous to behold." She held her breath as the phoenix landed on a lantern hanging from a metal sconce high above and began to preen itself. She had promised it a better home. There was none better than this.

"How marvelous!" The Queen clapped her slim hands

together in glee. "We have many wondrous things here at court, but never before have We had a phoenix of our very own. Well met, my lady," she cried to the bird. "You are most welcome here." She snapped her fingers at some servants, sending them off to fetch treats for her new pet.

"Well met to you as well, Baba Yaga," the King added. "You and your small apprentice are most welcome too."

Barbara let out a breath she hadn't know she was holding. She suspected the rest of her visit was unlikely to go as smoothly, but at least it was off to a good start.

Babs tugged on her shirt to get her attention, then pointed unobtrusively to a spot in a nearby corner of the throne room. The three children from the other side of the doorway sat together, playing in a desultory fashion with a pile of bejeweled toys, tended by a dark-skinned goblin nanny not quite as big as the largest child. They seemed subdued and a little vague, far too quiet for youngsters of their age. What little cheerfulness Barbara had felt fell away at this reminder of the price of her failure.

The Queen shooed away those clustered around the throne, clearly not in the mood to encourage gossip. This left Barbara and Babs standing isolated in a sea of silent disapproval in front of their majesties.

"Well, Baba Yaga?" the Queen said impatiently. "What news have you for Us?"

"I have not made as much progress as either of us would wish, Your Majesty," Barbara said. "But I came to the Otherworld to gather some very special ingredients for a spell I hope might solve the problem."

"*Might* solve it?" the King said, a frown tugging down the corners of his mouth. "That does not sound very optimistic."

Probably because she wasn't feeling very optimistic. But now was neither the time or place to admit to it.

"It has been difficult to make any progress," Barbara said. "This is, as far as we know, the first time such a crisis has ever occurred." She thought for a moment. "Of course, if it had happened before and another Baba Yaga found a solution, we would have no way of knowing, since things would have returned to their proper course."

"You are giving Us a headache, Baba Yaga," the Queen said. Her amethyst eyes narrowed. "Surely you must have something definite to report."

"Well, I can tell you that Maya showed up on my doorstep and threatened to harm Babs if I didn't stop poking my long nose into her business," Barbara said. "She was quite upset that you had accused her of having something to do with these Human children being brought to the Otherworld in defiance of your laws."

The Queen waved her fan through the air. "We did, of course, speak to the rusalka. Your accusation was too significant to ignore. Needless to say, she denied everything, and no one in Our court would admit to dealing with her. Without proof, We had no choice but to let her go."

"And did you give her permission to use one of the doorways to return to the Human lands?" Barbara asked.

The fan fluttered to a rest. "We did not," the Queen said. "When did you say she came to see you?"

"Yesterday evening, Your Majesty. Time flows strangely at times in the Otherworld, but she was angry with me because of your questioning, it must have been after you spoke to her."

"How very interesting," the Queen said, sitting back in her throne. "If she was not given Our leave to pass between the worlds, how then did she arrive upon your doorstep? Clearly this is one rule broken for which you do have proof."

"Moreover, my love," the King pointed out, "the rusalka made threats against young Babs, a Baba Yaga in training. This too is against our laws."

"So it is." For a moment, the Queen almost seemed incline to let Barbara off the hook, at least temporarily. But then she shook her head. "It is not enough. Breaking Our laws in one way, or even two, does not establish that she has broken them in others. Should she return to the Otherworld, she will certainly be punished for crossing the borders without permission, and for menacing a child under Our protection, but unless you can somehow tie her to the theft of these Human children, We will not be involved further."

"But Your Majesty," Barbara protested. "Surely you can take my word for her guilt."

The Queen and King exchanged weighty looks and Barbara

felt her heart sink down to the toes of her high heeled leather boots.

"Majesty?" she said quietly.

"Brenna came to see Us," the Queen said, her tone suddenly distant and cold. "She has cast some doubt on your stability. And your loyalty."

"I see," Barbara said. She had expected something like this. What she hadn't expected was for the King and Queen to actually listen to Brenna. "What did she say, exactly?"

"She accused you of trying to influence Beka against her, something no Baba Yaga would ever do with another's apprentice," the King said. "This is a very serious charge. How do you respond?"

Barbara took a deep breath. "I am afraid it is quite true, Your Highness."

The Queen's expression grew even grimmer, and ice began to frost the roots of the throne. "You admit to this?"

"I admit to trying to protect my friend and sister Baba Yaga," Barbara said. "I believe Brenna is actively harming her, both psychologically and physically. In fact, it is my fear Brenna has found a way to steal Beka's life energy, and probably her share of the Water of Life and Death as well. I did try to warn Beka to be on her guard. Alas, she doesn't think her mentor is capable of such great evils. I, on the other hand, know better."

"This is a terrible accusation, Baba Yaga," the Queen said.

Her fingers were clenched so tightly around the shaft of her fan, her knuckles were white. "Surely you are mistaken."

"Have you seen Beka lately?" Barbara asked.

"We have not. Brenna has not brought her to court in recent days."

"I wonder why that is," Barbara said, sarcasm edging her voice despite her best efforts to remain composed.

"Brenna denied all wrongdoing," the King said. "Moreover, she insisted—quite adamantly—that you were either insane, or plotting against Us, or both."

"I see," Barbara said in a calm voice. "Then I suppose it comes down to which one of us you trust. You clearly cannot believe us both."

The Queen's fan snapped in two. Gazing up at the monarch's ethereally lovely face, Barbara saw something she had never seen before. Uncertainty.

"This troubles Me greatly," the Queen said. "We do not know *what* to think, which is most upsetting. There has never been a situation like this one. If We had not gotten those glimpses of another timeline when We held your ring, We would probably be considering doing something quite drastic to resolve the issue." She tossed the two broken halves of fan onto the ground. "If you cannot settle this matter quickly, We assure you that drastic is still very much on the table."

CHAPTER SEVENTEEN

Barbara dropped to one knee and bowed her head.

"I have always served Your Majesties faithfully and to the best of my abilities," she said in a quiet voice, feeling an eerie calm stealing over her. "If you do not trust me to continue to do so, you may strip me of my powers and my title right now."

She waited, head down, unable to see the expression on either of the monarchs' faces. It was out of her hands now. She would accept her fate without question. There was a moment's qualm, thinking about Liam, and all she had lost. But if she couldn't change the timeline back, maybe she could find a way to build a new life with him as a mere Human. In some ways, that would make things simpler, although it was hard to imagine a life with no magic.

She might actually have to learn how to cook.

The thought of Beka being left at the mercy of Brenna was

more worrisome than any personal concerns, but that too was beyond her control without the support of those who wore the crown.

A small, cold hand snuck into hers, as Babs waited to hear their fates. Despite their fragility, those little fingers leant her strength, and she thanked the goddess for sending her such a gift. She could only hope that if she was declared to be unworthy of the title of Baba Yaga, the talented girl standing next to her would be allowed to continue her studies, even if it meant that Barbara lost her too.

The very thought made her heart clench in her chest, and for a moment she forgot to breathe. The world began to spin ever so slowly, and black spots danced before her eyes.

There was a moment of silence, and then, finally, the Queen spoke, her tone crisp and clear.

"Stand up, Baba Yaga," she said. "Of course We trust you."

Barbara let out a puff of stale air and got to her feet, not quite as gracefully as usual. She gave Babs' hand a squeeze before letting it go and facing the couple before her.

"But Brenna," Barbara started to say.

The Queen held up one white hand. "Can be very persuasive, it is true. And this situation is odd beyond even Our own broad standards for that word." She cast her violet gaze over the various unusual members of her court, all standing at a distance just far enough away to be out of hearing, but not too far to observe the proceedings. Odd was, at best, a generous word for the wide range of Paranormal creatures that peopled the Otherworld.

"It is not so much that We doubt your veracity," the Queen went on. "There were, as you have pointed out on previous occasions, very good reasons why We encouraged Brenna to retire in the first place. Her behavior had become erratic, and there were some indications that she had developed an unhealthy desire for power beyond that suitable for her station."

The Queen sighed, looking unusually vulnerable. Despite her delicate beauty, no one ever made the mistake of underestimating the fierce and deadly thorn hidden beneath the soft petals of that particular rose. In all the years Barbara had been coming to court, starting when she was a child younger than Babs, she had never seen the Queen waver in her strength and resolve. Until now.

"Then what is the problem, Your Majesty?" Barbara asked. "I don't understand."

"The problem, my dear Baba," the Queen said, "is that if the allegations you make against her are true, then We have made a terrible mistake." Next to her, the King looked grim, but did not disagree.

Barbara had to lock her knees to keep from kneeling again, more out of shock than any sense of humility. The Queen *never* admitted she was wrong. Barbara would have bet on all three moons falling out of the sky before such a thing would happen.

"I wouldn't say that, Your Majesty." Not if she wanted to keep her head, anyway.

The Queen shook her head. "You would say exactly that, Baba Yaga. And have done so, but We were unwilling to listen. Instead, We have allowed this wrong to continue, rather than to admit Our own misstep."

The King took his consort's hand, but his eyes were centered firmly on Barbara. "Perhaps We have become complacent, these many years of ruling without any serious challenge to test Our wisdom. It would appear that We have made an error in judgment."

"If all you say is true," the Queen said sadly, "then We not only erred in sending Brenna back to resume her role as Baba Yaga, but also did a grave disservice to young Beka. She should not have been punished for losing her supply of The Water of Life and Death—not if Brenna was responsible for stealing it. Even if Brenna is not purposely causing Beka harm, as you say she is, *We* have caused harm with Our actions, for which We are filled with profound sorrow and remorse."

Barbara had no idea what to say. If she disagreed, it would appear insulting and disingenuous, since the royal couple was finally admitting she had probably been right about Brenna all along. But if she agreed, she risked offending them even more. Not to mention that it was unnerving to see the Queen so genuinely distressed.

There was a moment of uncomfortable silence as the Queen's words lay heavily in the air. Then a small clear voice spoke up into the void.

"Sometimes I make mistakes too," Babs said kindly. "I am still not very good at living in the Human world. When that happens, Barbara always tells me that no one gets it right all the time. She says that as long as you are trying your best, you shouldn't be upset with yourself. All you can do is to learn not to make that mistake again, and if you made a mess, try and clean it up to the best of your ability."

Barbara held her breath again as she waited to see how the Queen would react, preparing to jump in front of Babs if necessary to defend her.

But after a long pause, the Queen leaned forward and said, "You are a very smart little girl. And fortunate to have such a wise mentor."

She held up her hand when Barbara went to speak. "We have made a mistake that put Beka in harm's way and allowed a dangerously out-of-control Baba Yaga to gain even more power. This must be remedied, and sooner rather than later."

Her stern gaze settled on Barbara, and there was no sign of the previous moment's softness. "You have three days to figure out a solution to this problem with the timeline. At the end of those three days, We will summon all the Baba Yagas, including both Brenna and Beka, and tell them to bring their Water of Life and Death with them so We might replenish it."

This was something the Queen did periodically, so that made sense. Barbara had no doubt that the rest of whatever Her Majesty had planned did as well. So why did she have a feeling she wasn't going to like it?

"Once they are here," the Queen continued, "We will strip

Brenna of *all* her magical powers, not just those which she acquired during her tenure as the Baba Yaga, as punishment for her crimes. Possibly her life will be forfeit as well—We have not yet decided. If, as One supposes, the Water Sickness is to blame for her misdeeds, it seems wrong to exact so serious a toll for an illness brought on by her long years of service. But she cannot be allowed to harm anyone ever again."

Yes! Barbara thought. Perhaps in this timeline, it wouldn't be too late to stop Brenna before she did permanent damage. The Riders would be safe. Beka, well, it would be a simple matter for the Queen to facilitate her physical recovery by giving the young witch a large dose of the magical Water. Beka's psychological recovery would be a more complicated matter, but hopefully having the Queen return the role of Baba Yaga to her would be a boost to her confidence. Barbara and Bella would do what they could to help as well.

"That is very good news indeed, Your Majesty," Barbara said. "But I need more than three days. I can't figure out this spell to mend the unraveled strands of time that fast. I'm only just beginning to experiment. I have to be cautious, to ensure I don't make things worse instead of better. I was planning to call on my sister Babas to help."

"Three days, Baba Yaga," the Queen said in tone that brooked no disagreement. "That is traditional, and more than fair. And you will stay away from Brenna, and neither see nor speak to the other Baba Yagas until you are all gathered here."

"But what about the children?" Barbara asked, looking over her shoulder toward where they sat, too silent and well-behaved. "If I can't fix the timeline, they will never be able to go home."

The Queen allowed the tiniest of sighs to escape her perfect lips. "That would be unfortunate, there is no question. And Maya will still be fetched back and punished if you can prove her involvement. But if you have not fixed the timeline in three days, We shall resolve all these matters and be done with it. The children will be found good homes in the Otherworld and stay here. But We will abide no more of this chaos and confusion. Your apprentice was correct. When One makes a mistake, One must correct it. If this means that timeline will continue on its current path, that is a small price to pay for setting other things right."

She waved one hand to indicate the audience was over.

"Three days, Baba Yaga. No more. We will be done with this."

There was clearly nothing more to say. Barbara and Babs made their way back through the throne room in silence. It was only once they were almost all the way back to the doorway that Babs spoke up.

"Did I say the wrong thing?" she asked in a small voice. "Telling the Queen what you said about making mistakes and cleaning them up?"

Barbara thought about it. "No," she said finally. "The Queen is right. We can't risk anything worse happening to Beka, or to anyone else. We'll just have to do our best to figure out a better solution in the three days we have left."

She could only hope they could.

Barbara spent the rest of the day doing small experiments with some of the spell ingredients. She was particularly intrigued by the more esoteric bits and pieces that Jazz had chosen, the ones that were only available in the Otherworld. The teen had scribbled some notes to explain her thinking, and Barbara found it fascinating to see how far outside the box (or at least, the box she was used to, based on tradition and her own training) Jazz had gone.

If nothing else, it was a good demonstration of why they needed to bring in new blood, like Jazz and Babs, who had minds that didn't work exactly the same way as those who had come before them. It made Barbara feel a little old, but also grateful to be witnessing the evolution of the next generation of Baba Yagas.

The three special items she had brought back from the Otherworld were all things that Jazz had gleaned from different spells in Bella's magical book and then used—at least in theory—to create something different.

Barbara looked at the vial of centaur tears. She only had twelve, and that was how many the original spell had called for. She didn't dare use up too many in her trials.

The spell in which Jazz had found them had been one for *Transformation*. Much of spell work was based on the principle of sympathetic magic, that is to say, like calls to like. Thus, one might use a candle to represent fire, or a bowl of water to represent the ocean.

Barbara's hypothesis was that the centaurs' very essence was that of transformation. Half horse, half man, they were therefore constantly in the state of transforming from one type of being to another. Since she was attempting to convert one timeline into another, she thought this theory might prove helpful.

The phoenix eggs were an even more powerful force for transformation, and also represented the continual mutability of life. As for the Kalpataru leaf, the ability to grant wishes was pretty self-explanatory. And since Barbara only had one, there was no way she could experiment on it.

So she took the more mundane components she was considering using, like rosemary and crystal quartz, and combined them with bits of phoenix egg and the tiniest fraction of a centaur's tear, and tried to get a feel for what might work and what might not.

It was not what one would call an unqualified success.

She'd tried taking a hardboiled egg and seeing if she could reverse the process magically, and return it to its raw state. She got close, once, but the end result was messy and made the Airstream stink of sulfur. Chudo-Yudo put one paw over his nose and eventually retreated outside.

After that, she tried unbraiding three strands of yarn and creating a spell to weave them back together again. She ended up with a knot that no amount of tugging at would undo. Not exactly the result she was hoping for. Although on the bright side, at least it didn't smell.

So it was with mixed frustration and relief that she heard the distinctive sound of Alexei's enchanted Harley. She really didn't have time for interruptions, but on the other hand, she wasn't getting anywhere and her temper was beginning to fray worse than the wool she'd been working with.

Alexei flung open the door of the Airstream and greeted her with his usual exuberance and a giant hug. (He was the only Rider who would ever have tried such a thing, and somehow, she never minded.)

"Baba Yaga!" he said. "It seems like years." He tossed a gaily wrapped bag in Babs' direction. "Hello, little one. I brought you something."

Barbara hoped that whatever it was didn't explode or make rude noises, He'd brought gifts that did both, back in their other life together.

"What are these?' Babs asked, unwrapping a package filled with brightly colored blocks. "And what does one do with them?"

"They are called Pegos, or something like that," Alexei said. "And you build things by putting them together in different arrangements. Or so I was told by the woman at the store where I bought them."

Apparently they were a good choice, since Babs immediately sat down and started puzzling out various combinations. They looked like fun and Barbara felt a strangely powerful itch to sit down and fiddle with them herself, but she had a feeling that Alexei hadn't come all the way back here to bring Babs a present. Although it wouldn't be the first time he'd done something like that.

"What's up?" she asked quietly. "Have you news?"

"I have a great thirst," Alexei said with a grin. "Also news, but with this dry throat, I am not certain I will be able to impart it…"

Barbara rolled her eyes but fetched him a beer anyway.

After he had downed half of it, he rested his massive body on the edge of the sofa, facing Barbara. "I don't have any definitive news," he said. "Just a gut feeling that Maya is planning something. I've seen her sneaking around the fracking site in the middle of the night, when there is no good reason for her to be there. Whatever she's up to, I think it is going to happen soon."

Barbara trusted Alexei's gut. After all, it had been around for thousands of years. Instinct plus experience made for an impressive skill set.

"Any idea what she has planned?" Barbara asked.

Alexei shrugged, a small seismic event. "Some kind of sabotage probably," he said. "Not sure what. But she doesn't strike me as the type to go small when she could go large instead."

So, nothing good, Barbara thought. "Anything else?"

Alexei hesitated. "I have heard the sounds of a child crying coming from the house at night," he admitted reluctantly. "I wasn't sure if you would want me to do something about it or not. It isn't exactly Baba Yaga business."

Barbara chewed on her lip, thinking. "Well, if Maya is going to do something that permanently damages the water system in the area, that would make it Baba Yaga business. Maybe. Plus an Otherworld creature kidnapping a Human child is definitely against the rules."

"If she has kidnapped him," Alexei reminded Barbara. "Maybe the boy's father is a willing accomplice. We have never gotten involved in Human custody fights before."

Barbara gave him a fierce grin, the kind that caused lesser men to suddenly decide they needed to be elsewhere.

"There's a first time for everything," she said. "Besides, I suspect that Maya is holding the boy hostage to keep control over his father, so it is less of a custody issue and more of a misuse of power. Not to mention that if I can prove that Maya is holding the child against his will, it would at least give the Queen a reason to punish her, which is something."

"So, we get to knock heads together and make trouble?" Alexei said. His glee at the thought of creating mayhem made his Russian accent even stronger than usual, so the "we" came out as "ve."

"Yes we do," Barbara said with only marginally less delight. She'd been feeling pretty frustrated about the entire situation, and the chance to blow off some steam and actually take action sounded pretty damned good to her.

She didn't, however, want to bring a small child—no matter how gifted that child was—into what might turn out to be a nasty confrontation. She pushed up the sleeve of her black tee shirt to reveal the tattoo of a white dragon with green eyes coiled around her right bicep.

Each Baba Yaga had her own way to summon the Riders when she needed them. Beka had two dragon earrings and a matching necklace she'd crafted herself. Barbara, however, had gone more traditional, and also had a tattoo of a red dragon with slanting golden eyes curled around her left bicep and a black Chinese style dragon with long whiskers drawn in intricate detail across her back and shoulders.

Now she stroked the white dragon and pictured Mikhail, his long blonde hair like strands of spun silk, the handsome features that reflected the kind heart inside, and his constant friendship over the years. "Come to me, White Rider," she said, murmuring the summoning chant that would bring him to her, and ignoring the tiny sting that came from the tattoo associated with him. "I need you."

"You want me to *babysit*?" Mikhail said an hour later. He hadn't been far away, and had come as soon as he'd gotten the summons. "You and Alexei get to go off on an adventure, and I have to stay here and babysit?"

Babs sat nearby, looking almost as indignant. "I do not need someone to sit with me," she protested. "I am not a baby."

Barbara sighed. She wasn't sure which one of them was being more difficult.

"Of course you are not a baby," she said to Babs. "No one thinks you are. Babysitter is just a term people use for someone who is watching a child. Which, despite your unusual abilities, you still are."

She turned to Mikhail. "And I am not about to take a child into a potentially volatile situation, so I need someone to stay with Babs."

Chudo-Yudo opened his mouth, sharp teeth on display, clearly ready to add his own protestations.

"Someone besides a dragon disguised as a giant white pit bull," Barbara added. "We all know that the two of you put together could probably take down a large army, plus a small group of telemarketers and a few insurance salesmen thrown in, but this is the Human world, and if someone happened to come by and find a supposed helpless ten year-old left alone with a dog, it could cause no end of ridiculous problems. None of which I have the energy to deal with right now. We got away with it before, but we're more public here."

Plus there was always the worry that Brenna might show up out of nowhere and make good on her threat to harm Babs, but Barbara didn't want to mention that in front of the girl, and possibly make her afraid. Barbara would have a quiet word with both Mikhail and Chudo-Yudo before she left about staying on guard against possible underhanded and/or evil attacks. In theory, the Airstream's protections should be enough, but Barbara wasn't going to take any chances.

"So Mikhail is going to Babs-sit, and Chudo-Yudo can watch over them both, and Alexei and I will try and be back as soon as possible. Any more questions?" Barbara glared at everyone. They all wisely remained silent. Mikhail bowed his head in agreement, perhaps picking up on her as-yet unspoken concerns.

"Excellent," she said. Then she gave Mikhail one of her rare grins. "I know you'd rather be in on the adventure, but you may find that taking care of a precocious magical ten year-old is more of an adventure than you think."

CHAPTER EIGHTEEN

WITH THEIR ENCHANTED MOTORCYCLES (HER ROYAL BLUE classic BMW had spent most of its existence in Russian fairy tales as a flying mortar and pestle), Barbara and Alexei got to Ohio faster than any normal Human could have. Even so, it was still after eleven when they crept up on the house where Maya and Peter Freeman were staying, just in time to see Maya getting into her flashy sports car. Barbara was torn—she wanted to go check the house to see if little Petey was there—but they didn't want to chance losing Maya, so they followed her instead.

Magical motorcycles can be quite silent when their riders want them to be.

Maya parked the car on a rutted back road that didn't seem to lead anyplace important and set off down a narrow track. Barbara and Alexei waited a few minutes to give her a head start, since it didn't seem likely that she would be going too far. Not in those heels.

"Any idea where we are?" Barbara asked quietly.

Alexei looked around, checking out landmarks and the position of the stars in the sky.

"I'd say we're north-northwest of the fracking site," he said in a thoughtful tone. "I didn't even know this road existed, and I scouted this area pretty thoroughly. But if my calculations are correct, then the main portion of the site should be about a half a mile away, over that small rise. I'm guessing that once we get about halfway down this track, we'll be able to see the tops of some of the towers."

"I wonder why she isn't here in broad daylight and parked right out front," Barbara said sarcastically. "Gee, do you suppose she's up to no good?"

"Considering that the last couple of times I followed her at night, she left her car by the side of the road not too far from the site, I'm thinking we got here just in time," Alexei said. "What now?"

Barbara shrugged. "That depends on her, I suppose." She *really* hoped the rusalka gave them a hard time.

From the top of the rise, they could look down on various mysterious pieces of machinery. Maya was crouched by something Barbara was pretty sure was a drill of some sort, although it was a lot larger than any drill she had ever seen. After a short period of time, Maya straightened up, tugging her short skirt back into place and wiping her hands off on a rag. She tossed the rag on the ground and turned around.

"*Blyat!*" she said, when she saw Barbara and Alexei standing right behind her. "Where the hell did you come from?"

"Tut, such rude language," Alexei said. "And you seem like such a nice woman."

Barbara pointed to the rag. "Littering *and* cursing. Really, what is the world coming to?"

Maya snarled at them and started edging away. Alexei's hand shot out so fast Barbara barely saw it move and settled around Maya's forearm like a band of steel.

"I don't think so," he said. "We just started chatting. You don't want to leave yet."

Maya glanced nervously at the equipment they were next to and gave what was probably supposed to be a charming laugh, although there was an edge to it that rendered it less than convincing.

"Oh, if you want to chat, why don't we go back to my house?" she suggested, trying unsuccessfully to loosen Alexei's grip. "It is so much more comfortable than this muddy old field."

"And yet here you are, in the middle of the night," Barbara said. She crouched down to look at the spot Maya had been fiddling with. A connecting piece seemed to be looser than it should be and was rattling fitfully. Even as she examined it, the noise got noticeably louder.

"Do you know, I think there is something wrong with this machine," she said in a pleasant conversational tone. "I have a sneaking suspicion that it might actually blow up." She turned to Alexei. "Does that sound to you like something that might blow up, Alexei?"

"You know, it kind of does," he said. "I'm guessing that would make rather a big mess." He grinned at Maya. "An even bigger mess of anyone who happened to be standing next to it when it went boom, wouldn't you say?"

"Yes!" Maya shrieked. "Now let me go. We need to get out of here."

Barbara shook her head. "I don't think so. Mind you, I have no love for the companies who desecrate the earth this way, and I'm almost sympathetic to what you're doing." She narrowed her eyes. "*Almost* being the operative word, since you don't seem to care who else gets hurt in the process, or even whether or not you make the problem worse instead of better."

Maya twitched under Barbara's basilisk stare, but didn't look the least bit remorseful. "They poison the water without hesitation, draining the power of any Paranormal creatures who depend on the natural waters here and in the Otherworld for their very essence. Why should I hesitate to exact my revenge?"

The machine gave a shuddering groan and they all jumped.

"Let me out of here!" Maya said through clenched teeth. "We're all going to die."

"I don't think so," Barbara said. "Although one of us might be looking at a considerably shortened lifespan for other reasons." She waved her hand at the equipment and recited a simple spell under her breath. The drill gave one last shudder and stopped altogether, smoke coming out of the section Maya had tampered with.

"Pity, but I doubt that particular apparatus is ever going to work again. Still, I suppose they'll be happier replacing it than they would have been cleaning up the mess you would have made." Barbara glanced around her at the rest of the site, shaking her head at the destruction of an otherwise beautiful spot.

"You know, since I'm here…" she nodded at Alexei to hang on to Maya and strolled around muttering to other bits and pieces of machinery. By the time she was done, the entire place was silent. Walking back to the other two, she dusted her hands off. "Waste not, want not," she said. "That will take them a while to get up and running again." Then she picked up the rag Maya had dropped and tucked it into the back pocket of her black leather pants. Barbara hated littering.

"Now we can go back to your house and have the rest of our little chat," she said to Maya. "You can consider the destruction of this operation a parting gift."

"Oh, you're going somewhere?" Maya said, perking up.

"No," Barbara responded. "You are. And I don't think you're going to be too happy about it."

Back at the house, there was a light on in the kitchen despite the late hour. Peter Callahan looked up when Maya entered the room and said wearily, "I don't suppose there is any point in asking where you've been."

"She's been at your fracking site, sabotaging your equipment," Barbara said cheerfully as she and Alexei followed Maya in. "I hate to say this, but you have lousy taste in girlfriends."

Callahan jumped to his feet, his gaze swinging wildly from Maya to the tall woman with the cloud of dark hair and the huge man wearing head-to-toe black leather.

"Maya, what the hell is going on?" Callahan said. "Who are these people? And what does she mean, you were damaging things at the site?"

"Oh, shut up, Peter," Maya said, any vestige of her charming persona completely gone. "You must have realized that every place you've been assigned since we got together, something has gone horribly wrong. Did you really think that was just an unfortunate coincidence?"

Callahan slumped back down into his chair. "Yes. No. I'd hoped so."

Barbara thought he was a far cry from the polished, arrogant man she'd met in the other timeline. Apparently life with Maya hadn't been easy on him. Pity.

"I don't understand," he said. "Why would you want to destroy my work? You're just a woman."

Okay, not such a pity.

Barbara watched Maya's shape waver as the rusalka considered showing Peter exactly what she was.

"Don't do it," Barbara warned. "You're already going to be in enough trouble with the Queen. I really don't think you want to make it worse." Allowing Humans to learn about the Paranormal world was strictly against the rules, and the punishment was swift and merciless.

Maya sighed. "You see what I have to deal with, Baba Yaga. I would think you'd be more sympathetic."

Before Barbara could say anything, Alexei held up a hand. "Do you hear that?" he asked.

Barbara listened. A thin, plaintive wail rose up from somewhere under the house, the distinctive sound of a child crying.

She was standing next to Maya before she'd even made a conscious decision to move, fingers wrapped tightly around the other woman's throat, lifting Maya up onto her toes.

"Where. Is. He?" Barbara asked through gritted teeth.

Maya made a choking noise and Barbara relaxed her hand a tiny bit, enough to the woman could get enough air to gasp out, "In the basement."

"I checked the basement," Alexei said indignantly. "There was no one there." It sounded like *der vas no von der*. Apparently he was upset too.

"Show me," Barbara demanded. She nodded at Alexei and jerked her head toward Callahan, although he didn't show any inclination to move. "Watch him."

Alexei gave the man a grim smile, and Callahan twitched.

Maya tottered on too-high heels down steep steps into a cement block basement. She stopped in front of what looked like a blank wall, sighed, and waved her hand. The illusion wavered for a moment and then fell away, revealing a small door with a padlock through its latch.

Barbara supposed she shouldn't be surprised that Alexei hadn't spotted it on a quick run through. Rusalkas weren't witches, but as Paranormal creatures they had their own abilities, and illusion was one they excelled at. How else to lure Humans to a watery grave when your normal appearance tended toward pallid skin, long green hair, and sharp teeth? On top of which, Maya had gotten a boost in power from her trades with the court nobles.

The crying had subsided to the occasional heartrending sob.

"Open it," Barbara demanded.

Maya gave her a snooty look, clearly still not understanding just how much trouble she was in. "I think the key is somewhere upstairs. I'll just go and get it. You wait here."

"I'm done waiting," Barbara said, and snapped her fingers. The lock fell to the floor with a thud. She swung the door open to reveal a small boy wearing ragged shorts and a stained tee shirt, sitting on a cot in what was probably intended as some sort of storage space. It wasn't even tall enough for Barbara to stand up. She restrained her fury—barely—for fear of frightening the child, but vowed that there would be a reckoning later.

"Hey there," she said in as calm a voice as she could manage.

"It's okay, Petey. I've come to rescue you. You can come out now."

When he didn't move, Barbara stooped down and went in to get him, glaring at Maya when she made a move toward the stairs. Together, they trooped back up, Petey nearly limp in Barbara's arms, his tear-stained face wetting the shoulder of her leather jacket.

His father stood up and reached for him, but Petey shied away, clinging to Barbara like a starfish about to be washed away in the tide.

"I'll take him," Alexei said, shoving Peter senior back into his chair with a little more force than was good for either the man or the furniture. At least one of them let out an alarming creaking noise.

"Hey," Alexei said in a surprisingly gentle voice. "Are you hungry? I just happen to have a cookie I was saving for later." He pulled an only slightly bedraggled chocolate chip cookie out of his pocket, and held out his arms. Petey went to him without hesitation. Children always seemed to know that the hulking mountain of a man would never hurt them.

Hands free, Barbara turned to Peter and Maya. "Neither of you gets a cookie," she said with quiet fury. "In fact, I'm not sure either of you will ever eat a cookie again. I hear toads don't much like them."

Peter Callahan sputtered. "I don't know who the hell you think you are, but I'm the victim here. This woman weaseled herself into my confidence and then took advantage of that by holding my son hostage so I would do what she said. She threatened to hurt him if I didn't keep my mouth shut."

Barbara gave him a hard stare. "Right. And it never occurred to you to break your son out and run for it?" True, the room had been hidden behind an illusion, but Peter had rented the house. He had to have known the room was there. She wondered if he had even tried to find and rescue Petey.

"I, uh, she was blackmailing me," Callahan said.

Barbara nodded, thinking of the nobles in the Queen's court who still hadn't admitted to Maya's involvement in their crimes. She must have had something pretty substantial to hold over their heads if that threat was worse than the Queen's current anger.

"She's good at that," Barbara said. Maya had the nerve to preen. "It's probably going to cost her that pretty head."

"Baba Yaga!" Maya endeavored to look pitiful. "I was just defending my kind from the desecration of the land he and his ilk have caused in the name of greed."

"Don't talk to me about greed," Barbara said between clenched teeth. "I know about the children you stole in Clearwater County and brought through to the Otherworld using an illicit doorway. And so does the Queen."

Maya subsided, head drooping. Peter, on the other hand, hadn't run out of bluster.

"All I want is her out of my life and to have my son back," he said with the confidence of a man who had never been thwarted more than temporarily. He held out his arms in the direction of the boy. "Petey, tell them you want to stay with Daddy."

Petey chewed the bite of cookie in his mouth and looked from Alexei to Barbara, and then to his father. "Want my mamma," he said in a whisper. Then more loudly, "I want my mamma."

Barbara nodded. She'd come across his mother's information while researching Peter senior. Well, Jazz had, which was nearly the same thing. The woman had been frantically trying to get the courts of the land to take her side. Luckily, she now had something better.

"I can give you his mother's address," she said to Alexei. "You'll make sure he gets safely home?"

"It would be my pleasure," Alexei said, magically producing another cookie. Trust Alexei to have snacks secreted all over his person, just in case he got hungry on the road. "Little boy, you trust me to take you home to your mother?"

Petey nodded, not even looking back at his father as Alexei carried him toward the door. Once there, the Rider hesitated. "Do you want me to stay, Baba Yaga?" he asked. "We can wait for you to be done here."

"I think Petey has waited long enough," Barbara said, making shooing motions with her hands. "If I can't handle a Human and a rusalka, it is time for me to retire. Go on."

She saw Alexei open his mouth to make a crack about her age, take in her general mood, and think the better of it. Wise man.

As the door swung shut behind the unlikely pair, Barbara looked at Peter Callahan with disgust. "I could turn you into something slimy, but really, that seems redundant at this point, So I'm just going to let your own company and the legal system deal with you as they see fit."

She shifted her gaze to the rusalka, who had been attempting to sidle in the direction of the basement. No doubt Maya had some kind of bolt hole prepared, in case things had gone wrong. But she hadn't anticipated "interference by a Baba Yaga" level of "gone wrong." Her mistake.

"You, on the other hand," Barbara said, "are coming with me. I am tired of explaining you to the Queen. Let's see how well you explain yourself."

She snapped her fingers, and an invisible but unbreakable net bound the rusalka's arms to her body and bound her powers, such as they were, at the same time. Barbara left the illusion of humanity, just because it would cause less trouble.

"I hope you enjoy long motorcycle rides," Barbara said with a smirk. "Because I intend to hit every bump I can find on the way home."

CHAPTER NINETEEN

BARBARA ARRIVED BACK AT THE AIRSTREAM WITH HER passenger more or less intact, although a lot less smug, and marched her through the door to find a frazzled looking Mikhail sitting on the couch, holding on to one bare foot.

"Those Jego things really hurt when you step on them," he said as soon as she walked inside. "I can't believe they let innocent children play with them." He glared in the direction of said innocent child, who was still up, despite it being way past her bedtime.

Barbara stifled a laugh. She'd seen Mikhail come out of bar brawls bleeding and bruised, and he hadn't complained nearly as much as this.

"I'm sorry," she said. "Your brother Alexei bought them for her."

"Oh," Mikhail said, subsiding. "That figures. They're probably some kind of weapon in disguise." He shook his head. "Did you know she will only eat sandwiches if you cut the crusts off of them? It took me three tries to figure that out. I had to eat a lot of rejects."

Barbara bit her lip. "I did know that, yes. Didn't you ask her what she wanted to eat?" She shoved the rusalka, still bound, into the nearest seat.

"Of course I did," Mikhail said indignantly. "She said she wanted a sandwich. She didn't say she would only eat them if they had precisely half an inch cut off around each edge. Or that the peanut butter side had to go on the bottom, and the jelly side on the top!"

There was actually a bright red jelly stain on his usually pristine white pants, but Barbara thought this was probably not the time to mention it.

"I'm sorry if I was difficult, Uncle Mikhail," Babs said. "It is only that I am accustomed to having things done in a certain way. It is not your fault that you do not know how to fix sandwiches correctly."

"Go to bed, little one," Barbara said, nearly shaking with pent up mirth. "Say thank you to your honorary uncle for watching you. We will speak more of this in the morning."

Babs, solemn as always, thanked Mikhail and popped into her bed, clearly not at all chastised.

"She's not an easy child," Barbara said, patting Mikhail on the shoulder. "You did just fine." She sobered at a thought. "I'm only sorry you can't remember what your own child put you through in the other timeline. It made this look like a cakewalk."

The White Rider pulled on his socks and shoes. "I wish that too, Baba Yaga. I see you achieved at least part of your goal." He jerked his head toward the rusalka, now back in her own form and dripping wetly on the furniture. "How did the rest of your mission go?"

"Well, we found the boy Petey, a bit traumatized but not physically harmed. Your brother is taking him to his mother as we speak. As for this one," Barbara kicked the rusalka none-too-gently on the ankles, "I'm taking her through the doorway and turning her in to the Queen right now. That is, if you're up to another hour or two of babysitting."

"Not a baby," Babs said from her bunk, although the blanketed form didn't stir.

Mikhail sighed. "Sure," he said. "But I'm keeping my boots on this time."

It was satisfying to turn Maya over to the Queen. Even more so when, upon seeing the rusalka captured and in disfavor, the three couples who had adopted the Human children she'd stolen stepped up and admitted her involvement. The Queen looked quite pleased, which was always a good thing, but for Barbara it was a bittersweet victory. The children were still trapped in the Otherworld, lost forever to the families who loved them, unless Barbara could pull a rabbit out of an increasingly shrinking hat.

Just how shrinking it was she didn't discover until she went to read *The Little Prince* to Babs, who was still awake when Barbara got back.

"I'm sorry," Barbara said quietly as she closed the book. "I know you like the way Liam reads it better."

There was a moment of silence, and at first she thought that Babs had fallen asleep. But when she looked, those big brown eyes were staring into hers, a tiny frown crinkling the skin between them.

"Liam used to read me this book?" Babs asked. "In our old lives?"

Barbara suddenly felt as though someone had sucked all the air out of the trailer. "Almost every night," Barbara said. "Don't you remember?"

Babs shook her head. "No, I do not," she said in a voice barely more than a whisper. "I remember the tree house and I remember breakfasts together, but I do not remember the reading." One tiny tear rolled down her cheek and Barbara brushed it away. She couldn't remember Babs ever crying before, not even the time when she'd fallen out of that tree house and broken her arm.

"It's okay," Barbara said. "Sometimes we forget things."

"Not Liam things," Babs said. "I always remember Liam things. Am I doing something wrong?"

Barbara gave her a swift hug, not sure which one of them needed it more. "Not at all, sweetheart. I think this is probably just the universe trying to fix itself. Something is broken and it is the nature of existence to try and mend it. In this case, it is the unraveled timeline. I have been trying to knit it back up the way it was. But I'm guessing that if I can't do that, the universe will patch up those unraveled pieces the best it can on its own. Your forgetting parts of your old time with Liam is probably a sign that the process is starting."

Babs' eyes widened in alarm. "Will I forget all the old Liam times? Will you, Baba Yaga?"

Tiny shards of pain dug themselves even deeper into Barbara's heart at the thought. If she forgot their time together, would she even know? Or would the memories of their love and marriage be washed away like a sandcastle left behind on the beach, reclaimed by the waves with no one there to see or mark the passing.

"I don't know, little one," she said. "I hope not. But the universe is a very strong force."

"You need to be stronger than the universe, Baba Yaga," Babs said fiercely, grabbing on to Barbara's hand with both of her smaller ones. "You need to fix it first, so we do not lose our Liam."

"We can build a new life with this Liam," Barbara said, her whole body aching with grief at the thought. "I'm sure it would be a fine life."

"But it would not be *our* life," Babs said. "Please."

Barbara pulled the girl into her arms and held on to her as if she could shield her from the pain to come. They clung to each other and Barbara cried her own never-before tears, hiding them in the darkness as she spoke a promise to them both. "I'll try my best. I promise. I'll try my best."

She just didn't know if her best would be enough, or in time.

Late the next morning, Barbara had finished up yet another unsuccessful variation of the spell she was aiming at (seriously, who knew yarn could explode?) when a knock on the door brought her work to a welcome stopping point. Waving away the smoke, Barbara opened the door to reveal a smiling Liam. Her day instantly got better, despite its frustrations and the depth of her fears.

"Hi," she said, almost shyly. She never quite knew how to act around him, since he looked exactly like *her* Liam, and yet this man was almost a stranger. "How are things going over at the house?"

"Pretty well," he said, stepping inside the Airstream and immediately wrinkling his nose. "Uh, is something on fire?"

"Not anymore," Babs said from behind the couch, where she was hiding from the worst of the smoke with her new toys, building something that looked a lot like the Queen's castle, despite the fact that there hadn't been that many pieces in the kit Alexei had brought her.

"Oh," Liam said, then looked closer. "That's really good, Babs."

"Thank you," she said. "I like to build things."

"I do too," Liam said. "That's why it is so much fun to work on your house." He turned back to Barbara. "The kitchen is done, for the most part, and all the bathrooms are in working order, although they could use a few cosmetic touches. Another couple of days, and you should be able to move in."

"That's great," Barbara said. "I look forward to living in a real house again."

Babs wrinkled her button nose. "But the Airstream is a real house, Baba. We always live here."

Barbara's heart skipped a beat. "Always right now, you mean."

The little girl shook her head. "Always always. It is our home."

More forgetting. But Barbara's dire thoughts were scattered to the winds by Liam's next words.

"I just wanted to come by and thank you for the pie," he said.

"Pie?" Barbara looked at Babs, but the girl seemed as clueless as Barbara. "I'm sorry, but I don't know anything about a pie."

"Really?" Liam raised his eyebrows. "Because there was a pie sitting on the kitchen counter when I got there this morning. I figured it had to be from you. I mean, who else would be leaving pies in your house?"

Barbara could think of a couple of answers to that question, none of them good. "You didn't eat it, did you?" she asked, holding her breath while also examining him for signs of imminent illness.

"Uh, no," he said, still seemingly baffled by her response. "I'd just had breakfast when I got there, and I was going to have some of the pie after my lunch break, but I thought I'd come over and say thank you first, and see if you and Babs wanted to share it with me. It's a pretty big pie."

"The better to eat you with," Barbara muttered.

"What?"

"Sorry. Fairy tale reference. What big teeth you have, grandmother." Barbara sighed. "Never mind. Let's go take a look at this pie, shall we?"

She, Liam, and Babs trooped over to the farmhouse, with Chudo-Yudo following behind. They walked through the back door into the kitchen, where just as Liam said, there was a huge pie sitting on the counter. It was a glorious creation, glistening with glazed cherries peeking coyly out through a perfectly woven lattice of flaky crust. Barbara couldn't have made one like it in a million years, even with a magical assist. It was practically irresistible, which was no doubt the intention.

"That is a very pretty pie," Babs said, standing on her tiptoes to smell it. Then she took three large steps back and pinched her nose shut with two fingers. "Bleh," she said. "That pie does not smell as good as it looks. I do not think you should eat it, Liam."

"No?" Liam bent down and inhaled. "It smells just fine to me. Just cherries and flour and sugar and such."

With her long sensitive nose, Barbara didn't even have to get any closer. She could smell all the things Liam mentioned, along with magic, and some acrid aroma underlying it all, plus just the slightest lingering hint of patchouli.

There was only one creature in the room whose nose was even more sensitive than hers. "What's in the pie?" she muttered quietly to Chudo-Yudo.

Chudo-Yudo padded over and sniffed at the pie, then cocked one furry white eyebrow and stuck a claw in to delicately carve out a small piece.

"Hey!" Liam said indignantly. "My pie!"

Barbara put a restraining hand on his arm. "Well?" she said to Chudo-Yudo. She wasn't worried about him getting sick from whatever was in the pastry. She'd once seen him eat an entire crop of Fly Agaric mushrooms, among the most deadly in the world, and only end up with a case of the hiccups. Dragon digestive systems were predictably tough.

He lifted the snippet careful to his mouth, chewed thoughtfully for a moment, then walked over to the back door and spit it out. "Pah," he said. "Arsenic, probably derived from cherry pits, although you'd think enough of them to be deadly would make the pie more bitter."

Liam swung his head from her to the dragon-dog and back again. "I swear, it sounds just like the two of you are having an actual conversation. Although what you could possibly get out of all that barking, I don't know. Is he some kind of specially trained drug-sniffing dog?"

"Something like that," Barbara said. "He can detect all kinds of poisons, including the kind hidden in your pretty pie. It's a very good thing you didn't eat it. It might not have killed you, but it would no doubt have made you very sick."

She could see the moment when the lawman superseded the handyman, if for no other reason than she'd watched it happen a thousand times in their previous lives together. It was as though a switch flipped behind his eyes and the mellow Liam was replaced by someone focused and analytical. When that look wasn't aimed at her, she actually found it pretty sexy.

"Why would anyone want to poison me?" he asked, mostly rhetorically. "And if they did, why do it here, instead of at my own house. Do you think someone wanted you to take the fall for this? Or was it aimed at you, and not me?" His glance fell on Babs, and he shook his head. "You don't think anyone hates you enough to risk Babs getting her hands on a piece, do you?"

"I would not have eaten it," Babs said decisively. "It smells of Brenna. I would not eat anything that smells of Brenna. She is a bad witch."

Barbara coughed. "We don't call people that name, Babs, remember? Although you have a point about the woman."

"Who is this Brenna and what makes you think she had anything to do with this? Why would she have anything against me? I've never met her, that I recall."

"I'm afraid her grudge is against me," Barbara said. "You would just have been collateral damage. She recently threatened to harm anyone who mattered to me." She could feel her face heat as the subtle admission slipped out. Hopefully he'd be so focused on the situation, it would go right over his head. "She is fond of a particularly strong patchouli scent, which you can just catch a whiff of on the pie, it you are looking for it." *Which the rest of them were.*

"Huh," Liam thought through the permutations of all that. "Not exactly proof that will stand up in court, alas."

"No, it isn't," Barbara agreed, thinking of another court entirely. "Circumstantial at best. Brenna would just say the she is not the only person who wears that scent, or suggest ever so subtly that if anyone wanted to blame her for something nefarious, that person would probably leave behind a dab of patchouli. Then she'd look at me sadly."

Despite the serious nature of the discussion. Liam had to hide a laugh behind his hand. "I take it you have gone up against this woman before," he said. "It sounds like you dislike her as much as she dislikes you, although I can't see you leaving around a poisoned pie because of it."

"Don't tempt me," Barbara muttered through clenched teeth. "I should have let Chudo-Yudo eat her when he suggested it."

The dragon-dog barked in agreement.

Liam patted Chudo-Yudo on the head and dug around in his jeans pockets until he found a treat. "He's a great dog," Liam said. "He wouldn't bite anyone."

"Don't be fooled by that goofy expression," Barbara said. "He's one hell of a guard dog. I only hope Brenna comes sneaking around when he is close enough to smell her." Something about her expression must have given away how serious she was, because Liam took an involuntary step backward before collecting himself.

"I guess I'd better keep bringing him treats," Liam said. "Stay on his good side."

Chudo-Yudo nodded assertively and Barbara rolled her eyes.

"In the meanwhile," she said, "if someone who looks like a harmless old hippie lady shows up, do not trust anything she says or does." The Queen had plans to take care of Brenna, but that didn't mean the crazy witch couldn't do all sorts of harm before that happened.

She held up one finger. "Wait here," she said, and ran for the Airstream. A minute or two later, she was back, a small black leather bag that dangled from a long leather thong clenched in her hand.

"I know you're going to think I'm crazy," she said, "But I want you to promise me you'll wear this day and night until I tell you it's safe to take it off. It shouldn't be for long."

Liam looked at it dubiously when she handed it to him, then made a face when he sniffed it. "Is that *garlic*?" he asked. "This poison pie lady isn't a vampire is she?"

Babs gave him a patient look. "There are no such things as vampires. Everyone knows that. You are just being silly. The bag contains garlic because it is a protection amulet, and garlic is a very protective herb."

She had been studying the magical qualities of plants with Barbara since they'd started living together. Each Baba Yaga used magic a little differently, and since the element of Earth was the one Barbara and Babs both connected to most strongly, they tended to use a lot of herbs and crystals.

Liam's expression became even more doubtful, if that was possible.

"Is this some kind of New Age thing?" he asked. "Because you know, I own a gun."

"That's nice," Barbara said. "But guns only work against threats you can see coming." She nodded down at the pie. "I know it seems wacky, but it will make both me and Babs feel better if you would just wear it. Please? I hate to think of you getting hurt because someone is targeting people I care about."

An unexpected smile lit up his face. *Dammit. She'd done it again.*

"Well, in that case," Liam said, lifting the necklace over his head and then tucking the small bundle down inside the front of his tee shirt. "I'll wear it. But I'd feel a lot better if you went into the sheriff's office and talked to Belinda Shields about this woman. The current sheriff is a useless twit, but there are still plenty of good officers at the department who could see if she has a record of violence. If she does, and you can prove she is stalking you, maybe you can get an order of protection."

Frustration creased his brow. "If I were still sheriff…"

"You'd still have to follow the letter of the law," said the woman who knew that better than anyone. "And until Brenna is caught in the act, there isn't anything you could do about it." *Fortunately, the High Queen of the Otherworld had no such restrictions. Barbara just had to keep them all safe until Her Majesty's justice took hold.*

"True," Liam said. "But then again, if I were sheriff, I

wouldn't be able to do this." He leaned in and put one hand on either side of her face, then kissed her so gently and so thoroughly it took her breath away.

"What was that for?" she asked as Babs giggled.

"That," he said, "was for caring about me enough that your nemesis would want to poison me. Although just for future reference, there are probably better ways to let a guy know you like him."

"Duly noted," she said. "Not that I expect there to be any need for that knowledge in the future."

"Duly noted," Liam repeated, grinning at her like a teenager.

"Coff. Get a room. Coff." Chudo-Yudo made a noise that sounded like it might be followed by a hairball if he were a cat and not a dragon disguised as a giant white pit bull.

So much for romance. Still, it would have to hold her for now. She gave Liam a stern look. "I mean it about watching your back. This woman looks innocuous, but she is pure evil."

"You watch your back too," Liam said. "I'm not the one she's truly mad at."

"Oh, I'm not likely to forget that," Barbara said. Nor was Brenna likely to let her. Romance would have to wait until this was all over and done with. Assuming they were are still around to celebrate then.

CHAPTER TWENTY

Barbara occupied the rest of her day working on her experiments, although she had Chudo-Yudo spend most of the afternoon sprawled casually under a shade tree where he could watch both the house and the Airstream, and she kept Babs carefully by her side.

Brenna had to have found another unauthorized doorway to be coming and going the way she was, but Barbara couldn't spare the time to go search for it. Unlike when Maya was using her doorway to carry Human children out of their world and into the Otherworld, which upset the balance between the two much faster than normal, it could take months before the mere existence of a random passageway would have enough of an effect for it to be noticeable.

It galled her to leave Brenna such an advantage, but Barbara was down to a day and a half to solve her problem, and she didn't have a minute to spare to chase down a crazy power-hungry witch who the Queen was going to deal with soon enough anyway.

The work had to come first.

But at midnight, she was throwing out another steaming, reeking failure when a familiar outline materialized out of the shadows. Followed by two more.

"Hello boys," she said, pretending she hadn't been so deep in thought that they'd caught her by surprise. "What brings you by at this late hour?"

"My mission is accomplished," Alexei said. "The boy is back with his mother, who was very happy indeed to have him returned. She is planning to start legal proceedings against the boy's father first thing in the morning. I think this deserves a beer, yes?"

Gregori bowed at Barbara, looking considerably less pleased with himself than his larger brother did. "I, on the other hand, must regrettably report the failure of my own task. Brenna slipped away from me. I'm not sure how. The woman is incredibly sneaky, even for a Baba Yaga."

Barbara inclined her head, acknowledging the compliment. "Well, I can tell you she was here at some point earlier in the day."

All three brothers made noises of alarm and concern, and Barbara had to shush them before they woke Babs, who was sleeping inside.

"We're all fine. We never even saw her. But she left a poisoned cherry pie in the house for Liam, and it was just good luck that he didn't eat it." She thought about what he'd said when he came to thank them and offer to share it. "Well, good luck and courtesy."

Alexei hummed a Russian love song under his breath, smirking. Then winced when Gregori kicked him.

"Either way, I don't blame you for not being able to keep track of her. After all, she's always got the excuse of being on some Baba Yaga mission to explain her comings and goings. At least if she's focused on me part of the time, maybe she'll leave Beka alone."

Mikhail stepped out of the darkness to join his brothers. "We think we would all be more affective sticking around here and keeping an eye on you and little Babs. Even your former sheriff, if that would put your mind at ease."

"It would, actually," Barbara said with relief. She'd never had any illusions that one small protection amulet, no matter how powerful, could stand against Brenna if she was truly determined to harm Liam. "But I want you to be on your guard as well."

Alexei roared with laughter. Even the normally somber Gregori smiled.

Mikhail just gave her his usual charming and cocky grin. "Really, Baba Yaga. You worry too much. She is one small, old witch. We are the Riders. We have seen dozens of her kind come and go. No offence."

"No offence taken," Barbara said, wishing she could laugh too.

But whatever memories she might be losing without being aware of it, the one of the sight of the three of them, broken and battered and barely clinging to life, still flared like a beacon in the landscape of her former life.

"But remember what I told you happened in my timeline. She used trickery and magic, and then turned your loyalty to each other into a weapon she used against you. Do not underestimate her cunning or the depths to which she will stoop."

Alexei wrapped one hugely muscled arm around her and kissed her on the top of her head. "Do not worry yourself, old friend. We have Mikhail for the cunning, and Gregori for our own stooping."

She looked up into his smirking bearded face. "And what do we have you for, *old* friend?"

"Well, someone has to drink the beer, and knock heads together, yes?" he said. And they all laughed.

Barbara gazed at them fondly, but she couldn't help but remember that if by some miracle she succeeded with her impossible task, she might never hear them laugh like that again.

Whose happiness did she chose? How could she be sure that this changed timeline wasn't was best for the most people, especially once Beka was out from under Brenna's thumb and able to grow into her own person? How could she take the Rider's immortality—and as ironic as it sounded, their innocence—away from them, when this fluke of magic had returned it, when that had proven otherwise impossible?

Was she being selfish to want her own life back? If nothing else, she was pretty sure after today that she and Liam would end up back together one way or the other. They wouldn't be exactly the same people, or have been brought together by the same common battle, but would that matter? Eventually, she probably wouldn't even remember that there had been any other reality. Maybe she should stop fighting the inevitable and just let it be.

But then she thought of the children who would never be able to go home again, no matter how well-treated they would be in the Otherworld. Thought of Belinda and her parents, aching from the void in their hearts and in their lives. She remembered the young couple she'd liked so much who had lost their home through no fault of their own, and the look on Liam's face when he realized that there was a problem he couldn't do anything about because he was no longer sheriff. Maybe he had built himself a reasonably good life, but didn't he deserve to have the job he loved, protecting the people of the area she'd become so attached to?

Then there were her sisters, who never met the men they were meant to be with. And the Riders, for whom being broken meant not just pain and sorrow, but their own journeys toward growth and love and the lives that suited them so well.

No, she thought, gazing at their laughing faces in the moonlight, they, all of them—her and Babs included—deserved to have the lives they had been meant to live. She just *had* to make this spell work and fix the timeline.

But by the appointed hour, she still hadn't managed it.

She had tried variations on the spell she'd created from what Jazz had come up with, using the most potent of ingredients, although she was still holding the Kalpataru leaf back. There would only be one chance to use it. If that chance ever came at all.

During a few of the most recent attempts, Barbara thought she could feel something trying to happen, but in the end they all fizzled out. She had come to the reluctant conclusion that it was such a huge magical working, it would require more power than even she could muster on her own. After all, the initial disaster had been caused by the intersection between two potent witches. It would probably take at least that many to fix it.

She wasn't sure if even all three Baba Yagas working together would have been enough to pull it off, but since she had been forbidden to speak to or see her sisters, there had been no way to even attempt it. Nor was she convinced that Bella and Beka would have agreed to help. No matter—time was up, in more ways than one, and she, Babs, and Chudo-Yudo were headed to the Otherworld, bringing her precious bottle of the Water of Life and Death with them.

She was also bringing along all of the magical supplies and abortive spells, just for the hell of it, but she suspected they'd be of as much use as the ornate decorative knife that hung at her waist. (The real one was tucked into her boot, of course.)

They were the first ones there, and the Queen's major domo ushered them into a clearing to one side of the castle. It looked like a cross between a throne room and a parlor, nestled in a verdant glen filled with wildflowers, its boundaries marked by concentric circles of orange and yellow ivy. Across the carpet of low, emerald-hued grasses, the King and Queen sat atop high-backed chairs carved out of amber with curving sapphire arms, and around the ivied edge of the circle, high-level courtiers either stood or sat in simpler versions of the royal couples' seats. Witnesses to what was to come, no doubt.

Barbara had never seen this particular space before, and she suspected that the Queen had created it just for this occasion. The setting might be bucolic and charming, but there were members of the royal guard scattered throughout the small crowd, and the circular nature of the area lent itself easily to the containment of magic in case things got out of hand. No doubt the Queen didn't want to risk the more delicate ornaments in her throne room if Brenna decided to argue her case more violently than expected.

Barbara, Babs, and Chudo-Yudo approached the Queen and her consort and bowed. The Queen looked stern but beautiful, at ease in her flowing gown of lilac silk with a matching amethyst tiara, necklace, and earrings that dangled nearly the length of her long, elegant neck. A delicate purple fan lay at rest for the moment on her lap.

The King wore black from his high leather boots to his embroidered velvet tunic, his simple silver crown adorned by rough-cut black diamonds. He too looked relaxed and unperturbed, and Barbara began to wonder if she had imagined the entire conversation about striping Brenna of her powers, or if the royal couple had changed their minds. Certainly no one else in the outdoor parlor acted as though they expected anything other than the usual entertainments of court.

"Greetings," the King said as the trio straightened up. "Lovely afternoon, is it not?"

"Yes, Your Highness," Barbara said. It was always a lovely afternoon (or morning, or evening) in the Otherworld, but Old World manners required a certain protocol. "I hope we find you well?"

"As well as possible, under the circumstances, Baba Yaga," the King said, his tone somewhat grim.

Barbara held in a sigh of relief. *Not* losing her mind, then. Thank goodness. Their Majesties were clearly putting up a casual front in hope of lulling Brenna into a false sense of security. It had certainly fooled her, so with any luck it would work on Brenna as well.

As they were greeting the Queen, Bella strolled into the clearing, followed by her dragon Koshka, in his usual guise of a gigantic Norwegian Forest Cat, his huge puffy tail arched high in the air as he walked. He and Chudo-Yudo exchanged affectionate head butts, and Bella flashed them all one of her brilliant smiles as she made her own graceful curtsey.

As far as Barbara knew, neither Bella nor Beka had any idea what was about to happen. The Queen caught Barbara's eye and gave a tiny tilt of her head in Bella's direction, accompanied by a raised eyebrow.

Barbara shook her own head. No, she hadn't gone against the Queen's orders and informed her sisters.

The Queen nodded, satisfied. "Ah, good, everyone is here," she said as Brenna, Beka, that and Chewie, their massive black Newfoundland dragon-dog, were ushered into the circular space. "And you all brought your bottles of the Water of Life and Death, as We requested?"

"We did, Your Majesty," Brenna said with a greedy glint in her eye. The pungent aroma of patchouli and potion-making preceded her, as if to warn the innocent that the witch wasn't far behind. "And your timing was as impeccable as always. With two of us using it, we have gone through our supply faster than usual."

"Is that so?" the Queen said, making a closer inspection of Beka. She exchanged a brief glance with Barbara, and tightened her lips imperceptibly. "Are you quite certain your apprentice is getting her share? She looks distinctly unwell."

Barbara thought that was a fairly epic understatement. Even in the brief time since they had seen each other, Beka had gone even farther downhill. Her skin was ashen, and her usually glossy hair was brittle and course looking. There was no sparkle in her blue eyes, which seemed sunken and dull over the dark smudges underneath them. Her usual cheerful blue and green silk skirt and tunic hung loose, as if she had lost weight.

Bella and Barbara exchanged grim looks. *If the Queen doesn't kill Brenna, I'm going to,* Barbara thought to herself.

Only someone as self-involved (or insane) as Brenna could have missed the warning in the Queen's tone, but it clearly sailed right over the older witch's head.

"Oh, she's fine," Brenna said. "You know the youth of today. No stamina. We've been working day and night on a potion I came up with to cleanse the seas. She's just a little over-tired. She'll be fine in a day or two."

"We are quite certain of that," the Queen said in a dry tone. She held out one slim hand imperiously. "But We will start with your bottle, certainly."

Brenna put it eagerly into the Queen's outstretched hand, and then waited, one toe tapping impatiently on the ground, for it to be refilled from the sparkling crystal jug sitting at the Queen's feet.

"There is one issue We wish to address before proceeding," the Queen said, putting down Brenna's bottle and picking up her fan. Around the circle, the more observant of the courtiers suddenly began to show more interest in the conversation.

"It has come to Our attention that there may be a problem with one of Our Baba Yagas," the King said gravely in his beautiful courtly voice.

Brenna endeavored to appear surprised, but smugness lurked not far under the surface. "Is that so, Your Majesties? How unfortunate." She cast a triumphant sideways eye at Barbara, her eyes glittering. "I did try to warn you."

"So you did," the Queen said.

CHAPTER TWENTY-ONE

BELLA GLARED AT BRENNA INDIGNANTLY, ALTHOUGH THE redhead had the good sense to throttle back her expression a bit before she turned to the Queen.

"Your Majesty, I know that Barbara has been a little…stranger than usual lately, but I can't believe that she has actually done anything that is against your rules. Brenna tried to convince me that Barbara had lost her mind, but aside from an unusual tale we can't prove isn't true, she seems perfectly sane to me. And as for suggesting that Barbara might commit treason against Your August Majesties, well, that's crazier than Barbara's story of unraveled timelines."

Beka took a step forward to stand next to Bella. "I agree with Bella," she said in a voice stronger than might be expected from someone who looked so rough around the edges. "Barbara would never, ever do anything like that. She's the best of us all."

Barbara had to blink a couple of times to clear her eyes of unexpected moisture. Having her sister Babas take her side meant more than either of them could ever know. Apparently she hadn't lost them after all.

"You misunderstand Us," the Queen said in a surprisingly gentle voice. "Barbara's loyalty has never been in question, at least not for long. As for her sanity, We would as soon doubt the moons in the sky."

Everyone looked up to make sure that all three moons (one still hanging crooked) were there before nodding in agreement.

"In fact," the King added, "We are quite convinced her assertion that time has gone awry is true, although it does not appear that there is any way to remedy the situation." He looked at Barbara and she shook her head sadly, clutching her useless bag of ingredients and tools to her side.

"But, but," Brenna sputtered. "Of course Barbara is the problem. I've told you."

"So you did, Brenna, so you did," the Queen said. "You also told us that Beka was getting her share of the Water of Life and Death, and that is demonstrably untrue." She waved her fan in Beka's direction, then used it to gesture both Beka and Bella back away from Brenna. They moved adroitly, not having to be told twice.

"Plus you lied about Barbara," the King added. "Who has informed Us of your treachery in the timeline she remembers, as well as your involvement in the poisoning and displacement of the Selkies and Merpeople, an event which took place in both timelines."

"As did your theft of the Water of Life and Death from your own former hut, after which you came to Us and suggested most convincingly that your replacement was too young and inexperienced to continue on as Baba Yaga, and volunteered to come out of retirement," the Queen said. The bitterness in her voice was so strong, some of the more delicate flowers began to wilt.

"To Our sorrow and regret, We believed you," the King said. "For this, We owe Beka a debt we will never be able to repay, although We shall begin, of course, by reinstating her in her position as Baba Yaga, with complete autonomy."

Barbara wasn't sure who looked more shocked by this statement, Beka or Brenna.

"But Your Majesties," Brenna protested. "You can't! I am the Baba Yaga!"

"You," the Queen said, pointing her fan in Brenna's direction, "are beneath contempt. You are a traitor to the crown and to all those you have sworn to serve. Your days as Baba Yaga should have been over long ago. We assure you, they are over now."

The color drained out of Brenna's face, and her hands clenched at her skirt so hard, Barbara heard the material tear.

"We do not know if you are a victim of the Water Sickness, or merely your own greed. Either way, your power is forfeit for these acts of treason. *All* your power. The natural magic with which you were born, as well as the power gifted to you by My potent Water of Life and Death. You will be left with nothing.

As mortal and weak as any other Human. What will happen after that remains to be decided."

"NO! Your Majesty, you can't! It's a lie. All lies." Brenna swiveled and glared at the three younger Baba Yagas. "They all plot against me because they are jealous of my skill and wisdom. I would never do the things of which you have accused me. I am innocent." Big fat tears rolled down her wrinkled face, but the Queen looked unimpressed by Brenna's theatrics and raised her fan.

"No! No! Not my powers!" Brenna's face grew red with rage, her brief tears already dried and forgotten. "I am the strongest Baba Yaga who has ever lived. The best! You can't take it away from me!"

A glimmer of an idea started to form in Barbara's mind. Hope suddenly bubbled up, like a potion in a cauldron.

"Wait, Your Majesty," she said.

"What?" the Queen said, looking baffled, but lowering her fan a fraction of an inch.

"What?" Beka and Bella asked in unison. "Why?"

Brenna stared at Barbara with suspicion. "Yes, why?"

Barbara ignored the rest of them, speaking only to the King and Queen. They were the ones she would have to convince.

"She's right," Barbara said. "At this moment, Brenna holds within her the most power any Baba Yaga has ever had. The magical potential even the weakest of us contains is huge, and she has not only been accumulating power for a great many years, but undoubtedly drinking extra of the Water, both that which she stole originally and Beka's share of their current supply, in addition to siphoning off some of Beka's power to supplement her own."

"Your point, Baba Yaga?" the Queen was not known for her patience, and she was clearly ready to finish what she'd started.

"My point, Your Majesty," Barbara said with a brief bow, "is that the spell I have been attempting to use to fix the broken timeline hasn't worked because it lacked the necessary power to undo the magnitude of changes that were created when the original timeline came unraveled. Those changes were brought about by the clash of two witches that resulted in a death. The amount of power this conjunction of raw energy generated was huge, possibly more than all three of the current Baba Yagas could bring to bear."

She stared at Brenna, who glared back with so much hate a lesser woman would have paused. Luckily, Barbara was not a lesser woman. Not by a long shot.

"But when you rip away Brenna's power—*all* of her power, original, earned, and stolen—it will generate more energy than any ten Baba Yagas could produce using a safe portion of our total magic. *If* I perform the spell at the exact same moment you reclaim her power and *if* you send it into the enchantment, it just might work."

Barbara gazed at the royal couple and held her breath.

The Queen raised one silvery eyebrow. "That is a lot of 'ifs,' Baba Yaga."

"Yes, Your Majesty." She didn't add that it was the only chance she had left. They already knew that.

The King looked thoughtful, his handsome face more somber than usual. "Even assuming you are correct, Baba Yaga, are you absolutely certain you wish to do this? If everything you have told us about the other timeline is true, there will be sacrifices as well as gains. The Riders will lose their immortality. Brenna will have died."

"What? What?" Brenna shrieked. "No! You killed me?"

Barbara smirked. "Not me," she said. "After we discovered you about to burn the Riders and Bella to death to fuel your insane immortality spell, Koshka here turned you into a charcoal briquette."

"Did I?" Koshka said, looking surprised and not a little proud. "Go me." A little spurt of fire shot out of his feline nostrils. Bella patted him on the head, only having to lean over a bit to do it.

The Queen cleared her throat delicately. "As Our beloved Consort was saying, this is not a decision to be taken lightly. You have settled into this timeline, for all that it lacks some of the things you knew from before. You and young Babs here have made a new beginning for yourselves. All of that will be lost should you succeed at casting this spell, and there is no guarantee that your old timeline will be exactly as you recall it. Magic is strange and unpredictable. No one knows that better than you, Baba Yaga."

Barbara exchanged glances with Babs, who had stuck close to her side through the entire exchange. The girl would be affected as strongly as Barbara by whatever decision she made. Babs just stuck out her chin in that particularly stubborn way she had always had, and nodded decisively. "Home," she mouthed silently.

Barbara sighed, casting a subtle smile around those nearest her in the clearing, all so precious (with one notable exception). "If I succeed, there are many good things that will happen as well. The stolen children will be returned to the families who love them. Bella and Beka will get back the lives they were supposed to have, with men who love them, magic and all."

The smile grew wider as it rested on Beka. "You are so much stronger and tougher in that other world," she said softly. "It was hard to get there, but you did. If this doesn't work, I know you'll get there in this one too." She turned to Bella. "And you finally get your fiery temper under control, more or less. You haven't set anyone on fire accidentally in ages."

"Cool," Bella said, slinging one arm around Beka supportively. "It's kind of hard to imagine being me but different, but I like the idea of getting true love. You've got my vote, for what it's worth."

Beka nodded. "Mine too."

"And what of the Riders?" the Queen asked. "They are not here to have a say, and they have the most to lose."

"They told me once that they trusted me to do the right thing," Barbara said. "They seemed quite intrigued by the new lives they built for themselves. Especially Alexei. He marries a woman who owns a bar."

Even the Queen laughed at that, a peal of lightness in an otherwise somber gathering. Alexei was notorious for his love of drinking, even in a court where there was always a party going on somewhere, day or night.

"More than that, though," Barbara went on. "As Babs so wisely said, and you reiterated when you told me you were resolved to deal with Brenna, if one makes a mess, it is one's responsibility to clean it up. I made this mess. I broke the timeline, and it is up to me to fix it. No matter what the end result, I have to try to make things right again."

The King and Queen spoke to each other quietly for a moment, the meadow so silent and still, you could hear the flutter of a bird's wing as it shifted in a nearby tree.

Finally, the Queen turned to Barbara and nodded once, briskly. "We agree, Baba Yaga. It is worth the attempt. You have Our full support. It will be as you have asked. Set up whatever you need. We cannot assist you, since this is a Human problem, but we will hold this space safe as you do your magical working."

She waved her fan clockwise around the circle, and the orange and yellow ivy burst into heatless flame, shutting all those inside off from the rest of the Otherworld. A few lords and ladies who had been standing too close to the outer edge took rapid steps inward.

Brenna made another effort to protest, but at another gesture from the Queen, a quartet of extremely large guards in silver armor moved to flank the disgraced Baba Yaga, and she subsided into incoherent and mostly inaudible muttering, glowing with the dim light of a stasis spell. Any efforts she made to fight its magical hold sputtered and dissolved instantly.

Barbara gave Babs a quick hair tug for reassurance and made the few preparations that were necessary. A large, perfect quartz crystal was placed toward the north, the shards of phoenix eggs opposite it in the southern quarter to represent fire. The vial of centaur tears—down to eight, which she prayed would be enough—went into the western quadrant, as a form of water, and in the east, one of the phoenix's bright feathers as a symbol of air. Four pure white candles, one for each element, were placed in each quarter, and she sprinkled rosemary around them all to form a circle of remembrance. The Kalpataru leaf she held in the palm of her right hand. She was as ready as she was going to be.

"You'd better come and stand next to me," she said to Babs. "I'm not sure what will happen if this works, and I don't want to take any chances." If she went back and Babs was somehow left behind in this timeline, Barbara wouldn't be able to bear it. There was undoubtedly some danger in bringing her into the circle, but there didn't seem to be any way to avoid that. From the look in her eyes, Babs was a lot happier to be by her side.

"We'd like to help too, if you'll let us," Beka said. She and Bella moved to join the other two. "We probably shouldn't be inside the circle itself, but we could help to guide and control the energy from out here, and add our own to boost yours."

Barbara nodded, tears of gratitude pricking at the corners of her eyes again. She gave them each a quick hug, just in case. She truly had no idea if this would work, or what would happen if it didn't. Maybe nothing at all. Maybe some unforeseen disaster.

For a moment, her resolve wavered. She clenched the fingers of the hand not holding the leaf and felt the cool metal of her wedding ring biting into her palm.

The hell with it. She was going to get her life back. She was going to get everyone's life back. Well, except Brenna. Tough luck.

She looked at the Queen and nodded her head, then snapped her fingers to cause each candle to burst into flame. The Queen aimed her fan at Brenna, who began to scream as a trickle of energy was slowly drawn outward, glowing like the light of a small sun. As the trickle grew to a stream and the scream to a high-pitched wail, Barbara held up the leaf and began to recite the spell in her strongest, steadiest voice.

"Transformation happen now

Change the wrong to right

Take away the dark mistakes

Return us to the light

Weave together what was sundered

Mend the broken threads

Undo the magic that was blundered

So that happily it ends

I call the power of the leaf

The power of rock and tree

Re-entwine what's come unraveled

As I will, SO MOTE IT BE"

She uttered the last words, practically shouting them to the sky as she poured all her desire into the leaf in her right hand. "This is my wish!" she added more quietly. "Please."

A shudder ran through the clearing, the air in front of her blurring and wavering. Through the haze, she could see the concentration on Bella's face, the sweat pouring down Beka's paler one. Beyond them, Brenna's body lay in a crumpled heap, as the Queen sent the glowing flow of energy directly into the center of Barbara's circle.

It was almost, almost, almost enough, but Barbara could feel the shiver that marked the moment before the spell collapsed. So close. So close.

Then a small hand slid into hers, holding on with a strength belied by its diminutive size. A rush of additional power ran up her arm, across her chest, and into her core, flowing outward into the leaf and the rock and the shards and the feather, out into the circle and beyond.

The shudder became an explosion, and everything turned to black.

CHAPTER TWENTY-TWO

"Baba Yaga! Baba Yaga!" The piping tenor voice brought the world slowly back into focus.

Barbara's knees trembled a little and she could feel the uneven earth beneath her booted feet. A deep breath drew in only the scent of trees and clean air, and she opened her partially closed eyes all the way and took a look around.

The Queen and her court were gone, along with the rest of the Otherworld. Barbara and Babs stood at the edge of the Human witch's yard, facing a house that lay in ruins, but clearly hadn't burned. It looked, in fact, as though a tornado had torn through it, ripping it apart log by log and flinging the pieces into the air like a giant's plaything. It reminded Barbara a little bit of Babs' new blocks, when they were strewn about between projects.

Best of all, they were not alone. Katherine Chanter stood staring at the wreck of her previously tidy home, her pretty face twisted in fury and disbelief, but clearly and unmistakably alive.

"She is not dead!" Babs observed, sounding cautiously happy. "That is good, right?"

Barbara shrugged. "Well, it is certainly good for her, although she doesn't seem to be in the mood to appreciate it at the moment."

Barbara wasn't sure exactly *what* it meant that things had changed from their original timeline. Hopefully it was an indication that the spell had worked, and undone all the harm caused by the violent confrontation that had precipitated all that followed, rewinding the unraveled pieces of time back into a less destructive whole. But there was also the possibility that they now stood in a third timeline, in which events had been altered to some extent, but perhaps not enough to have mended the most important broken pieces.

"What the hell happened here?" Katherine turned her attention away from her shattered cabin and aimed it at Barbara instead. "What did you do to my house?" She looked confused, as if she couldn't quite remember how things had gotten from point A to point B.

"You showed up at my door," Katherine said, pointing an accusing finger at Barbara. "And you shoved your way inside and demanded I stop making my wonderful elixir." She shook her head as if to clear it. "You're the Baba Yaga."

"I am," Barbara said. "One of them, at least. And yes, I did all of that. Your so-called elixir was messing with time, which is completely unsafe and against the rules." Nobody knew that better than she did, that much was for sure. "So I stopped you."

She glanced around the clearing and was pleased to note that all the plants which had previously shown signs of unseasonal coloration or growth seemed to have gone back to normal. There were no berries on the raspberry bushes, and all the leaves were their proper tones for the time of year. Another change, but surely a good sign.

A low growling sound drew her gaze back to Katherine, who was making a noise that sounded surprisingly like Chudo-Yudo in a bad mood.

"You *stopped* me? You stopped me?" The woman's voice went up an octave with each repetition. "You stopped me from making a magical potion that would keep me and thousands of other women looking young? You stopped me from getting rich from all my hard work? What gave you the right?" That last one came out as a shriek.

"She is the Baba Yaga," Babs said calmly, having finally let go of Barbara's hand. "It is her job to stop bad magic."

"I don't care if she is Harry Potter," Katherine said with a sneer. "I am not going to let her ruin my life's work." She thrust her hands out in front of her and started muttering in Latin.

Oh, not again, Barbara thought, preparing to put up a shield. At least this time maybe the house wouldn't explode, since it was already lying in a heap.

But nothing happened. Katherine glanced down in disbelief and snapped her fingers. Not so much as a spark.

Babs giggled. Barbara was—just for a moment—tempted to join her. Instead, drawing on her superior maturity, she flipped the woman the bird and then looked down at Babs.

"I think our work here is done. Shall we go and see if everything else has turned out as well?"

"Yes please, Baba Yaga," Babs said in a quiet voice. Her brown eyes held a mixture of fear and hope that Barbara was fairly certain was mirrored by her own amber ones.

They walked down the road, Katherine's loud curses following them until they were out of earshot.

"You know," Barbara said. "You could call me Mama. Or Mother. You know, if you wanted to. You don't have to though."

Babs gave the matter some thought, her sneakers scuffing up the dusty soil. "I believe I would like that. Mama." She thought some more. "But sometimes I will still call you Barbara, or Baba Yaga."

"Whatever you like, little one," Barbara said, feeling inordinately pleased. Liam would be pleased too. She hoped. If he was at the end of this road, waiting for them. Dread gnawed at her soul like a jackal gnawed on the bones of its prey. Please goddess, let him be waiting.

Every footstep closer made the terror rise higher in her throat so that by the time the Airstream came into sight, she could barely breathe. What if he wasn't there? What if it had all been for nothing? She tried to pull herself together. She'd found him once, and then again. She'd just keep doing it until they were together. But, oh, how she wanted him to be there.

For a moment, it looked as though her worst fears were true. The silver trailer gleamed in the sun, but there was no one near it.

Then the door opened and Chudo-Yudo bounded down the steps, followed by the most precious sight in the world.

"Hey," Liam said, looking just the way he had when they'd left. "Did I just hear an explosion? Is everything okay?"

Barbara raced across the parking lot and threw herself into his arms in an uncharacteristic display of emotion. "It is now," she said, kissing him soundly. She pulled back to take a closer look at his astonished—albeit delighted—face.

"At least I think it is. How are Belinda and Mary Elizabeth? And Mrs. Ivanov?"

Liam took a step back and stared at her with a bemused expression. "Um, fine, I suppose. I haven't talked to them since we left." He held her at arm's length, one big hand on each of her shoulders. "What's going on, Barbara? You're acting a little odd."

"Even for you," Chudo-Yudo put in. "And you have to act pretty damned odd for anyone to notice."

"Oh, shut up, you big furball," Barbara said, but she leaned down and kissed him on his soft black nose after she said it.

"Really odd," the dragon-dog said, but his tone lacked its usual bite.

"It's a long story," Barbara said.

"Very long," Babs agreed. "And very strange."

Liam laughed. "Why doesn't that surprise me? Are you going to tell me all about it?"

"Later," Barbara said. Right now she didn't even want to think about it, or how close she came to losing almost everything. "Right now, we have a family vacation to take."

She turned to Babs and knelt down to put herself at the same eye level with the girl. "Unless this was too much of an adventure for you, and you want to go home. We can always take a trip another time."

Liam raised an eyebrow, but withheld comment, clearly trusting that she would explain later.

As always, Babs took a moment to ponder the decision. Barbara thought it was probably one of the great ironies of the universe that a woman who tended to simply take action—usually with a certain forcefulness—had ended up raising a child who always thought things through first. She could practically hear the gods laughing.

She didn't really mind, all things considered.

Babs looked from her to Liam and back again. A tiny hint of a smile played around her rosebud lips.

"You know how sometimes when I work very hard to accomplish a difficult task, you say I have earned a cookie?' Babs said finally.

"Yes," Barbara said.

"I think seeing Niagara Falls is our cookie," Babs said decisively. "This adventure was very hard work."

"What adventure?" Liam asked, a little plaintively. "I'm pretty sure I'm missing something here. Something big."

Chudo-Yudo sighed. "We're not going to like this story, are we? I mean, when we finally get to hear it."

"Don't worry," Barbara said. "It has a happy ending. That's the only thing that matters."

"So should we get back on the road?' Liam asked, clearly resigning himself to remaining in the dark for a while.

Barbara considered his question, and gave him a smile that smoldered with such intensity, it made the sun feel cool in comparison.

"Not quite yet," she said, not taking her eyes from his. "Chudo-Yudo, why don't you take Babs for a nice walk? See if you can find the sprite who brought us here and tell him that the problem is solved. I'm sure it will put his mind at ease."

"A walk," Chudo-Yudo repeated.

"Yes," Barbara confirmed. "Maybe take about an hour."

The dragon-dog rolled his eyes. "Come on, kiddo," he said. "I know when we're not wanted."

He and Babs started off in the direction they'd seen the sprite take, either that morning or many days ago, depending on your point of view.

As they moved away, Barbara could hear their voices drifting back on the wind, one low and deep, the other high and light.

"There is going to be kissing, is there not?" Babs said.

"Yes, I think so," Chudo-Yudo said in a disgruntled tone. They both made disgusted sounds as they disappeared through a stand of trees.

Liam got a glint in his eye. "*Is* there going to be kissing?" he asked. He flipped a lock of sandy hair out of his face and straightened up at the thought. Barbara enjoyed watching his muscles move under his tee shirt even more than she usually did. Absence really did make the heart grow fonder.

"Yes there is," she said. "I'm going to kiss you as though I had lost you forever and miraculously got you back again."

"That long story sounds as though it is going to be pretty interesting," Liam said, one side of his mouth quirking up in a grin.

"Not half as interesting as what I'm going to do to you as soon as we get into that Airstream," Barbara said in a husky voice.

"I love it when you're wickedly dangerous," he said, then scooped her up in his arms and carried her inside. Their laughter echoed through the clearing, and then there was silence.

More or less.

ABOUT THE AUTHOR

Deborah Blake is the award-winning author of the Baba Yaga and Broken Rider paranormal romance series and the Veiled Magic urban fantasies from Berkley.

Deborah has also written The Goddess is in the Details, Everyday Witchcraft and numerous other books from Llewellyn, along with a popular tarot deck. She has published articles in Llewellyn annuals, and her ongoing column, "Everyday Witchcraft" is featured in Witches & Pagans Magazine. Deborah can be found online at Facebook, Twitter, her popular blog (Writing the Witchy Way), and www.deborahblakeauthor.com

When not writing, Deborah runs The Artisans' Guild, a cooperative shop she founded with a friend in 1999, and also works as a jewelry maker, tarot reader, and energy healer. She lives in a 130 year old farmhouse in rural upstate New York with various cats who supervise all her activities, both magickal and mundane.

OTHER FICTION BY DEBORAH BLAKE

Novels

WICKEDLY DANGEROUS
WICKEDLY WONDERFUL
WICKEDLY POWERFUL
DANGEROUSLY CHARMING
DANGEROUSLY DIVINE
DANGEROUSLY FIERCE
VEILED MAGIC
VEILED MENACE
VEILED ENCHANTMENTS
REINVENTING RUBY

Novellas

WICKEDLY MAGICAL
WICKEDLY EVER AFTER
WICKEDLY SPIRITED
DANGEROUSLY DRIVEN